ALSO BY AKIL KUMARASAMY

Half Gods

MEET
US BY
THE
ROARING
SEA

FARRAR, STRAUS AND GIROUX   NEW YORK

MEET
US BY
THE
ROARING
SEA

AKIL KUMARASAMY

Farrar, Straus and Giroux
120 Broadway, New York 10271

Printed in the United States of America
First edition, 2022

Title-page art by Thomas Colligan.

Library of Congress Cataloging-in-Publication Data
Names: Kumarasamy, Akil, 1988– author.
Title: Meet us by the roaring sea: a novel / Akil Kumarasamy.
Description: First edition. | New York: Farrar, Straus and Giroux, 2022.
Identifiers: LCCN 2022020655 | ISBN 9780374177706 (hardcover)
Subjects: LCGFT: Novels.
Classification: LCC PS3611.U5 M44 2022 | DDC 813/.6—dc23
LC record available at https://lccn.loc.gov/2022020655

Designed by Gretchen Achilles

Our books may be purchased in bulk for promotional, educational,
or business use. Please contact your local bookseller or the Macmillan
Corporate and Premium Sales Department at 1-800-221-7945, extension
5442, or by email at MacmillanSpecialMarkets@macmillan.com.

www.fsgbooks.com
www.twitter.com/fsgbooks • www.facebook.com/fsgbooks

10 9 8 7 6 5 4 3 2 1

MEET
US BY
THE
ROARING
SEA

A mother is a slippery thing: she brings you into the world and then departs. All your mother has left for you are these rough-cut memories that both sting and shimmer when held too closely.

In one she sits next to you and asks you to be grateful that she is dead.

You clench your teeth and she tells you to spit out your anger.

It will lessen the pain, she says, *embracing what hurts.*

You don't look into her eyes because they are entrances to all these unsaid feelings, regret and longing, and you are afraid of how her face might crease into pity for her weak, sad daughter.

Aya, do you know which came first, mother or egg?

You live in your mother's, your grandmother's, your great-grandmother's house in Queens. It's a Ghost House, filled with your mother's archive. Old rotary phones from Atlanta line the living room wall. Stacks of magazines tower over the

3

dining room table. Flowers wither in milk jugs. Your mother's mind is this collection of ephemera from the near past that you haven't touched since the funeral. She possessed a spatial muscle memory: take three steps west of 1930 rain boots and then jump into the swamps of Florida. It was a shorthand of things, people, places, and years you had mapped out in your mind to navigate childhood, and now, without her, meaning has floated away as if she possessed a gravitational force that held together everything, even you.

Nothing has moved. The picture of Bud Powell and Thelonious Monk sitting in Mary Lou Williams's Harlem apartment rests on a cupboard in the hallway. The trumpet mouthpiece owned by Freddie Hubbard in a silver bowl on the end table. A letter written by John Coltrane to his wife underneath a recorder full of pennies. You were never certain of the authenticity of any of the objects. All you had was her word, worth no more than paper money: a belief you had built your life around.

Your mother would play a record by Alice Coltrane, and you would lie on the carpet and move your arms and legs in the shape of an angel until you safely arrived in 1970. You would think of your grandmother Claudette Williams, a backup singer for a short-lived group called the Awakening, meeting your grandfather Luis Martinez, a quiet postman. According to your mother, Luis Martinez wore his father's red zoot suit at the wedding. Once your mother slipped and described his suit as mustard, and when you corrected her, she looked at you suspiciously, her nose tightening as if something were burning. You tried to make the suit mustard in your mind but you couldn't. All you could see was a smudge of red, the color solid and unforgiving. Often you have a sensation of a phantom memory, something that was true but is no longer there. It throbs just above your collarbone.

In college you were a hopeless student. Somehow you managed to make it out with a degree in machine learning with a specialization in natural language processing. Your intuitive understanding of syntax and algorithms made your mother believe that you would be a polyglot, fluent in an assortment of languages like Arabic, French, Khmer. But in your first year of school, you barely woke in time to catch the train for class, and you might have slept through the years if you hadn't lived at home with your mother, whose sudden enthusiasm for your formal education involved finger-lifting you from bed and concocting a protein-rich breakfast, as if she were trying to make up for all those mornings and rituals that she missed over the years.

For the foreign language requirement, you were late to enroll in an elective and ended up creating a "slot machine" program to choose among the three remaining courses. It didn't matter to you. Did you really need to learn to communicate with people in another language when you were training an algorithm to comprehend all permutations of sounds?

On your thirty-seventh try, you hit the jackpot. Tamil Tamil Tamil!

When you looked it up, you found out it was a classical language of antiquity. All together you counted two hundred and forty-seven letters. Some of them were shaped like fish. On the last day of registration, you signed up for the class and felt strangely like your mother, like you were reaching deep into a past that wasn't really your own.

There were five students in your class, but you were the only one who continued over the years. You have no clear explanation for why you decided to stay, but your body followed a Newtonian impulse—*an object in motion will stay in motion*—until you stumbled on the manuscript.

Your aunt Zee calls you at home and asks you why you're not at work. You tell her you took the day off and she seems nervous about your response, picturing you at home doing nothing by yourself. Her daughter, your cousin Rosalyn, lives with you now. She's twenty-two and you're twenty-six, which gives you some authority but not much. Your mother's sudden death, two months ago, has cemented your aunt's need to be on guard.

Just don't make me worry, okay? your aunt says.

I'm earthbound, you say, and wait until she sighs and says she loves you and so does Uncle Roy, even though he's not talking anymore. You wait for her to hang up.

Space traveling was your aunt's euphemism for what you were up to during your two-week disappearance after your mother's passing. It was true, in a way, because you were traveling through space, drifting, letting your body go.

She doesn't like to hear about that time, which, in her mind, occurred long ago, light-years away.

Before you started working at ML Consulting, you taught at a government-sponsored learning center focused on increasing machine learning literacy. You had a cross section of NYC students with various levels of attentiveness: Louis, in his forties, grinding his teeth methodically as he checked the time; eighteen-year-old Patricia, napping with one eye open because she was trying to make sure information sank into her subconscious; and Aisha, straight out of college, spending half the class on emergency calls.

It paid poorly, but you still can remember the speech you gave to each incoming class: *How many of you take showers? Dry your hair? Brush your teeth? Buy food at the grocery? All this data is collected and stored. Your everyday living accumulates to your carbon score. We all know what it's like to receive a fine for exceeding the limit. We are living in a more thoughtful and conscientious age. Don't you want to be part of that? Helping the world become more functional? We are not individuals but behavior patterns. What if using a certain temperature of water makes your skin cells shrivel up and age more quickly? Because of the inordinate amount of data being collected, we can make all kinds of correlations. Don't you want to be part of how that world is built?*

It was meant to be inspirational, but you always mangled up the script from the handbook and punctuated it all with a sigh. Now, at MLC, you train AI models and have a decent wage. You hardly need to interact with people. After your abrupt absence, your boss, Petrov, didn't question you, simply looked into your eyes very earnestly before assigning you double the work. He likes to remind the employees that MLC is an empathetic environment, not like one of those body shops, where companies hire a bunch of foreigners and squeeze all the life and sweat out of them with the promise of a residency sponsorship. Instead, you work in only a partially exploitive system, with health insurance benefits that ensure your body can continue working.

You are a pro MO$ coder. The dollar sign is your addition, because the language oozes money. In a parallel universe, you work in a finance company or at a start-up, leveraging your life. Your mother is still alive in that universe, but you never see her. You don't have the time.

Books don't interest you. Nothing in English registers. When your old Tamil professor reaches out, he sends you a line from the manuscript you first read years ago—*There's a way beyond mortality*—and the line worms into you until you're on your knees, searching under your bed for your copy, which you find in a shoebox.

The manuscript is untitled with no known author. Some might call it a collective memoir, not fully fact or fiction, about a group of female medical students, all of them under the age of twenty-one, not quite doctors or mystics. Written in the late 1990s, it was discovered only in 2001, when a young police officer in Rameswaram was rummaging through evidence boxes. Newspapers allude vaguely to the incident: "Medical College Suspends Classes Indefinitely."

You once saw it referred to as a "secret minor classic." It has never been translated. And you think maybe that is for the best. Some texts should remain elusive. The girls in the manuscript wouldn't want to immigrate to English. But as you focus on the shape of each word, you feel this undefinable need to try.

When you go to bed, you think of this manuscript that no one will read, about a movement that no one really knows. It comforts you, all this accumulative uselessness. Your mother, a devout internationalist and anti-capitalist, who took pride even in a bird shitting on a car—*nature striking back against modernity*—would have appreciated it. She boycotted retail stores for years because she saw brand names and discounts as euphemisms for domination and poverty. In your closet, you still have your iconic sweater, which you wore between the ages of fourteen and seventeen. It's mostly all yellow except for the last few inches, where your mother ran out of the yarn and had to go with teal. You were forced to wear it during the school year because you really had no other option. It was ugly and embarrassing and your mother's shield, warding off those who lacked a true, far-reaching eye.

According to your mother's wishes, she was cremated, her ashes tossed into the Ohio River, near where your great-grandmother was born. Silver minnows nibbled at the cloud.

Your mother's youngest sibling, Bobby, placed a hand on your shoulder. They wore a patterned floral dress your mother made for them years ago. It was too modest for them, with its high collar, full sleeves, and long draping bodice, but it had Bobby's favorite colors—a turquoise with streaks of umber—and they loved your mother.

My sister was churchly without going to church, they said to the small gathering. *She always wanted to be a mother without having to be a wife. For her, memory was a solid thing, something that could be treasured and passed down.*

Your mother wanted to time travel and brush shoulders in another century with Claudia Jones and Emma Tenayuca. Instead she kept an archive made of ordinary things she imbued with history. For twenty-eight years, she jumped between temp jobs, doing everything from testing the shelf life of spoiled food to administering databases. She was rich with ideas, which did little to help with the bills and the ever-increasing household carbon score. One way or another, she went on trips for weeks at a time, going on *digs*, as she called them. When she returned with stories of her travels, and freshly unearthed additions to the archive, you'd sit beside her, smiling, like you were not unmade by her absence. Together you'd watch a spider weave a web in the dark corners of the kitchen.

On Mother's Day, while other children programmed cards with hearts and roses, you designed an algorithm of thirty-two baby spiders bursting out of their eggs and encircling your mother's name. It looped over and over again. As you grew more excited with each rebirth, your teacher came over to your station and placed one hand over her mouth. *Oh child.*

It's strange that you can't remember your mother's reaction to the card, only the act of creation. The dampness of your hands. The breathless feel in the hollow of your throat, a brief space of suspension. You sometimes wonder if that's how your mother felt when she held you for the very first time.

You drifted for two weeks after your mother's passing. Followed the grassy edge of the highway or rode the train to some unknown city, where you slept among the birds. You carried with you a photograph of your mother and a lighter with the image of the Virgin Mary that supposedly belonged to Grace Lee Boggs. You told everyone you met that your name was Grace Lee. An older man who seemed to drink more cream than coffee looked closely at your face. *Aren't you too dark to be Chinese?* he said.

He frowned and you saw his gums were blackening. You smiled back. He smelled like used magazines, and part of you wouldn't have minded if he sat beside you and told you a story. He beamed you some e-credit, and as you turned your head, you caught the few words he threw over his shoulder. *Wretched girls.*

You didn't shower, and your skin turned mossy. Dirt is natural except on the human body. Let it seep into you and the flesh turns undesirable. What kind of girl doesn't want to be desired?

You could sense people's fear like heat as they passed you. They never got too close. Like you were a castle carrying a moat that no one dared to cross. A slight girl only five feet tall, you sat on a bench and everyone scurried. You scraped some pigeon shit as you stretched your legs, settled into the throne of your body. Flexing your right foot, you felt this sudden instinctive power, waiting to be harnessed.

The longest you have gone without looking at your reflection is two months. You wonder what beauty looked like thousands of years ago, in the murky surface of water, in the unfathomable reactions of other faces.

You live a few blocks away from the Museum of Sound. In one exhibit, called the Time Capsule, patrons are submerged in complete darkness, except for a small square of light by the placards. As you listen to each recording, your body disappears. You hear babies wailing as women coddle them in various languages. Pieces of conversations from disco clubs around Greenwich Village. Wax cylinder recordings of nursery rhymes played on Edison's phonograph. There is a booth of emotions, where you can hear people around the world express love, fear, hatred, embarrassment across the decades. Your favorite is a couple from the 1980s. From the placard, you know that one of them is dying, and this day they are discussing something ordinary like the cake they're baking but continuously digress into stories about friends, long-winded memories of the years they lived in Paris. They never finish making the cake. The last words are spoken by the one who's dying: *What's next?*

And then there is silence for twenty seconds. In that brief stretch of time you feel yourself coming apart, stripped down to bones, grateful for the darkness.

~

At home, in the archive, you find a paper with a line in your own handwriting: *If there is any substitute for love, it's memory* —*Joseph Brodsky*.

You read it like it's a clue to your existence. What happens to a mother, if all the stories she told are untrue? What is the life span of a phantom memory?

For the past week, your mind has been on the manuscript, circling one dead girl. Mole on her right cheek. Necklace of scar tissue. A ripe-eared millet.

She appears in only a handful of pages near the end, but you can't stop thinking of her. Overnight you feel her taking you over. Like you're the ripe-eared millet with a mole on her right cheek. The teenager reaching out one last time. *There's a way beyond mortality.*

To translate means to carry over, to move from one place to another. In your solitude you find yourself picking up each foreign word like a stone you might use to make a path back home. You write and rewrite until they are polished little monsters. *We were eighteen the summer of the drought.*

Instead of sleeping, you pace up and down your mind, and somewhere in your wandering, you find an empty room you hadn't noticed. The door is jammed, but still you can hear them, in the silence, your mother, the girls, whispering, and she's telling them, you, to listen, keep still, because she knows the secret to remembering.

We were eighteen the summer of the drought. The cow's milk tasted of water and the harvest had shriveled to half-formed things. Onions the size of chicken eggs were pulled from the ground, and lentils the color of the sky, the same bright blue as the dye from the garment factory. At Saint Mary's Hostel, we survived off boiled peanuts and rice porridge. The single meal was meant to last us the whole day. The hunger was a lesson in the human body, and on our first day of anatomy class we all looked drained and hollowed out like the skeleton hanging in the front of the room. Seventeen girl specimens.

Alone for the first time in our lives, we walked from the hostel to the canteen, our backs hunched and arms tight across our chests, and the older girls would look at us wordlessly while passing, their gaze like the steady surface of a mirror. We'd feel them willing us to look, step closer, reveal what we did not even know of our true natures.

Sitting side by side, the older girls ate with a patience we had yet to fully understand. They chewed on a single peanut for twenty minutes, moving their mouths so slowly, as though they were chanting. Sometimes they left their porridge outside the gates for a street dog, or they searched for the hungry before sundown, walking barefoot down the streets. To us, it seemed like they survived eating nothing at all.

We had come from all different villages and cities across the state to the recently established medical college, only twenty-nine kilometers from the Island. Our parents were told we would get first-rate medical training because of the geography. How many first-year students were able to operate on patients? Our parents knew of the civil war on the Island but with a distant recollection much like their memory of the old epic poetry we shared, written in the same tongue, when ancient kings ruled the land and nothing as elemental as water divided dynasties.

For them these were like fables, old wives' tales, useless musings that brought only more hunger. We were mostly average students, who scored high enough to enter medical school but not enough for a government scholarship. With the opening of the medical college by the refugee camps, our parents prayed at the temple, the mosque, the church, thanking the Lord for the misfortune of others. As long as people suffered, we would be employed. When they spoke of the refugees, they expressed an oversaturated pity, their voices clotted with satisfaction, and before they could turn away, we saw the faint outline of a smile crossing their lips, as if they found a dark-edged pleasure in the image of us holding knives and needles, poking and prodding with our young, inexperienced hands.

The refugee camps dotted the shoreline, and at night when we heard the ocean we could picture the kerosene lamps lighting square shanties, walls held together by the spit of longing. The third-year students told us that in their first year there was an epidemic of gangrene in the camps, and when they ran out of anesthesia, at least four girls needed to hold each patient as they stuffed cotton into the mouth, rubbed alcohol on the sickly limb, and prayed as they cut down through the skin, scraping into the bone.

Some of us had never seen a dead body, but the older girls said we would be used to those soon enough. Out of every ten patients in emergency care, eight passed on, while two lived a little longer. Patients wanted one more day, a couple of weeks, some years, which is all a life really is anyway.

One afternoon we noticed a line scrawled in the margins of Sangeeta's biochemistry textbook: *There's a way beyond mortality*. It was a used book but we couldn't find the name of any previous owner. Instead we studied each chapter, searching for answers, and at night we dreamed of that secret hatch door in the body, the hidden route to salvation. The boys already believed themselves invincible. Instead of studying, they went deep diving for pearls, never returning empty-handed because luck was on their side, even if they brought back only seashells or a bottle of toddy. Perhaps fearlessness was the elixir to ward off death.

Our girls' hostel was less than five hundred meters from the college but the boys' hostel was much closer, practically adjoined. The boys woke only a few minutes before class and arrived red-eyed with their hair uncombed and in the same trousers they had worn for weeks, smelling again and again of yesterday. After class they ate quickly in the canteen, joking with us, savoring some crude line to forget their hunger.

At night they stayed out, sometimes jumped on an empty boxcar following the tracks to another town. We watched as they howled through the evenings, their slim bodies alarming us with only jealousy, perhaps, as we returned to Saint Mary's at curfew, with Madame Sarojini counting our names on the sign-in paper and checking our tardiness against the clock. A single old television with a knob and metal antlers waited for us in the common area, the floor covered with a green sheet where we sat side by side with our legs folded. On nights when the electrical current was out, we played games of rummy, passing the candle and holding the flame close to our faces, the hot wax dripping against our fingers as we glimpsed our cards and our features, all our doubts and worries, glowing in a brief flash visible to everyone, before we slipped back into dark anonymity. During one of these nights, the older girls told us that we needed to wake early, before sunrise. When we rose the next morning, we bumped into one another, still dreaming as we stood in the courtyard in our nightgowns while the senior student Baseema looked us over. "You're going to need to separate yourselves from your egos," she said, and looking at one another—tall, short, fat— the sun slowly blinding us to the world above us, we saw our shadows spread across the dirt in a single black mass.

Radical compassion was what the older girls called it. We were practicing to become not only doctors but saviors, bodhisattvas who were drawn to suffering and embraced it. Above the doorway of the second-floor hall was a quote by Khalil Gibran, painted in thick cursive. *Your pain is the breaking of the shell that encloses your understanding . . . It is the bitter potion by which the physician within you heals your sick self.*

Therefore trust the physician, and drink his remedy in silence and tranquility. Madame Sarojini would walk under those words every day, never lifting her head. How much of the world went unnoticed by us?

We exchanged class schedules, pretending to be one another. Sonya was Parvati, Radha was Urvashi. Anatomy traded for organic chemistry, and entomology swapped for another animal equivalent like ornithology. At first our professors didn't even notice that we were becoming one another. Only after Avvaiyar required that we speak in pure Tamil three times a week (Mondays, Wednesdays, Thursdays) did the professors look at us like we were a pack of imbeciles, as we replied to their questions in a manner we imagined our kings, warriors, and saints must have once. We were sent one by one to the dean, who couldn't get a handle on our names, which we kept changing, slipping further and further away from ourselves. "English only, please," he demanded as we explained how the refugees spoke pure Tamil, unlike ours, which was all mixed with English, and he rubbed his head, placing two fingers against his closed eyelids as if to correct his vision.

We were learning two different systems of knowledge, one structured by a clinical understanding of the body and the other ancient, known before knowing. At night we congregated in the common area and turned on the television, black-and-white static lines chopping up the screen along with music. We weren't really watching, instead listening to one of the older girls, either Baseema, Avvaiyar, or Leela, speak in a soft whisper, all the while straining our ears because we knew what was spoken dug below the surface of this world. There was much suffering and dying everywhere, and we needed to reach a new consciousness to be of any use. Regular medical training would not be enough. "Like Siddhars living in the forest, half naked, turned inward so deeply, we will uncover enlightened perfection, but unlike the Siddhars, we will circulate ourselves with the people. They will be our forest, our shelter," Avvaiyar said, and we felt a sudden fear of being apart from this world and vulnerable to it.

You sleep for only a few hours, sunken in your mother's mattress. In the morning light a congregation of objects greets you: a rocking horse, two birdcages, eighty-six video cassettes, three globes, a percussion set, a vacuum cleaner, a pair of tennis rackets, a boom box. The TV shrieks from the living room. For a moment you almost forget where you are, wander into the hallway expecting to find a group of girls, and you simply make out one snoring, her naked legs dangling off the couch's rim, her white lab coat covering her like a blanket. On TV an episode from *Soldiers' Diaries* rages along.

Your cousin Rosalyn finds the noise soothing. She says it reminds her of the womb, but you think it's probably related to her father. Almost a year back, without warning or explanation, her father stopped speaking. He was a military man, won a few medals during his service, and for the past ten years worked as a contractor for a manufacturing company that creates hybrid appliances. He used to drink beers and chat with his buddies into the evening, his laugh landing like a shovel. The last time you saw him he wore his fisherman's hat and sat in a red plastic chair in the garden, staring at the toxic flowers.

On TV a soldier eats a sandwich, pausing now and then to wipe the mayonnaise from his lips, as he recalls his last mission. His face is as soft as cream pudding, and before you turn it off and salvage what is left of your ever-increasing carbon score, he looks straight at you and says, *There are two kinds of people in the world. Those who let things stick to them and those who don't.*

For work you dress in the color scheme of a tree. One day you hope your colleagues will mistake you for vegetation and forgo all efforts at conversation. Lately they have been gifting you flowers with downturned, commiserating expressions.

You are highly proficient and have little ambition, making you an ideal employee. When your boss, Petrov, passes your desk and gives you a thumbs-up, you mirror him, which is much easier than saying what you actually think. Today he's happily sunburnt, his skin almost matching his final ring of hair.

On your last assignment you trained a model to respond to customers' issues about their washing machines. The AI was competent, repeating strings of words that it didn't even understand. Could an AI really comprehend why someone cried for three hours when the washing machine couldn't remove the period stain from a favorite dress?

Once, for a model that was instructed to associate accents with specific countries, you labeled the training data with fruits instead of countries. You are from Papaya.

If you were more precise, you wouldn't have written *radical compassion*, it would be *suffer beyond for caring*, but you sensed something was lost in that translation. You struggle with the word *suffering*. Two weeks ago, when you cut your finger chopping garlic, you stood there, letting the blood drip out of you. Your hand, a distant scene, you watched, and as the tired viewer, you feigned interest, half-heartedly asked, *Does it hurt? Will you make it through?*

The movie you watch with Rosalyn is about a woman who befriends her ex-lovers, who happen to be ghosts. The twist at the end—which you saw coming—is that she killed them all.

Rosalyn has already watched it three times, but watching it with you, she says, is a new experience. As you stare at the TV, you sense her examining you, each crease and twitch of your face a revelation, and you purposefully smile through the gory scenes, like the part when the protagonist reaches into a dog who has swallowed her ex-boyfriend's heart.

Rosalyn's taste lies somewhere between romance and horror. It shouldn't surprise you her favorite TV program is that old reality show, *Soldiers' Diaries*, condensing a day's worth of violence into a nightly hour-long program for families to consume—a boy's arm getting blown off or a baby being blinded by shrapnel or an elderly man's face turning pulpy with bullets.

So what do you think? she asks when the credits start rolling.

Still digesting, you say as you chew on the final scene of the film. The protagonist sits under a cherry tree with her latest ghost ex-boyfriend and they both weep—his tears ethereal—and hold hands.

I'm not saying she's not a serial killer, Rosalyn says, *but you need to think of the subtext of the film, which is really about a woman's search for wholeness.*

She removes her ice helmet, almost out of charge, so she sinks into the couch, surrendering to the heat. The windows are open, the night air warm and congealed with an occasional spark from a siren. The house is one of the few relics still standing. Without the usual installations and devices— not even an outdated A/C to spritz out recycled cool—it's wasteful, a carbon score hazard. Your monthly carbon payment is possibly double what you should be handing over to the government. It never seemed to bother your mother, who paid only on the last possible day, when a power cut threatened. She disapproved of the nature of efficiency, all the hidden costs, and while you carry a hint of her mistrust, you still want to believe in this system tracking your accountability, so on a personal level you can feel like you're doing your part to ensure that life proceeds on this planet.

At midnight, when the theme song of *Soldiers' Diaries* comes on, you know it's time to retreat to your translation. Helicopters chop up the horizon in a propulsive beat. Young faces flash across a desert landscape.

What's the name of that dead girl?

You pause. *Which dead girl?*

In the book you're writing.

Oh, it's Yaadra.

She nods and repeats the name to herself, the letters stretched out. *You know, I think you're in love with her.*

With who?

Yaadra.

A dead girl?

Uh-huh. Rosalyn shrugs, her eyes fixed on the show. *Falling for someone is never rational.*

The TV is a translucent screen as thick as your thumb. It hangs like an invisible portrait, where data can flow in and out of the house. Your mother would have hated it. She kept an early version, a massive black box from the twentieth century, in the closet, where she also stored her shoes and coats. Something in the machinery was broken, so she never used it and most likely wasn't interested in fixing it in the first place. For her it carried symbolic value—*Do you know who owned this? What they used to watch while eating dinner?*—and you'd watch your image, the silver face of a girl trapped inside the glass.

According to Rosalyn, every cell in your body remembers. She picks up your hair follicle on the counter like a worthy specimen. She's eating a slice of toast with sunflower butter and dried pineapples. It still surprises you that your young cousin is an associate researcher at a laboratory known for the regeneration of appendages and the growth of third eyeballs. Their latest endeavor—an Alzheimer's drug—sounds strangely prosaic. But Rosalyn assures you it's not your usual kind of medication, and from the way she grins, with only one side of her face, you're afraid to ask more questions. Her supervisor, who goes by V. F., is known for bizarre creations like winged frogs spawned from embryonic stem cells, and you wouldn't be shocked to find out that he named himself after a childhood hero, Victor Frankenstein. Sometimes you imagine your cousin and V. F. in the laboratory, bloody gloves on their hands and streaks of lightning illuminating their hunched figures as they work on something perfectly diabolical before breaking for lunch, where they sit side by side and eat leftovers and ponder morality and God.

Rosalyn picks up a teacup holding a baseball from the table. Next to it is a hammer and a stack of travel magazines from the 1960s. It's an unsaid rule: don't move any of the objects. To be honest it took Rosalyn a while to figure out how to hopscotch around the house without disturbing the decorum of things, but she's gotten used to it, and, after all, she's not paying rent, and freeloaders can't be choosers.

She tosses the ball up in the air and it doubles in your perception. What did your mother say about it? Baseball and tea are both imperialistic goods. You blink until it blends into one solid object.

On a Saturday afternoon you meet a ghost in real life. You don't know it at first as you shoulder your bag of groceries and

Rosalyn details the anatomy of a human heart, but your body tingles and you step back to reverse time and the milk slips out and puddles on the ground by your feet and a colony of ants takes shelter but there's nowhere for you to hide as the heat pins you to the sidewalk, so you're staring, wide-eyed, across the street to a house you know from a dream of childhood and she's standing there, her hair the color of magma, and her mouth caught between words under the lights and the cameras. Saleha. Sal.

Rosalyn looks it up, the accident. The first article refers to it as *The Trolley (a.k.a. Self-Driving Car) Problem.* On a detour, a self-driving car meets another self-driving car in what seems to be an inevitable, fatal accident. In one car, fifty-eight-year-old Mr. Ahmed with early hearing loss and a heart murmur and Mrs. Ahmed, fifty-one and diabetic. In the other, thirty-four-year-old Ms. Lockwood and her three-year-old toddler.

The manufacturer, Solintel, said the cars exchanged data and attempted to make the best decision. Medical histories and demographic information were included. Pakistani, Muslim, heart condition, diabetic, Caucasian, Christian, baby eczema, and so on.

The company involuntarily confessed these details through a leak. In the past year, there have been a number of accidents with similar results, and the CEO of Solintel responded that race, age, wealth, and religion had in no way impacted the decision-making process of the cars. These were tragedies, simple as that.

The comments at the end go on for pages.

Baby + Mum > Two OLD PEOPLE

What's the problem? Our cars work just like how our drones work. With minimal casualties.

Would a non-white baby have lived???

AI IS GOD

Rosalyn closes her eyes like she's overloaded but then she begins whispering: *I remember them, Mr. and Mrs. Ahmed, and that girl Sal down the street, who you used to hang out with when you were a kid. She made those weird collages with like hair strands and nail clippings.*

Rosalyn looks at you, momentarily satisfied at her memory-retrieval capabilities, but then the news sinks into her and she's wiping her eyes, saying it's the saddest thing she's heard, and you're not sure why she's getting sentimental about people she has seen only twice in her whole life, but she's staring at you, waiting for your face to respond, and you remember the time many years ago when you visited her family out in that lonely stretch of Pennsylvania and the four of you went out to dinner and outside the restaurant she spotted a mangy three-legged dog that was clearly abandoned and she wanted to help it, but no one would listen, and throughout dinner, she kept talking about this ashy dog that no one cared about, and her food went cold and she refused to eat, and later you heard the sad rumbling of her stomach as she slept, and you can still sometimes hear it if you listen closely.

This is the story your brain has about Sal:

You and Sal were childhood friends.

Sal went off to college.

You reached out.
Silence.

Unlike your mother, you don't safekeep memories. What
you remember of your father can fit in a child's palm. You
once found a picture of him squashed inside an old Oxford
dictionary between *junk* and *juxtaglomerular*. He was dressed
in a pirate suit and had a hook hand, beside him a woman in
a princess outfit who wasn't your mother, and a young boy
in a ninja costume, who wasn't you. Later your mother pro-
nounced him dead and ripped up the photo. In your mind
he is sixty percent dead and forty percent alive. In a state of
uncertainty. You're a high-probability orphan.

There's an interview with Sal on the TV, but you don't watch
it. Instead, sitting on your mother's bed, you translate, writing and rewriting sentences, as if you too could improve
yourself through willful effort. From the living room, Rosalyn shouts out lines from the program and by the time it
reaches you, it's thinned out, all fizz. *She was an art administrator in Boston . . .   data is the breath of AI systems . . .
glitch . . . loved her parents very much . . . first solo exhibit in
some fancy place called Martoykowikkiii . . . she dyed her hair
orange in protest . . . what must it be like to be famous because
your parents died . . . and why did you lose touch again?*
    In Tamil there are two kinds of first-person plurals. You
can't make any distinctions in the text, but you've felt it in
English. Petrov saying *We* when he wants to feel more au-

thority but less blame or your mother using it to include everything, both the inanimate and you. There's comfort in reading the *We* in the text over and over again, the warm shelter of belonging somewhere, even if it's only in your imagination.

A futurist visits the office for a general assembly. He asks everyone to fill out a virtual questionnaire about their expectations for the future.

Rate your satisfaction with the present: 3 out of 5

How do you rate the amenities at your home? 3 out of 5

Would you want to move away from New York City? Undecided

Do you think the future will be better than the present? Okay

What is your level of excitement for the future? Enough

Breanna peeps over to stare at your answers and says you sound dispassionate about everything.

Being unbiased is good, no? you say.

She shrugs and blots her face with an oil-cleansing wipe. She hands one to you, and you proceed to squeeze your pores until your face is a desert landscape. Your cellular memories sopped up in the cloth.

The futurist is a bald man who wears the pin-striped suit of a salesman. Breanna tells you he looks like her husband, and you squint, trying to remember the picture at her desk of him and their son, but they come out looking like blobs.

The man is named Luke, not after the Jedi, he clarifies

for the audience. Some people don't get it. Petrov laughs his face into a beet.

Luke projects images of New York City. Standard photos of a subway station at midnight and Central Park at the height of summer with hydrants flooding the streets and kids jump roping, their shadows butterflying across the asphalt. Images of a young woman hanging her legs outside a fire escape and waving at the camera and then shots of her messy bedroom. A plant dying in the corner of the room. It all makes you feel slightly nostalgic for a past you didn't have.

Luke asks the audience to close their eyes and then he commands everyone to awaken to a better New York City. The streets are brighter with a silicone-like shine. Houseless people have disappeared. The subways look sleek and efficient, everything more streamlined, especially homes.

You stare at an image of a teenage girl smiling in her techy room, chatting through a chip in her index finger. The house bot has prepared her coffee and breakfast. Her blinds open precisely at seven in the morning. On a mobile ReadyPress stand, a school outfit hangs, freshly steamed, courtesy of the house bot.

Can you now imagine the future? Luke says, and waits for the slow, stomach-rumbling midday applause.

Azizi stands up, raising a hand. *Whose future is this? I can't imagine this girl's room in my village. Please label it properly as a Western future. Not for everyone.*

Half the crowd has already snuck out of the room.

Luke projects his business card on the wall. Underneath

his title is a quote: *We had the internet of things. Next will be the internet of beings.*

You thank Luke telepathically and tell him not to join the dark side.

Outside the office you watch the gyro man, Yusuf, have a heart attack. You are third on line and your initial thought when you see him pause from his work, his hands on the counter, moments before crumpling, is of your own hunger. Along with his other faithful customers, you carry him to the sidewalk and blow on his face. By the time the ambulance arrives, you're holding your hands in some kind of prayer, repeating a question from the manuscript. *Who is he to you?*

He once showed you a photograph of his family—his wife and two daughters—that he kept taped on the back wall of the truck. The girls gave each other bunny ears, squeezed next to their young mother, who was crouched low to their height with her matchstick neck and light eyes. Without turning away from them, he said, *It's nice, no, to have a family?*

The soldier falls asleep on top of a half dozen eggs and wakes up plastered in embryonic goo. It's supposed to be a prank and the other soldiers around him laugh and point at his sheets, but he's in a state of complete disorientation, clawing through the bleached shrapnel of shells and liquid with this dilated look in his eyes like he's being born on live TV, which isn't the case because *Soldiers' Diaries* is a delayed reality show, released three years after filming for what you assume are security reasons. But when you're watching, it feels alive and timely, as if the troops could be part of any mission in one of the many stabilization zones.

It came out five years ago, but you missed it, along with everything else remotely popular. There was a period when you tried getting on all the devices and streams, bursting out thoughts and images, projecting versions of yourself to strangers and almost-friends, but you found you were drained of something vital because deep down in the kernel of your existence your mother planted her misgivings for the world around her.

According to Rosalyn, you're a rarity, a coder who is stuck in a different age. When you watch *Soldiers' Diaries* with her, you sometimes sense a shift in her tone, as if she's talking to a child or one of her lab experiments, and she's introducing you to something you've never seen before, but then as effortlessly as blinking her eyes, her voice returns to her usual cadence, and she recites lines along with the characters, who are playing themselves, and in the late hours of watching, when sleep weighs on you, she sounds like she is also part of the cast.

She tells you she's not fond of the Egg Incident. Max didn't deserve it. She finishes a beer and opens another one.

In the handful of episodes you've watched, nothing exceptional has stood out. The camera takes are choppy. The story lines are poorly strung together. The soldiers are not even particularly attractive. And the title, *Soldiers' Diaries*, has a skin-squirming effect. Still, with all these shortcomings, the show has a cult following, won a few awards, and has you unexpectedly hooked.

Maybe it's the utter lack of artistry, the images unframed, the lighting poor, which gives the show a level of authenticity. When someone's arm explodes from rocket fire, does anyone expect the shot to be centered? From what Rosalyn has shared, you know two cameramen were killed, one producer had a leg amputated. The creator was twenty-three years old. It was the first show that was permitted to film in a stabilization zone. The behind-the-scenes delirium is palpable while watching, and it feels like no one, including you, is entirely sure why they are where they are or what the point of it all is.

After two episodes your cousin lowers the volume, and you think she's about to tell you something important, maybe to do with the memory drug, but she only blows the air between her front teeth. The sound like a far-gone train.

And in the darkness, seventeen girl specimens sit cross-legged on the floor watching TV, the glow lighting their faces. One by one they turn and ask you if you've seen her. The ripe-eared millet.

It was a lucky accident, bumping into her alone, not a single news crew around, Rosalyn says, and looks down into her empty bottle. *And I just said your name and she invited us over.*

In your dream, all the soldiers are robotic deer. They graze on a grass patch and in two hops are blown up by a land mine. Then a deer with dark red eyes turns its laser vision at the neighboring village and blows it up. Still, they look sweet, with their gunmetal heads.

You stop the cassette and return it to its cover, labeled 177. Your mother was a diligent recorder of dreams, labeled each tape with important details like *teeth falling out, turned into a plant, fell into a black hole.* For her, dreams were the best way to examine one's subconscious, and you recall hours of her sitting alone, listening to her own voice, like it was a dear friend she hadn't heard from in a while. On a few of the tapes your childhood dreams are recorded next to hers, but growing up, you didn't listen to them, even when she was away. They stayed in the swamp under the bed.

You choose a tape titled *goodnight bird* and after the initial static your mother's voice springs forth, filling the entire room. She describes the dream in a neutral voice. She walks to the grocery story in the middle of the afternoon and on her way back, out of nowhere, a giant bird begins to chase her. She can't identify the bird precisely, but she's certain the bird is of an extinct variety. What strikes her the most is the unbearable terror she felt, though thinking back, she supposes the fear might have been misguided. What if the giant bird was seeking help from her?

You turn off the tape before she's finished. It would be so easy to unspool the film into a meaningless pile. An outdated form of technology like a cassette offers a level of privacy—who could be bothered?—and insurance of no data trail.

On Dream #177 you write: *Soldiers' Diaries Late Night w/ Ros.* This is the third dream you recorded. What pattern do you see? Well, you're not in them.

~

The first time you meet Ricky Lee, your new colleague, he tells you, *MLC is not the worst place to work, trust me,* and there's something in the way he says it, the massage roll of his tongue, *trust me,* that makes you unexpectedly relieved, and the feeling lingers until you return to your desk with your burnt coffee and untrained models, the flowers gifted from your coworkers hunched together, littering petals, and you count them, the months, the years you've worked there. It's not the worst place, is it?

Later in the bathroom you sit half naked, a hundred feet from your coworkers, and your body oozes. Head bent, eyes closed, inside the confines of a stall that could really be a confessional, you wait for that feeling of lightness.

Your old Tamil professor now lives in Germany with his daughter, who works on artificial intelligence for a delivery company. When you call him, he's pouring powdered formula into a bottle. He keeps missing, making plumes.

Are you okay, Professor?

His face looks splotchy on the screen.

Yes, yes, dear, it's just that I didn't think I would have to be a substitute father again at the age of sixty, he says, and collects his breath like he might run out. *My bloody son-in-law runs off and leaves my daughter alone with a baby. You know, I was a single father, and now I'm back being a father to my daughter who won't even get out of bed and this little crying baby who wants to suck my tit.*

You're struck by his usage of *tit,* which you first mishear as *teeth*. Both of you grin at each other through the punctured silence.

You breastfeeding now? you say.

Someone has to do it.

Your professor's name is Socrates. The first time you heard it you thought he was playing a joke, but he explained it quite naturally: the rationalist movement had taken over his great-grandfather's generation and led to the proliferation of names relating to Greek philosophers, which were passed down into posterity. *There was an idea that no belief was sacred, and everything could be challenged*, he said. He went to school with a Plato, who bullied him ruthlessly.

You don't end up discussing the manuscript. Radical compassion means that tomorrow works too.

You never invite guests over to the house. It's not a rule, but you know they will feel uncomfortable. Whenever your aunt Zee visits, she sits in the living room very carefully with her purse on her lap, eyeing the objects in the room like she's afraid to wake them. It must be difficult for her since she grew up in the house and remembers it differently. Occasionally you wonder if she's bitter that your grandmother left the house to your mother and not to her or Bobby. Fortunately for you, you're an only child. The house, the debt, the residual memories are all yours.

～

Rosalyn brings over strangers at night, and in the mornings you find them walking around the house, wide-eyed and half-dressed, blinking in the startling daylight as if the house is a museum, except nothing is off-limits for them to reach out and touch—the chunky rotary telephones lining the wall, bowls full of whistles, sheets of piano music pinned to cork, miniature ceramic figurines seated high on cabinets like angels. This time a young man sits at the kitchen table, drinks coffee, and looks at the manuscript. Rosalyn eats her usual toast. You stand out of frame, right on the edge between dreaming and waking.

What does this have to do with her again?

Well, she's translating it.

I understand that, but is she like part Asian or Tamil or something?

It's a language. Anyone can learn a language.

I guess grief makes you do weird things, doesn't it?

On your way to work you pass a man in a wheelchair who carries a sign around his neck. SUPPORT A VETERAN.

He says loudly that he was stationed in Attawana. He pats his ribs as if this imagined city is located somewhere inside him. He shows you his arthritic fingers and silicon knees. His legs don't work. He says his liver is engorged, lungs embossed with tumors, but his kidneys are perfectly shaped. With these final words, a sprinkle of spit wets your arm.

Sorry, you say, and walk straight into the deli, holding the door for the next entering customer. You don't touch the spot on your left arm, the flecks of liquid still visible. The bathroom is out of order, and as you pick up items for lunch, you are oddly aware of the weight of that arm as if it's an extension of the man sitting outside, who you recall most clearly through the outline of his injuries. He talked to you and everyone at once, and you avoided staring, out of politeness, you think, the nakedness of his need on that crowded street, the discomfort in your glands as you walked even closer to him, tossed an apology—which he might not have even heard—that was more for your sake than his.

At the register, the woman in front of you doesn't have an ID, so the clerk scans her eyes, and she winces slightly. You rub your own, remembering the prick of the red light, the momentary dizziness. You haven't felt it in a few years. Because you make sure not to forget your ID. When it's your turn, you hand over the stale meatless sandwich and color-less drink and mouth, *Sorry, I don't want these anymore*, and walk out empty-handed. You look down both sides of the street, but the man with his sign who was once stationed in Attawana is gone.

Petrov considers himself a kind man. He knows your finan-cial difficulties stemming from your mother's recent pass-ing, so when he calls you to his office to offer you one of the more lucrative projects, which will include a pay hike, you can only muster up half a grin, but you're sure it's enough for Petrov to fill out the rest since he expects you to be grateful, and secretly he's grateful you're so capable and undemanding.

On his desk he has a half-eaten burrito and a new oxygenating cactus. *Have you heard of Nim Chimpsky?* he asks.

Noam Chomsky?

No, I mean the chimpanzee named Nim, raised by humans, he continues. *What I'm saying is what you'll be doing won't be much different.*

I will be raising a chimpanzee.

It's just an analogy, of course. You will be training and fine-tuning the model as usual, except this model is more versatile. The client, IntraVan, considers your role to be more like that of a caretaker, raising a unique child. They're more interested in seeing how well this new model learns. He coughs and moves his oxygenating cactus closer to him. *If a client is willing to pay, it is not our duty to judge their purpose or lack of purpose.*

On your way back to your desk you find Ricky leaning in his chair, his hands behind his head like he's watching clouds. His hair calcified into spikes. Music leaks from his ears.

What are you listening to? you ask.

"Chia Pet."

That AI-generated song?

He lets you listen, and you find it syrupy and trite and can't resist humming along.

I want to be your Chia Pet for love, he sings, and then laughs. *Where did the AI come up with this crap? Oh, I forgot, from us.*

You play the song as you wait for Rosalyn. She's late from the lab, and you stay up, seated by the window in the dark. The TV is off, and that's why you can make out the vibrations, an insect-like thrumming, of the things around you. In the heat your thoughts slow and you can smell the smoke, the burn of metal in the breeze. On a Thursday evening your mother was starfished on the kitchen floor in a bright green sweater with her night socks, dying a domestic death. And months later Sal has returned home. There is no connection.

You take a deep breath. All this time you think you have control, moving along a straight line, from one point to another, but really you're spinning with the earth, so deep in that vortex of girlhood.

Of the senior students, Baseema, Avvaiyar, and Leela were the professed leaders of the movement. They had arrived at the principles independently, all searching through their suffering for transcendence. Baseema had spent a year slowly dying from jaundice. It was said that the bilirubin glow of her eyes made her look like a wild cat, fevered and untamed. Avvaiyar had forsaken her family because of their wealth, while Leela had been exiled because of an unsanctified pregnancy, though she had miscarried on the bus two months after the discovery. The death of a dog crushed under premium tires and her future child dripping into her underwear are forever linked. The story went that on a Wednesday afternoon, the three of them had skipped eating at the canteen and walked instead near the beach, where they found a man dying on the street, struck by a Mercedes-Benz. No one had stopped to aid him out of fear that they would be blamed, since only the guilty would have blood on their hands. Together they carried the man five kilometers to the hospital. Baseema held him by the shoulders and could remember his face so clearly, the cut on his lips, the mouth full of too many teeth, the wingspan of his brows: the older brother she had never known. Avvaiyar shared his blood type, A positive, and gave everything she could. The nurse had to stop her because she was willing to give up her life. It wasn't enough, though, and the man still died. Perhaps that was where radical compassion began, an unknown man dying and three young girls weeping over the corpse. "Who is he to you?" the doctors had asked.

There was never a formal text on radical compassion. To that extent, it had no clear goals of proselytization. We circulated into the public our own beings, the teachings archived within us. Moving beyond metaphysical abstractions, radical compassion was a living practice, and unless we became it, we were useless. Avvaiyar was the most stringent of the group, with almost Jain-like principles, refusing to harm anyone except for herself. She would not kill even a mosquito and on an overnight train she would give up her seat, spending nearly sixteen hours on her feet without complaint. She wanted to brush up against what the body needed and what it could do without. For her, radical compassion was an experiment with the body's limits. Could she possibly dilute sleep, stretch it out over a day so she could close her eyes a few minutes each hour and still be well rested?

Baseema was more dutiful with her studies. She saw radical compassion as an accompaniment to traditional Western medicine rather than a departure. The philosophy, she insisted, would deepen our relationships with our patients, which would better equip us to truly diagnose them, tend to the source of pain rather than just the symptoms. She did not see radical compassion as a revolution like Avvaiyar did, but she respected Avvaiyar, called her a daring and unguarded visionary, though what she had really meant to call her might have been closer to reckless. More subdued and unassuming, Baseema preferred not to lecture about radical compassion but rather to wait for us to approach her with questions, all the while warning us against any teachings or hearsay. Do not follow blindly, she'd say with a smile on her lips. Unconsciously we would bow our heads and in response she would bow lower to show us she was not our teacher. The Siddhars wanted to destroy the normalcy of the self, and we could sense in Baseema a joy in the mundane. We wondered how easy it would be for her to live a traditional path, working at the hospital, becoming a wife and then a mother, bound to her own earthly matters. Baseema had chosen to work the maternity ward, and after hours, we saw her standing by the window near the newborns, her hand pressed against the glass. Radical compassion required us not to squander our love on a child or a husband, when we had the world to heal.

Leela, who almost had a baby, had sworn off motherhood. She smoked long menthol cigarettes to make her womb even more uninhabitable. For her, radical compassion meant liberation. Though she no longer prayed at temples, she went once a month, each time she menstruated, as a means of transgression. Ecstatic over the impurity of her body, she waved at the priests, pressed ash into her forehead. "Only we women can transform from pure to impure," she had told us, and then paused to trace the belly of Ganesh. "There's a place within you that no one can touch, beyond good or evil."

While Avvaiyar wanted to deprive the body to discover its capabilities, Leela wanted to feel everything, find the outer limits of sensations before she exploded. In their own ways, both of them sought to intensify their energies in this life-time and then in death. The land where Siddhars were buried released a magnetic pulse that even birds could detect, but looking at our scrawny arms, the cages of our ribs, we could not imagine such power emanating from our bones. Our skulls seemed too ordinary, nothing more than heavy paper-weights, which Shakespeare might have called ugly, for the only beauty we could imagine was the possibility that one day our skulls might contain a nest of mice burrowing and mating with their small, ferocious love.

The night before quarterly exams, Leela instructed us from their past exams. We learned how to cheat properly. Selfish-ness had no part in it. In our classes no one stood out, and the bell curve disintegrated into a cluster. After we finished our exams, we learned that a local bus had swerved off the expressway. Thirty-two people were killed, and Baseema, on duty that evening, brought home two pairs of hearts in glass jars from the hospital. Burned and poisoned with gasoline, they floated like dark talismans.

"One belongs to a child," she said, "the other is from an old man."

We imagined our hearts somewhere in the middle, drift-ing between two points of death. We thought the child's heart would be soft and supple like a boiled egg, but it was tough and firm as Avvaiyar cut through the flesh with a kitchen knife, pressing down with both of her hands. As we held sections of the child's heart, one of the first-years, Parvati, started weep-ing. *Remember, the form transforms but the essence remains.* For the rest of the week we had the smell of raw heart on our fingertips. The boy's blood had seeped beneath our skin and left us with the delirious feeling of half living.

The refugees continued to cross the sea and we tried to map out the violence, the peaks and the falls, through time. When does a war begin? Is it with a public declaration broadcast in the morning hours in the president's voice, or is it more private, watching your village burn down, your family slaughtered in their sleep by salaried soldiers?

On Sundays, our free days, we visited the clinic near the refugee camps. It was a single room meant to treat minor ailments, but over time nearly eighty-three refugees had died in that room; seventeen were born. Enough lives had passed through the rectangular space, only ten by twelve meters, that it might have been a small broken wing of a hospital.

We divided the day into one-hour shifts. The senior students watched over us as we diagnosed symptoms, proposed remedies. For the examinations, the youngest arrived first, colicky infants in their mothers' arms. We weighed and measured the poor things, as light as birds. In the room, lit by three bare bulbs, we were students pretending to be doctors. When we ran out of medication, we became apothecaries. Sitting in the hostel kitchen the night before, we mixed teaspoons of turmeric powder and crushed neem leaves. If we needed to harness the deep power of the mind, we handed plain capsules to those patients we could not help and told them how their pain would leave the body with one swallow. Looking at us, a bunch of adolescent girls, they drank up our words like we were the goddesses from their dreams who led them from the Island to these quiet shores. Belief might be the cure of the stronghearted, but it is the poison of the weak-minded. Our biochemistry professor, Mrs. Natarajan, was told she had six months to live because of a black mark they suspected was a tumor in her lungs. She told us about the black mark every day during class. Other professors advised her to take a leave of absence but she refused because she couldn't handle any more change. As she stuttered on and on about the black mark, we noticed how her posture shriveled, her mouth curved inward into a thin horizon. She died within three months of the doctor's prophecy. But during the autopsy, the doctor discovered that her lungs were tumor-free. All along she had been healthy.

With radical compassion, we knew how to empty ourselves in order to let someone else in and feel their pain so deeply until it was our own. Sitting in our rooms, we took turns, entangling our senses with our roommates'. One girl would prick her finger with the tip of a needle, until a clean drop of blood surfaced, while the other watched for the slightest of reactions, the stretch of a lip, the shudder of an eyelid as the hand trembled. The floor stained the dark color of nectar. We never inflicted the pain on our partners but watched as they lit matches against the soft, rubbery skin of their elbows, pulled out hair follicles from the crowns of their heads. The body was perishable, we learned again and again, and as we offered up pieces of our flesh, any shallow notions we had of beauty left us. Hunger had already carved us into crude stick figures. We were training like Pavlov's dogs, Leela would say, wetting a finger with saliva to show us that liquid of pleasure and hunger. As doctors, we should not fear the pain of others, we must embrace it, make the pain our own to find the remedy.

We felt the saliva in our mouths, the questions lingering unspoken in that pool of longing.

As relief during the drought, the government gave out color televisions to the poor, the star-hungry, anyone who wanted to plug in for nourishment. It was a campaign gesture by the newly elected chief minister, nicknamed the Artist, who had spent years in the film industry before taking up politics. She was called a visionary for wanting to bring technology to everyone, even those in far-off villages, hidden by sugar cane and water buffalo.

It was Pavitra who made the suggestion about the televisions. Quiet, with her hair cut right below her ears, she looked like the young boy her father had always wanted. None of us had ever questioned the senior girls. In our hunger, they gave their meals to us, and we ate and watched them, craving to know the fullness in their faces. When Pavitra raised her voice as we sat in the common area, she sounded far away, as if she were cupping her mouth trying to reach us through the distance. "How can we be vulnerable to the world if we have not seen it?" she said, and we felt a sudden yearning for everything childhood had denied us.

From the beginning, Avvaiyar was against it, but Baseema and Leela saw the televisions as perhaps only instruments for amusement, a way to make Madame Sarojini pay with her electricity bill. Or perhaps the older girls were curious themselves, secretly drawn to these idle comforts. There was an extravagance in our smiles as we measured the empty space in each of our rooms. *How many televisions can we fit in Saint Mary's Hostel?*

On Election Day, standing in lines that coiled through alleys, we waited under the thrill of the sun, the heat pressing against us and the tide of laughter, delirious and seductive, pushing us forward. The mandate was one television per family. Because our families lived in villages and cities hours away, we each became the last of our tribes, sole inhabitants. Altogether, sixty-three distinct clans with sixty-three identical televisions in a single building with only one spare generator.

We hid them in plain sight, with only a towel or an old shawl draped over their square shapes. The distinct fear of discovery kept us staring at a blank screen, brand new but still coated with a fine dust, our faces dull and somber in the reflection. In the quiet of our rooms, they stood as solid shrines, containers of unseen meaning.

Who would know what would arise from that void? Surely, the older girls anticipated only an artificial exchange, an amusing, short-lived diversion for the senses. How could they have known we would find the fixed borders of our egos and liberation all at once? Consumed with our own suffering, we would follow a path of fire that would lead us to that secret hatch door we had longed for all these years.

On a Saturday evening, hours before curfew, we heard the buzzing of hundreds of indecipherable voices spreading from the halls of the fourth-year students, and before long the whole building chattered in a low hum. Maybe it was only a matter of a minute before the power was cut or the circuit blew, but in our dark rooms we sensed within us a deeper, irrevocable pleasure, stirring under the surface.

We heard stories of families sitting cross-legged only an arm span away from the screen. Empty-bellied, they savored each image, not blinking once in case they missed an advertisement for Detox soap or fairness cream, the sweet-smiling lady waving at them to buy Shivani biscuits that they could not afford. Facing the bright square window to another life, they could fall asleep, full of their desire.

Because we did not want to raise suspicion, we arranged a schedule with twenty-two-minute intervals where we could each watch separately from our own television. All over town televisions blazed twenty-four hours a day, but we hungered for our own specific allotment, the sacred portion carved out especially for us, where we could lie half naked in our rooms and memorize those oversweet, overacted lines, or chronicle the news stories according to their distance from us. Some evenings we blindfolded each other, reenacting an old episode or news event, forgetting where and who we were. Sometimes we were men and we slapped our partners or tugged at their clothes suggestively to reveal soft bodies. Or we were the young Muslim teenagers shot by the police, and unlike their actual, quiet, unknowing deaths, we died elaborately, arms waving, necks arched to the heavens, as we swore and cursed the officials and their descendants. Throughout the day or night, there was always at least a single television on and this way we felt nothing was missed, that someone had kept watch while we were away, as if collectively we were sixty-three pieces of the same being.

Avvaiyar was the only one who refused to collect a television. She said it would make us suffer more, and we didn't believe her. It was simply a projection of images, we assured her, naming the function of the machine in our most clinical voices. Child's play, really, nothing more than shadow puppets prancing around a lantern.

"What then is reality?" she asked, and left us to our thoughts as she headed to the library. She had named herself after the ancient Tamil poetess, most likely to avoid any allusion to her family's wealth or high caste. Her father was the owner of a popular brand of textiles, his surname often projected on billboards and on the television, especially in the late afternoons. The name Avvaiyar connoted no caste, no age, and no singularity. In all of the images of the poetess, she was depicted as an old woman, gray-haired with a walking stick. We were to forget she was young, drinking kallu with a curse between her lips. Young women were not allowed to be wise. Our Avvaiyar was slender, her hair never plaited. Dressed all in white, a virgin widow who never married, she carried the burden of multiple lives, remembering the past with the clarity that belied her age.

In the library almost all the books were in English except for two ancient Tamil palm-leaf manuscripts preserved in a glass shelf, the etchings faded, nearly indecipherable. From Avvaiyar, we knew how the British burned the palm-leaf manuscripts to warm their horses, how the brigade of General Van Goens lit their tobacco with them. Our own ancestors let the manuscripts rot in dark places, mashed the literature into pulp. Avvaiyar spoke to us mostly in pure Tamil and we wondered every so often if she was only playing a character. Having lost all sense of self, she was open to becoming anyone. Like Dheeran Chinnamalai, who fought the British so valiantly that the generals wanted to spare his life if he would prostrate himself and serve the British Crown, but he refused and so hanged from the gallows. We didn't remember the local kings, but we could tell you stories of Babur and Akbar, the Mughal emperors we read about year after year in our textbooks though they never ruled our state. Remember, she'd tell us, British soldiers, the color of moon wax, first landed on our southern coastline. Valiant death awaited us too.

Besides history, we were forgetting the origins of our words. Avvaiyar reminded us, pulled apart the collage of images. *The-Mill-of-Words* meant *Dictionary*. *Letting-Go-of-the-Hand* was *Give up*. *Distant-Scene* was *Television*.

We tried to remember it was only a Distant-Scene as we shared with one another what we had watched at all hours of the day. Ten car crashes on Monday. Two floods in South America on Tuesday. The oldest man in the world passed away on Wednesday. On Thursday, Aboriginal land in Australia was retaken. Friday, a heat wave killed six people in Portugal. On Saturday, the peregrine falcon was officially removed from the endangered species list. Sunday, five trekkers died attempting to climb Mount Everest.

We wished we could see others with the clarity of a television serial. The story already written. And like faithful devotees, we followed the characters through betrayal, love, revenge, knowing them in ways they could not conceive. We were like fruit flies, worried over them, sucking at the invisible pollen of their being. During quiet moments of their private heartbreak, we were sobbing, rubbing our eyes over some untrue event. The electric current ran across towns, cities, countries, buzzing with a kinetic energy we wanted to harness.

The television was an unblinking, blind eye, an ever-changing box of images. And we controlled it. The channel and volume buttons fit neatly into the space of our fingertips, and we felt then, so keenly, the minute, potent force of our own will and indecision. With only a single bulb in our rooms, the televisions brightened our space, washing us with light in the middle of the evening. The images on the screen carried a vitality, an almost translucent glow. When we saw the image of a chair, somehow an actual chair looked plain, dulled by reality. Lifeless. Of course, none of us expected to speak to our furniture, but we were aware of a slight shift in our bearings. Even after we turned off the television, our eyes kept returning to the blank screen, wondering what we were missing, as if our everyday lives had become more muted.

n Sal's home you turn into your silent uncle. Eat one stale cookie after another. Sal apologizes for not having anything else, and the thought of her mother buying them before she died makes you feel slightly ill. Sal wears her father's Green4 jumpsuit, the lightning bolt emblazoned on the front pocket. When she catches you staring, she says she always thought he would die from his work, inhaling those noxious fumes that promised thick grass and edible food.

She shrugs and wraps her arms around her knees. *I have ended up being wrong about so many things. I should be the last person to make predictions.*

You have avoided looking at her. Instead, you eye the pistachio-colored walls, still remarkably ugly, and the furniture unmoved but worn with stains—it all matches the miniature version you've kept unknowingly in your mind, except she's no longer the girl you first met when you were eleven, and in the near decade she's been out of your life, your cells have shed and regenerated. When she finally catches your gaze, you see you're both different people. Strangers on a molecular level.

Rosalyn asks to see her art, and she leads the both of you to the basement. On the wall is a line from Grace Lee Boggs: *You don't choose the time you live in, but you do choose who you want to be, and you do choose how you want to think.*

You scribbled those words with her on her fourteenth birthday. She doesn't mention it, so you don't either. You're a little surprised her parents didn't paint over it with the pistachio color. It feels like you're seeing cave drawings from a prehistoric time. With each step, you sink deeper into another stratum of extinction.

Sal shows a door she plans to paint with the statistics of data-related deaths. People will open the door while wearing their virtual eye stamps and enter another galaxy of existence. She's still in the conceptual stage. It's for her first solo exhibition.

Besides the sofa bed, everything has been pushed to the corner of the room, letting Sal's work consume the space. On her desk, you find a page ripped from an artist anthology. It's about T. L. Baddin, who created a maze of emotions, where participants moved across a spectrum of feeling from shame to joy with a combination of sensory activators. The work is described as an *overwhelming sublimation.*

Against the wall, there is a series of paintings of the female figure trapped inside various mundane objects like teacups and knives. They almost look like still lifes, but you notice a human flourish: the edges of the papers are ripped, and the red borders have a bloody depth. They are labeled Judith #1, Judith #2, Judith #3, and so on. There are fifteen of them.

You really have it in for Judith, Rosalyn says.

Oh yeah.

Is she a real person?

Well, my partner, maybe ex-partner, not sure.

Is she an artist?

No.

You stack paint cans into a pyramid and find a polyester sheet to protect the carpet. In the corner you hear laughter, Sal and Rosalyn whispering together, eyeing you.

You open your mother's wardrobe full of books instead of clothes. You pick one with a thick red spine titled *Angkor: Saving the Ruins* and flip through it. After you finish, you pick another, this time a novel, W.E.B. Du Bois's *Dark Princess*, and you read the first fifty pages of the romance between an aspiring black doctor from Virginia and a purple-haired princess from India. Together on a transnational journey, they struggle to end the domination of Western nations, upend capitalism and colonial rule.

Without much effort, evening approaches and the stack of books stands like a watchtower. Moonlight shimmers into the gutted wardrobe. You reach inside and touch nothing but wood and your world.

Writing is another way of fasting. You can't eat or talk or listen to anyone. You're silent and alone but in conversation with a group of girls: *Why is your syntax so elliptical? Does nothing ever end? Is there a single author? Is this a testimony, a final note, written to no one, everyone? Do you think I'm misin-*

*terpreting your words, making them more my own? Do you even
want to be saved from obscurity?*

You call Socrates, but he doesn't respond, and out of a
certain desperation you call Rosalyn and then Aunt Zee;
Bobby is deep in some forest studying elephants. When no
one picks up, you try Uncle Roy, who answers, you think,
but you're not sure. You breathe into the phone, until you
hear something like life on the other end.

At college you worked at a suicide prevention center. It
looked pretty bleak, with linoleum floors and fluorescent
light that jaundiced your skin. On your team there was
Grumpy, Dopey, Bashful, Sleepy, and Happy. The names
didn't fit. You were nicknamed Sleepy because you mostly did
night shifts and slept in the day. Your face didn't show it, and
you sustained yourself with frequent naps during the week.

The building was old, from the early 2000s. A labyrinth
of cubicles that let everyone squirrel away. The conversations were recorded, and the phones were outdated so you
didn't have the option to video call. Some people would
request to see a friendly face before they died. Mostly the
callers were lonely. One graduate student hadn't spoken
to a single live human for over a month and she was sus-
picious that you were an automated robot. *Prove you're human*, she said, and you recited poetry, told her about your
day and coursework. *That can all be programmed*, she said,
show me that you're really human. It was your first week, and
you wanted to transfer her to someone else but you needed
this job and didn't want to seem inept. Probably because of

your nerves, you just started hiccuping and apologizing, *I'm sorry*, and when the line went silent, you murmured, *Please be alive still*, dispensing an emotional entreaty, which went against protocol. But then, from the pits of a whale's belly, she emerged. *Thank you.* You weren't too sure if all the expulsions and stammering of your body made you any more human. She hung up and you hoped that was not the end for her. There were no follow-ups.

Your old coworker, the fifth dwarf, Happy, was fired after working at the center for two years. They deactivated his ID and didn't even let him collect his belongings. Everything was shipped to him. In an afternoon conference, the oversight board, which consisted of a woman in her eighties with a hearing aid and a fresh graduate with an eye patch, played the recordings, referred to as "The Love Chats." Over the course of a week of mandatory retraining, you listened to the ten-hour conversation between your coworker, Happy, and the young man, Caller #347, he was falling in love with. Caller #347, or David, said he planned to die that night. He had tidied his things and called his mother but she didn't respond, so he thought he would call here before he ended it all. His words were careful and slow like he was standing on the ledge of his voice. Happy stayed calm throughout the first half hour. He asked David about himself and the people in his life. Then, somewhere around the forty-five-minute marker, there was a shift. David described an incident when he was eight—he had tried to drown himself by sticking his head into a toilet bowl—and in the middle of the story, Happy's voice cracked as he said, *Oh no, you poor thing*, and he began laughing, and David said he was supposed to save him and not ridicule him. *Why do you keep thinking you're shit, sweetie?* Happy asked, and David returned the question: *Why do you keep listening to this shit?* Then they kept repeating *shit* to each other like it was the loveliest word. Happy was known for using endearments that might be deemed overly affectionate. It was his style, but even Happy knew he could stray only so far from protocol. Around eighty-seven minutes in, he snapped out of it, remembered he was in his cubicle and David was teetering over some black hole. *Can I call you tomorrow?* David asked, and Happy said, *Yes, please.*

That was how it started. He called at the same time and Happy made sure he was at the phone. It went on like that for over a week until the oversight board stepped in. David's number kept coming up in the logbook. A frequent caller was always tagged.

The pair of administrators paused the recording at certain sections to make sure everyone understood the breach in protocol.

Your voice was in my dreams last night.

Were you trying to make it shut up?

It helped me sleep.

I bored you that much.

Not in the least.

Mr. Eye Patch stopped the recording and wrote on the board, *FLIRTING*, and then crossed it out. *Think of how many people who weren't helped because of this*, he said. *You need to be aware.* It was like that for the rest of the retraining. As much as you wanted to block the administrators out, you wondered if they possessed a keener sense, beyond hearing or sight, that you couldn't access. Even Happy didn't seem to know he was in love when they dismissed him. And it almost felt unethical to dissect feelings that someone didn't realize they possessed. Maybe nothing would have come of those feelings. You always knew the conversations were recorded and no longer belonged to you, and maybe that was true for everything, all your actions, words, purchases.

The day after Happy was fired, David called and asked to talk to Happy. When they said Happy no longer worked at the center, David asked for a personal phone number, which they refused to give him. He hung up, never called back. You wonder if, after all this, he felt like dying out of love.

Whenever you have a new project at work, you name it. Usually, the name comes quite naturally, you'll hear a word in passing or while reading the news something will catch your attention. It's a ritual you started from your first day and provides, you think, a physical anchoring to an assignment. Today you scan a story about a man living on a houseboat on the Hudson in preparation for the city turning into Atlantis.

For your lunch hour you slip off your shoes, sit cross-legged in your chair, and eat a spicy eggplant sandwich. You're in a partial state of meditation: closing your eyes, chewing, and waiting for the perfect word to drop in. From this emptiness, a voice asks, *Do you mind if I join you?*

It's Ricky, his hand already pulling over a chair. He brought with him a greasy slice of pizza he must have picked up outside the building.

I can't seem to prepare myself for the future, he says, and takes a bite. His skin is slightly pale and erased. Because he doesn't look well, you momentarily forget yourself, the self-consciousness you normally would have felt by the intrusion. You hand over a commiseration chocolate, gifted from one of your coworkers, and he eats it right away, telling you it has raw, floral undertones. Like bee vomit.

Nearby you sense Breanna watching the two of you, tucking away this information for safekeeping. She once mentioned the bareness of Ricky's desk—no pictures or extraneous things—and then his overt disregard for his colleagues, the failure to engage in normal human chatter like, *Hello, how are you, your hair is wet, did it rain, the weather is unpredictable, let's talk about what's outside of us because we can't talk about what's inside.* She shook her head. *I wouldn't trust him. He's not planning to stick around long.*

Ricky tells you about his past gig: he trained a specialized AI program at a research hospital to analyze images from medical scans to identify malignant cells. It wasn't so hard to mislead, he admits. A slight alteration of an image led to dramatically different results.

The real difference between machine error and human error, he says, *is that no one gets in trouble when AI makes a mistake.*

The image of Mr. and Mrs. Ahmed blinks in your mind, and you resume eating your sandwich. The vegetables taste charred and rubbery. Lately you've heard more jokes about the meaning of AI—Appearing Intelligent, Artfully Idiotic, Archangel Incarnate—usually followed by a tentative, knowing gasp of laughter as if renaming something made it more manageable. How else to survive the great, invisible forces pulling everyone closer into this claw of convenience and efficiency? You pause and stare at your half-eaten sandwich.

Ricky touches your arm, maybe sensing your thoughts. He points at the news article you pulled up and tells you he wouldn't mind living on Atlantis because he likes swimming. You shake your head and tell him you were looking for a name, and this must intrigue him because he nods like he understands, and you go on to explain the new assignment without giving away too many details except calling it *strange* and *alarming*. He leans back, thrumming his fingers against his chin as you wait in anticipation.

Ah, he says, and pauses for suspense. *How about Bogey?*

Bogey?

Like the Bogeyman. I think every culture has a variation of that childhood monster.

You test the word out loud, and it morphs on your tongue into *booger,* sounding somewhat childish, disgusting, and cute.

It has a ring to it, you say, and he nods, summoning the creature with three incantations: *Bogey, Bogey, Bogey.*

The name doesn't change anything, but somehow it makes you feel better.

Downtown at the gallery space, you read the wall text twice: *T. L. Baddin resurrects the ghosts of all the individuals who impressed their bodies against these objects, capturing different states of being—sitting, lying, sleeping, fucking.*

A cremated table fills the seats of a couch. A cutting

board transforms into a desk. A door lies horizontally as a table, fitted with light bulbs. You spend an hour peering into cracked open chairs and metallic frames of beds.

Sal walks the perimeter with artist friends who judge the pieces they pass with eye rolls and sharp exhales. In a few weeks everything will be cleared out for Sal's solo exhibition, but right now they must imagine into a space still cluttered with someone else's vision. You stare at a lamp converted into a talking chair and almost give up. Rosalyn was also invited to ruminate on art, but instead she's lying on a couch, miles away, in a coffin-like stillness as she prays for a miracle: for the clinical trial of the memory drug to proceed without further delays. You had not been aware that they were already testing on humans.

This one should be called A Scene of a Crime, Maurice says, looking up at the albino couch suspended from the ceiling, pierced with metal blades, titled *Ahab's White Whale*.

He moves toward you, balancing his weight on one leg. He wears a tie as a belt and his skin as a shirt, printed with all kinds of ink designs. He reveals to you that he's broke, surviving off packaged noodles and his ex-girlfriend's pity, but in the same breath he says there are college courses designed around his installation pieces, students send him fan mail, asking for career advice and remedies for their disappointed parents. He puts an arm around your shoulder like an old friend and says, *Sal's show is going to be fuckin' brilliant*, but the way his mouth twists, eyes glaze over, makes you think he's feeling something else.

Some people are really lucky, he says into the distance, where Sal and Eric measure a wall with their bodies.

Maurice has known Sal since college, right when the two of you lost touch. According to him, she smoked more than she ate, lived off any stray praise, and managed to conjure artistic value in her blackout vomit projections. He calls those her glory days and squeezes your shoulder tightly, and you feel a pulse of energy run though you like the sudden flickering of lights on a night road, filled with nothing but promise.

Maurice pulls his arm away and rolls his eyes at the exhibit. In the center of the room, he stands right below the albino couch as if planning his future death.

Ladies and gentlemen, he shouts, *do you think an artist should milk every experience for art?*

No one responds. From the other side of the room, Sal and Eric turn their heads.

He begins to clap as he moves toward them and when he's only an arm's length away, he says: *Are you truly processing these deaths? Or just capitalizing off them? Wouldn't it have been more tragic if that toddler did die?*

By the time you find Sal, she's squatting on the curb and smoking. The air smells of chlorine. You sit beside her, your knee bumping against hers. She's taller but seated side by side you can't really tell.

Are you okay?

She nods and blows clouds, you breathe in the leftovers. The sky darkens and the street swells with people.

When you return home, Rosalyn is watching a particularly disturbing episode of *Soldiers' Diaries.* A blond soldier named Cherry chews gum as she talks to the camera. She never uses the word *torture*, only *tactic*, even when producers question her again and again in the span of the episode. The viewers are never allowed into the interrogation room, but Cherry speaks freely about it as she reclines in a chair. Her last case took four hours. *If you're lucky, you can get them with just a lap dance*, she says, *make them feel enough guilt to start chatting.*

The producer persists on the line of torture and she says, *Look, if there is no visible mark on the body, then there is no violence being committed.*

The episode cuts to follow a female translator who assists in Cherry's interrogations. She doesn't actually seduce any of the prisoners, only communicates the threats and other things. Like after stripping one of the prisoners, she was told to tell him his cock was the size of a baby's pinkie. She felt uncomfortable, but everything in a stabilization zone is disorienting. *People are blowing themselves up, schools are being bombed, nothing makes sense*, she says. *Who am I to say if a man should be stripped and made to crawl around like a dog?* On one difficult case, Cherry reached into her underwear and smeared fake menstrual blood on the prisoner. Through secondhand reports, the audience is told this works extremely well.

Two female soldiers, Michaela and Sandy, listen to taunts from their male comrades as they play a game of table tennis. They don't visibly seem to mind the hollering and continue their conversation uninterrupted as if no one is calling out and asking them about the wetness of their pussies. They seem bothered only when asked directly by the producers about the abuse they face in the military.

The episode ends with Cherry making a fruit pie. It's for the mother of one of the prisoners. She wears a frilly apron and curtsies for the camera. She sucks on a fig and turns to the producer, who continues on about torture.

Do I look like a threat to you? she says, licking some of the filling.

Rosalyn turns off the TV and raises her head to take a sip of her beer. On the coffee table is a knife your mother said belonged to a distant relative of Sonny Rollins. Close up, the blade looks cheap, the kind of thing you could lose in someone's belly and no one would care.

If the drug doesn't pass the study, you say, *it wouldn't be the first time that happened, right?*

Rosalyn shrugs and then lets out the mousiest burp. She cups the air around her. *When his wife came to the lab, she was so pregnant. It looked like she'd eaten a five-year-old child. He didn't even mention it once, that he was going to have a baby.*

Her supervisor V. F. is fifteen years older, his body pillowed with flesh. Rosalyn had told you on more than one occasion that he was married, and you had always assumed she was making fun, silently asking, *Who would tie the knot with him?*

She sits up like she might take the knife and stab the couch. Instead she finishes off her beer and peers into the depths of it, her disappointment poised in plain sight.

Socrates calls you back and says he's glad to speak to a grown adult who is not related to him, and you notice he's wearing a clean button-down shirt without a trace of vomit. In the background, the baby wails and he sighs, clearing out the air.

Adults are not as good at vocalizing their needs, he says, and goes on to tell you that his grown daughter is still in bed sleeping. She is often asleep when you call. It has been a few months since her husband abandoned her. Only once did she pop up on the screen. At first you thought it was Socrates's dead wife, from the dewy eyes and shriveled face. She waved at you with a half-open palm.

He asks you about the manuscript. He can tell you're working diligently on it because you've opened multiple dimensions in the text, sometimes writing a single sentence six different ways, leaving him no choice but to behead them as he plunges onward.

Don't you want to be kinder to an old man forced to raise a baby?

You shake your head. *I'm afraid of misinterpreting them.*

It's a risk every translator takes, which some readers take for granted, he says, and pauses to readjust his voice. *Well, most readers are not even aware of the existence of the translator, and to be fair, the mark of a good translation is for this crossing between languages to feel seamless. You should never think you're reading a translation.*

The last translated book you read was a Japanese tale from the perspective of an earthworm. It was unexpectedly moving, and, of course, bizarre, but only on your second read did you run into the translator's note, confined to one page, at the beginning of the book. She stated that the original story possessed enough humor to kill a horse but admittedly she could not match the charismatic tone. It was a succinct apology, given preemptively.

Self-doubt so plainspokenly delivered, you could see the flesh of it. You sat still as a rush of heat passed through you. A wind of embarrassment mixed with something coarse. The note was unnecessary. She should have stood by her words irrevocably, rejecting the impulse of vulnerability that critics would surely associate with her sex. Wiping your eyes, you reread the book and the text carried a new aura, her presence lightly hovering, a hand over her mouth concealing a laugh. It struck you how every translation was born out of a relationship, in some cases between the dead and the living.

Socrates waits for your face to fill up his screen with your full attention. *Translations are essentially approximations of the original. Certainly, I've read translations that reinvent the original text in astounding ways that go above and beyond the source material. But that's not the purpose of a translation and neither is pure fidelity.* He leans in closer, so you can see only a left eye and the side of a nostril. *In each translation exists a sliver of space for another book, everything lost in the migration, and only in very good translations do you feel this unknowable texture beyond the realm of words.*

You nod, hoping for him to continue, but he doesn't, and meaning is suspended somewhere between countries. He disappears and you can make out the corner of the sky through the window, a triangle of slate.

After a few moments, he begins speaking though you still can't see him. He reads out loud headlines from the morning news like "Peace Missiles Fight Terror" and "Learning to Survive through Protozoa" and says how grim everything looks but that, reading your translation, the girls stretching a few nuts to last a day, he's reminded of the possibility for the world to sustain us, and as you try to interject about the ending, his mind has drifted elsewhere, absorbed in the tumult of a diaper emergency.

What happens when the translator's note becomes larger than the translation: Does it turn parasitic? Do you become too aware of the human behind it?

Underneath the manuscript are your jumbled feelings. Two paragraphs written under severe self-doubt sit next to a few days of loneliness, which bump into a full page of inebriation. No one will know, you also struggle to remember. That your mother is dead.

On your desk you find accessories from IntraVan. Stress balls that change colors when squeezed. The company motto stitched along the circumference: VANGUARDS OF INNOVATION. There are also T-shirts with a matching logo. The only person wearing the T-shirt is Petrov.

You begin like you normally do, stemming and chunking the data. You start off with children's books with simple grammar patterns like *Girl feeds ducks* and *Man smiles at child*. You're no longer agitated by the fact that an epoch of training runs so quickly you can't even blink before it's done. Petrov called it unique for a reason, and maybe this is the reason: Bogey's a voracious eater. Its neural networks can be trained for both speech and visual capabilities. In the bathroom you record yourself singing a lullaby and upload it along with an archive of nursery rhymes. To teach it to see the world, you start feeding the tagged visual images from the training archives—everything from a box to a tree. In the test environment, you analyze some results. It has identified a chair as a dog and a truck as a whale, and the latter you partly understand.

By lunch, when Ricky shows up, you're exhausted.

How's our monster doing?

Delightfully bad.

That's the most we can hope for. He combs his hair with his fingers. Near the back of his neck sprouts a spider-shaped birthmark. When he asks you to go out for a drink after work, you stare at it like it's a sign.

Your mother liked the term *white noise* because it revealed what might go unnoticed, the oppressive possibilities of sound. In the crowded bar you must sit very close to Ricky to hear what he's saying. He has ordered a bacon cheeseburger with fries, a meal with a high carbon index. As you watch him eat, the saliva collects in your mouth. You, the vegetarian, don't have much moral high ground. You refrain from meat to reduce your carbon score to save money, not the planet. While you follow the rules, Ricky breaks them, intentionally exceeding his monthly limit and accumulating so many fines that you're surprised he still has credit. He's like your mother in that way.

After three low-impact beers, you are pleasantly buzzed.

If the government really cared about our carbon score it would tell us to reduce the number of children we have, but it doesn't, because all it cares about is surveillance. Ricky licks the grease on his lips. *What do you think the government is really doing with our carbon score monitoring data?*

You look at him thoughtfully. *I suppose they are training an AI with our CSM data so one day it will rule us all and know whether we prefer American cheese or Swiss.*

Just wait, he says, and wipes his mouth. He is improbably skinny for his level of consumption, so you sometimes wonder if he has a tapeworm or a wormhole leading all his excess calories to another Ricky living through a famine. At times you feel like he is hiding away, deep inside a bunker, waiting for the end of the world, and there is no room for anyone else.

We like to give a human's fate to an AI to adjudicate because it seems fairer, he says, *but really, inside the machine is a tiny, flawed alien who we think is a god that we can't possibly begin to comprehend.*

Like humans are easy to comprehend?

He grins and takes a sip of his beer. *I know who you really are.*

Who I am?

You're one of those AI whisperers, aren't you?

He moves closer on the bench, and you smell the distinct woody fragrance of his cologne, probably AI designed.

I saw how you adjusted the optimization algorithm for the Missing Persons program, matching voices that have aged. Not many people have that kind of intuition, he says, and stretches his arms behind his head. *I'm a third-rate coder but I'm fine with that. Do you remember that saying—success narrows, failure frees? I think I must have taken it to heart at an early age. I have tried so many things, even studied fermentation for a while. I'm not afraid to be bad at something. When you become successful, you stay in the small realm of your talent and never venture out.*

You sip on your beer. *Are you saying successful people are like narrow AIs that can only perform one specialized task?*

Please don't go comparing AI to humans. It never works. I would love for the day to come when androids exist and humans lose all sense of purpose, but right now a general AI can't even compete with a toddler.

So you aren't afraid of the singularity?

He grabs a few peanuts from the bowl and cracks them. *Am I afraid of robots ruling over us? Well, there's colonialism and slavery, so I think most of the world already knows what it's like to be ruled over.*

You nod and raise a glass. You're on your fifth drink now, you think. Both of you have lost count. In the dimly lit room, everything begins to lose objectivity. Hands, glasses, tables, spoons blend together. Ricky's head has the pleasing shape of a winter melon.

The form transforms but the essence remains, you say.

He crushes a peanut shell in his fist, and you inspect the ashy fragments as if they contain a secret of existence. Soon enough you're telling him about the translation, radical compassion, and a girl named Yaadra. As he listens, he stretches his head back and closes his eyes. They stay closed even after you finish speaking. Your mother used to play

the keyboard with a dark cloth bandaged over her eyes because she was sharpening her senses. It was the first time
you thought deprivation could be a strength. When your
mother left on her trips, you imagined she was training you
for this moment, this future departure. Telling you to close
your eyes, find her without sight.

You first read this manuscript in college, right? he says, flick-
ing his eyes open. *What do you think attracted you then?*

*I don't know. I was feeling lost. I even started working at a
suicide prevention center, trying to get out of my own head. The
manuscript just happened to float along at the right time.*

Ricky props his head on his hand and stares at you side-
ways like he can see through your thoughts.

The root word of compassion *means suffering, there's no es-
caping it,* he says, and then empties his drink. *I had my first
dream in four years last night.*

Are you sure you haven't been dreaming?

He looks amused. *I'm positive.*

*Maybe you are just one of those people who can't remember
their dreams.*

No, I'm certain I have dreamed of nothing for a while.

Did something traumatic happen four years ago?

He shakes his head. *Nothing very unusual. I broke up with a
girl I was seeing, my brother's wife had a baby, and my childhood
dog died.*

That might be it.

Dog dying?

*The past disappearing, and your brother moving toward the
future while you're not able to manage the present.*

Because of the breakup?

You nod. *You might have liked her more than you thought.*

That's a theory, he says, and closes his eyes. *I can't even remember what she looks like. It's as if someone scratched out her face in a picture.*

Do you keep in touch with her?

She left to live abroad soon after we broke up and she was married for a year and then divorced. We don't have much contact, but she still sends occasional Christmas cards to my parents. She was younger than me and very smart. I'm not sure if I deserved her.

Across from you, two people make out discreetly, the red light from the exit sign flickering across their faces.

Ricky leans back, staring at the ceiling. *After a while I think it's cruel to be with someone you don't love as much as they love you, or at least about the same amount.* He picks up his empty glass. *There is a thrill in being desired. For someone to hand over the keys to their well-being and for you to walk freely in and out as you please, throwing your legs on their weaknesses, criticizing their choices, them keeping quiet through it all as you linger by the doorway with the promise of staying.*

What did you dream last night?

He covers his face with a hand. *I don't think I can tell you.*

Why not? Was it a sexual fantasy?

That would be more normal, he says. *I can't remember the details, only this ridiculous thirst when I woke up. I drank seven glasses of pineapple juice and then sat in a patch of sunlight. I don't know how to say this, but I just craved yellow.*

Was it a nightmare?

I pissed in my bed. I haven't done that since I was five.

Piss is yellow, you offer, *well, most of the time.*

He smiles and you sense yourself mirroring his face. There's something elemental to his presence like water moving between states. Any coldness, you think, is a means of conserving energy. At the end of the night, you wish him good dreams, and when you return home, you reach under the bed for your mother's tapes.

In Dream #98, Philippa Schuyler appears. From what you recall, she was her parents' experiment. Their solution to the race problem in 1932. Josephine Cogdell, a white Texan journalist, and George Samuel Schuyler, a black writer from Providence, were testing the conditions of creating a model human being. From the looks of it, they succeeded. At age four, she was said to have an IQ of 180. By then she had penned musical compositions, at an earlier age than Mozart. At fourteen, she debuted with the New York Philharmonic Orchestra. And besides her playing, newspapers remarked on how attractive she was—"the right amount of mixing"—and how Chopin seemed to be "the master" best suited for her. She held titles like Dame of the Order of Honor and Merit of Haiti and Decorated with the Order of the Lion of Judah of Ethiopia.

She was a Leo. She died at the age of thirty-five on a helicopter in Vietnam, trying to save some orphans.

Like Josephine Schuyler, your mother ate raw foods, even slabs of steak, the year of her pregnancy, and she watched carefully for a trace of precocity in you that never fully arrived.

In the dream, Phillipa stands by the window. The curtains are drawn open. It's nearly midnight. *Play me something*, your mother says, and they sit side by side, the perfect mother and daughter.

The man in the living room smells of piss and his feet are bandaged with plastic foam, glowing in the morning light. On closer inspection, you notice he's wearing a jacket with no zipper. Some of his teeth are missing. Wisps of corn-husk hair quickly receding. And even under the cake of city grime, you can tell he's white. The TV blubbering next to him.

You grab an empty bottle from the kitchen counter by the neck and feel your mind working out an algorithm. Threat or no threat. You can see his ribs, his whole skeleton rising to the surface. He seems to be staring down at the globs of his hands, but maybe he's sleeping. He doesn't move.

From the bathroom, Rosalyn grabs you by the arm. *You know him*, she says. *This is Cheeze.*

You look hard at this man, supposedly named Cheeze, who you supposedly know.

He's from Soldiers' Diaries *and has nowhere to stay.*

You watch him, waiting for something to open up inside you, and then he turns and you see his sad eyes, a deep synthetic blue. It's him.

The government released a statement that effectively suspended any processing of refugees for the indefinite future. "It's a privilege to exist on our soil," our chief minister said. Since the refugees were not citizens and had no voting power, they were not given televisions, but because we were nearing the beginning of the international cricket season, cricket bats and balls were distributed to anyone who appeared to be under the age of seventeen. Years ago the country's prime minister was assassinated by someone who could have been a refugee, and in response, the chief minister had designated all refugees as potential criminals and spearheaded a campaign to paint the national flag on everything, even supposedly tattooing it on her upper bicep, discreetly hidden underneath her blouse, to show her devotion.

She was the mother of us all, a patron saint.

Madame Sarojini added a photograph of the chief minister to the hallway and told us we were lucky to be ruled over by a woman respected by all men (no mention of the sickly and disabled, who must writhe on the floor to genuflect).

"One of you might even grow up to become chief minister

of the state," Madame Sarojini announced, staring at our skinny, bone-shriveled faces. She had forgotten that our chief minister was first a heroine on the cinema screen, gyrating across the hearts of everyday people who dreamed of the Swiss Alps and everlasting love that could survive a truck rolling off a bridge or a fight with ten gangsters.

We too longed for such excitement. Outside the tedium of the classroom, we watched the boys dressed in their fitness clothing, laughing and cursing as they played cricket in the late afternoon. In between pitches and runs they turned to us, flexing their muscles and whistling at us, *Girl, look at this*. The sight of their bodies in motion, the revelation of muscles, kept us returning to the matches. We hadn't known that Govind, sitting quiet in class, arms crossed, his face shrouded behind a textbook, was the fastest boy in school. The possibility of hidden abilities electrified our imagination, and we watched attentively, peeling back layers of each individual, until finally what we saw were a bunch of English boys prancing around the field with milk cream mustaches.

We knew of no sport besides cricket, and we wondered when we got into this practice of forgetting. Our fascination with cricket was a colonial instinct, as Avvaiyar would say, and we counted runs with the precision of a government official reporting to the Queen. If they were toad lickers, we would have followed their custom, hallucinating in the back seat of a rickshaw as we drove into the sea.

During our breaks, we took the boys' cricket bats and used the wickets as bases in the fashion of American baseball. We had watched it on television, first on a Tuesday at nine in the evening. Instead of a straight line, the court was diamond-shaped, and some of the players had rotund bellies. Nine players on each team. They spat and beat the ground with a thick, round wooden stick. It was like cricket but not, and we loved it.

Gloveless, we caught the ball with our bare hands, letting it crack open our skin. Calluses bloomed from our fingertips. Our flesh formed a thick, protective layer.

We felt devious using the instruments of a British sport to play an American one. Winning was never a matter of points but an exercise of our spirits. What did we know of the rules except three strikes and you're out, or the theatrical slide from one base to the other, fingertips outstretched to graze against the four corners of in and out, life and death?

To the boys, we appeared idiotic, players of a perverse cricket.

"This is why they shouldn't have a women's league," they said, but they kept watching us, alarmed and perhaps intrigued by our relentless bodies.

Unlike the stiff shape of us in class, on the field, our limbs flailed and contorted in unexpected and unflatteringly geometric ways. We'd fall with our asses pointed in the air, the crude formation of a triangle. Or in catching a ball, we'd arch our backs into parabolas, curls of pubic hair sprouting in the sunlight. Knees bent into diamonds and slim rectangles of girls sliding into home base, calves mossed with dark hair glistening.

On television, the women were clean and spotless with a fluorescent glow. No mustache fuzz, no pimples under the chin, and even their voices sounded like prepackaged biscuits.

These women had chubby faces, but not too chubby. They looked happy, probably because they had the right kind of chubbiness.

On menstruation week, Saint Mary's Hostel usually smelled of a copper womb. Our fertility was especially potent to Madame Sarojini, who at the age of fifty-eight was keenly aware of the impossibility of her own body producing children, and she sprayed the halls with the strong scent of hibiscus and lemongrass. "Bloody girls," she'd say under her breath as we passed, waving at her with our unclean hands. A layer of blood in the toilet reminded us we were baby-less beings. Relinquishing a godly power we did not fully understand, the creation of life. But after the drought, when we had little fat or blood to spare, it took the stray spotting in our underwear to recall our female bodies.

Leela kept a palm-sized notebook of quotes, which she called the Book of the Dead. Radical compassion had no hymn-book, no written text, but at the end of every lesson, Leela would open up to a page and recite a quote. Never-ending, it seemed, as she turned each page and another appeared. She did not register value distinctions between the thoughts, but Avvaiyar always left before she spoke. At first, we had assumed she had some prior obligation but night after night, her disapproval became quite clear through her absence. She did not want to be tainted by the words of Max Planck or Heidegger.

The evening when Baseema struggled to untangle a piece of red yarn to show how the chaos of thoughts in our minds

made us useless, Leela opened the book early and read the
words of Joseph Brodsky: "If there is any substitute for love, it's
memory. To memorize, then, is to restore intimacy."

She closed the book quickly and turned to Avvaiyar, who
was not prepared to meet her gaze, and in that moment, we
sensed an invisible piece of yarn between them, knotted and
fragile, as if by trying to unravel each other they would find
themselves. Later we would return to this moment of recognition as a silent declaration of both war and love. Doesn't every
rivalry possess the seed of an unconsummated love?

Avvaiyar straightened her face and proceeded to leave,
and Leela stood there watching her. After we all left, Radikha
rushed back to get her tiffin box and said she saw Leela leaning against the wall, two tear streaks along her cheek.

On the banister of the staircase near the second floor, there
were two names carved into the interior of the wood. When
you slid your hands against the rough curves, your fingertips
blushed. Nagaswary and Arun. Her name coiling around his.
She had left the school three years earlier after deciding she
did not want to study medicine. We heard about her because
she was the only student not to complete her training. As she
left, she had marked her name and a boy's, a lover, perhaps.
With her writing, she had stealthily let him inside the hostel
where he had not been allowed. In passing we unconsciously
rubbed against the pair, these unassuming relics of love. It
was foolish to search for eternity in external things, Leela had
told us. But after one girl cut her finger near the etching, the
stain left the peculiar feeling of life. Most of the time we kept

our hands to our sides and our eyes closed purposefully as we crossed the threshold to the next floor.

Tragic love stories like Romeo and Juliet, Bajirao and Mastani interested us simply for the intensity of longing. A kiss like a burst of flames. The thousand knives of heartbreak. We did not crave the beauty of the actresses on television, with their smooth, round faces and curvy hips, but we wanted what the body allowed, the sensation of being.

Watching television, we felt the ache in our mouths when the hero kissed the heroine, never on the lips, but somewhere far off like the pale palm of her hand. She held him there, sealing his lips, holding him still. At night when we slipped out of our clothes we examined our bodies, some still prepubescent with chests as flat as ironed linen. Anatomy had taught us the dual functionality of the body. A bird's cloaca provided both sexual pleasure and execratory relief. Tracing the rim of the inner ear with a wet tip of cotton left us delirious, with a momentary glimpse of the orgasmic. We feasted on our desires secretly, crumbs we held on to in the middle of the night when hunger kept us awake. Some of our older sisters had married early and wrote us letters filled with recipes for meals they could no longer cook because of the missing ingredients. Chicken Chettinad: *chicken (1.3 kg), 1 onion, sesame oil (2 tbsp), 2 tomatoes, ginger (10 g), garlic (5 g), 3 dried red chilis, cumin seeds (1 tsp), coriander seeds (1 tsp), fennel seeds (2 tsp), turmeric (1 tsp).* We chewed on the words until nothing remained.

Craving meant suffering. Made from equal parts of pain and pleasure, and like trained dogs we leaned in toward pain, held our own cheeks when our friend was slapped. It was pleasure that the older girls warned us against, said it would leave us with soft bellies.

We were becoming doctors. Soldiers of Salvation.

Remember.

At the clinic, Dhivya treated a young refugee who had wounded his leg during the war. He limped slightly to his right side, and out of some askew need for balance, he smiled too widely to the left, like he was stumbling on a private joke. He was missing his index finger on one hand, Dhivya told us, and now and then we'd catch her bending her own finger, making it disappear. He had lived in the camps for five months, arrived with his younger brother, the two of them making a living selling betel leaves.

The senior girl assigned for that hour fell ill, and she had not bothered to find a replacement. Of all the hour sessions, Dhivya had chosen the evening hour between seven and eight, for she must have known without knowing that they would meet. Unsupervised, she stretched out his limbs and he talked about the pain coiling up his leg and settling in his knee. Sitting down on the table, he reached her full height. She faced him, placed her hands on the sides of his face, and traced his pressure points, her eyes holding his. She would remember his bone structure, could re-create him with precision in her dreams. Everything too fine to shatter pieced together. Cheekbones constructed with the broken curves of porcelain teacups.

He was three years older than her. Vignesh Prakash with his nine fingers. She knew so little about him, no more than the betel leaf he offered her before he left. As she mourned a loss she couldn't name, we would tell her that he was no different from any other young man and she was not special either. But she searched for him tirelessly, with her palms out for stray facts, collecting what would neither nourish nor relieve. Just enough to keep living. She learned the police picked him up from the camp to question him, believed he was an ex–rebel fighter. He had enough injuries to convince them, and tucked inside the stitching of his cot they had found a dagger the length of his missing finger. A stack of Archie comics was also confiscated.

We told her she was not Dhivya. He was not Vignesh Prakash. There was no beginning and no ending.

Standing in the courtyard of Saint Mary's, we watched the boys pass by the gates in their almond-colored uniforms, their hands slapping the metal lightly as they whistled between laughs. The boys lingered, eyeing us through the rectangular spaces, their faces pressed so deeply against the bars that they seemed willing enough to break through their skulls to find a way inside. Often, they simply called out compliments on the shine of a braid, the flowers adorning our hair, the pattern of our uniforms. Looking at them, we felt interchangeable, our sorrow discreetly hidden as we turned away.

Radical compassion was beyond the realm of love, a state of consciousness where language lost meaning.

Though we longed to exist in that space beyond linear time, each morning we washed our faces and brushed our teeth, all these habits of the living. Enclosed in a classroom with the professor groaning, her hand scraping the board, we sat at the edge of our seats, losing oxygen, ready to faint.

Starvation had reoriented us. In one afternoon, eight students were gummed to the floor, but before they were carried off, Param sneezed, and the professor, watching the boy rub his nose, began to doubt the students' embrace of gravity. She instituted a two-finger ear-twisting truth test. The number of collapsars declined.

After class, before meeting the older girls for our lessons, we sometimes would lie in the courtyard, the dirt chalking up our skin, and we would pretend to be things connected to nature. We would finger the earth, plant seeds, sucking our mouths dry as spit trickled out.

We had read that a healthy human body was roughly sixty percent water, and we knew that after all these months under an unforgiving sun, we had forgotten our aqueous existence.

We felt more like the paper origami we folded in our breaks throughout the day. Thin brown squares susceptible to becoming anything. Waiting for the washroom, we would count our breaths with each crease, crafting animals we had never seen, pandas and tigers.

Over a few weeks we constructed in the common area a thousand-and-two sheet kingdom, an Eden, with water buffalo and three-toed sloths and winding rivers.

We tried to remember a time before our own, before the infestation of plastic bags, when we used to have forests, when nothing was wasted, when the only utensil needed was your own hand.

Avvaiyar called our activities childish and wasteful. One morning we found a stack of flattened paper on the television in the common area, our universe undone.

At night, during quiet hours, when we watched television

with the volume low, we closed our eyes and opened them to catch images in sustained blinks. A man stood by the doorway in one blink, and by the second blink he was clutching his chest, bent forward. The stories on television were often too ordered to lift us from the ordinary. We wanted time to move backward. A grown man turning into a baby. Or the unfathomable, a miniature woman swimming in a bowl of curd rice. Still, we couldn't look away, the black boxes emitting a force we had no name for. We knew that starlings, with their fragile bones, could feel the magnetic field of the earth, the force as thin as a needle guiding them north. Maybe we, too, sensed the invisible pull of far-off things.

Avvaiyar wanted to rid us of all these external distractions and staged a Tirumular Yogam, where we competed to reach beyond our minds, ascend levels of consciousness. We crossed our legs and fasted from dawn to sunset, focusing on our breathing. The goal was to exist without breathing at all, merge with death in the living form. Walking to class we often saw on the roadside shrubs growing from rotten trees. Green sprigs bloomed from dead roots. We struggled to be that leaf pushing through the decay to the other side. Deepti was the only one of us who was able to slow down her heartbeat and her breathing. Once every minute she inhaled. After the older girls disqualified each of us, only Deepti remained with her eyes closed and her head turned upward, the stem of her neck bright against the fluorescent light of the common area. We felt her energy pulsing within us. Passing by her, we would hold a hand by her face, unsure if she reached immortality, beyond the laws of time and death. But on the second day, with her forehead spotted with sweat, she simply fainted, falling forward on the grass-colored sheet. We woke her with a rag drenched with precious ice water, the liquid collecting in the cup of her collarbone. She could not remember her higher state and did not believe us when we told her how she stretched her breathing.

Deepti had lost both of her parents at a young age and we wondered if this gave her a natural affinity with the dead. Loss cut through reality like a knife. And that was why Siddhars who gave up everything, even the clothes on their backs, were rumored to have the ability to levitate a half meter above the ground and to control the movement of water. We wondered if we were capable of such miracles.

We heard that Leela moved into a higher consciousness through coupling. In her first year, it was said that Leela fell into a trance so deep her skin turned into a pale blue hue. It was said she could outdrink men and one evening earned almost a month's worth of tuition fees after she drank a whole bottle of whiskey without wincing, as if she had trained her body to process the liquor like water. Last week, after the celebrations for the chief minister's birthday, Leela brought a guest over to Saint Mary's. The girl was dressed in a plain green salwar with dark red leggings, a shawl covering the rim of her face. Bowing to Madame Sarojini in the front entranceway, she took small, deliberate steps up the stairway through the hall. Under the archway of Gibran's words, we saw the girl tip her head back as the shawl and tendrils of hair dropped to the ground. Leela embraced the short-haired figure by the mouth, her fingers clasping behind the crouched neck. Leela smoked long menthol cigarettes and we once believed this habit part of her alluring charm but really it was an excuse to linger outside, veiling her secret trysts. We could not imagine Leela in the earthly act of sex. She had once referred to men as vehicles to the road to enlightenment, and with her we knew intercourse would become a ritual, the union of the divine, where, at the height of pleasure, there must be withdrawal. The semen must reverse its flow for consciousness to fall apart. In her absence we searched her room for signs of her human condition, a wet patch on her sheets, strands of hair, any revelation to hint at the intimacy of deep release. We were startled by the nakedness of her room, plain white walls and an unadorned cabinet, with only the wire of the television sneaking from under the bed to disturb the order of things. We unplugged the television she had hidden behind the bedpost. She must have watched as she slept, the images flashing beneath eye level. Holding the tail of the television, we pulled it out from its dark lair and placed it in the center of the room like a dead thing we had killed. Part of us wanted to rid ourselves of these Distant-Scenes that left us craving more. As we stood above the television, we saw the reflections of our own faces, and we waited, our hands limp and aching, in anticipation of what was to come.

Cheeze was a secondary character in *Soldiers' Diaries*. He appeared only in a handful of episodes. Early on, viewers learn he's from Minnesota, grew up on a farm, and loves his dog Cookie. In episode fifteen, he spends a good five minutes picking at a scab on his arm. Near him, a twelve-year-old civilian boy nibbles on a Galaxy chocolate bar. It's not clear if Cheeze is speaking to the camera or to the boy. Cheeze talks about his dog Cookie, mainly. He is lonely and misses the smell of wet fur and grass when he and Cookie would run down the field and jump into the creek, waking the dragonflies. Besides this snippet from the episode, he mainly fades into the background of the main cast.

You look between the young Cheeze on the TV and the nutrition-less face staring at the ceiling. Years have passed since *Soldiers' Diaries* was released, even more since it was filmed.

It's him, Rosalyn says. *I'm sure.*

She found him on the Upper East Side on Park Avenue, asking for e-credit outside Plasme, a high-end recycled plastic clothing boutique for people who probably don't even have a credit limit. Because nothing Rosalyn says makes sense, you ask her to bring him to the grocery store down the block and after you say you're buying the man two premade sandwiches, his eyes are scanned. His name comes out as Dustin Creed, and you're relieved, looking at Rosalyn and then at the man formerly known as Cheeze.

Cheeze is not his real name, obviously, Rosalyn says, and shows you the list of names at the end of the show. *See? Dustin Creed.*

Outside, Cheeze huddles near the ground with his two premade sandwiches. His chest is exposed. It's slightly chilly.

We can't just take a semifamous houseless man back with us, you say. *That's not what you're supposed to do.*

Yes, we are supposed to just leave him on the sidewalk, where he can starve or be murdered.

There are thousands of houseless people in the city.

Remember, a few months back when you wandered the streets, space traveling or whatever, like you didn't even have a home?

Rosalyn, we are not bad people.

Radical compassion is just an idea, right?

Cheeze sleeps on the couch. He snores and reeks but for the most part he's quiet. For the first time in years, you sleep with the door locked.

Baseema lifts her red yarn, showing you the chaos of your mind. You head to work before Cheeze or Rosalyn wakes up. Alone in the office, the sky still murky, you fiddle with a sentence until it feels right: *Everyday life had become predict-*

*able, desolate, and in our search for transcendence, did we hope
to find refuge in a glowing box, where life was more visceral and
complete, by opening our eyes rather than closing them?*

As a patch of sunlight creeps into the hall, you walk over
to Ricky's desk and drop into his chair with your hands behind your head, humming to yourself. His space is sparse
with only a company stress ball you left during one of your
lunch breaks. You squeeze the ball, watch it change colors.
The emptiness stretches around you like a cocoon. You close
your eyes and spin. On the third revolution, you catch sight
of your own desk, and it looks overgrown, an accumulation
of untended years. One of the cabinets is slightly open,
stuffed with papers. Then there are rotting tangerine peels,
spoiled coffee in an MLC mug. Condolence flowers are
hunched and withered in the corner. For some reason you
have kept them.

Right now in your life there are no safe zones. A stranger
is lying on your couch at home and at your desk the inexplicable Bogey is waiting to be trained. Last night in your grog-
giness you made your way to the bathroom and suddenly a
dark shape appeared from a nightmare and said, *Hello, I'm
Minnesota Cheeze*, as you slammed the door shut.

What are you doing sitting over there?

Nothing, you say, shielding your eyes against the sun.

Breanna shakes her head and puts her things down. Un-
buttoning her thin jacket, she tells you how she found her
teenage son smearing a clear powder on his face like an ath-
lete greasing up in preparation for a game. Most of the time
he's simply sitting in his room, chatting and coding with
his friends. But this morning he seemed possessed, walking

over to her with a determination she had rarely seen as he reached for her, rubbing the powder on the corners of her eyes very delicately, like he was wiping away tears. He told her that changing a few pixels in an image was enough to fool an AI. Facial-recognition programs might think you're someone else. *Be careful, Mom.*

When your child is worried over your safety, you know you should be afraid, she says. *What if he joined some deranged underground hackers?*

Her usually braided hair is loose, and she gazes distantly out the window, forgetting her morning routine. She doesn't look like herself.

You ask her if she wants coffee, and she doesn't hear you. The air between the two of you has turned solid, nothing travels through it. Back at your desk, alone, you repeat, *We are not bad people*, and Bogey waits, full of potential, to be anything.

Even in the close quarters of the house, you avoid direct eye contact with him. What you catch are glimpses: a scar running along his left arm, a pus-filled trail; a black smudge on his neck, which could be a tattoo; chest hair turning red in the sunlight; an earlobe folded like the crease of a page; clear fingernails darkened around the rims in perpetual night; and an unassuming smile twisted into a knot.

A splash of pimples on your cheeks. Six on the right, seven on the left. There's an almost symmetry as you stare at the mirror. It's nothing lethal, but you blame him. His presence clogging up your pores. Your mother's house smells like a stranger.

Your body is only a reflection of your mind, Rosalyn says, and counts the small monuments. *Thirteen negative thoughts are being swept out.*

How long is he staying? Are you expecting him to become our third roommate? Our carbon score is turning excessive.

He's in mourning. We have to be understanding.

Who died?

Cookie. You know, his dog.

When you see Sal, you are overly self-conscious, your cheeks are warm. She's moving the furniture into the backyard, and you carry out an end table and a rocking chair. The grandfather clock is lugged between the two of you. After an hour of sweating through your clothes, you sit outside on a plump cushion resting under the roof of the sky. Your glass of juice is untouched and sweetened by two dead flies.

I'm going to sleep here from now on, while we have our visitor, you say, and stretch out your legs, suddenly aware of how little you have slept.

He moves in and you move out. Well, you know you're always welcome here.

She's staring at you, and you instinctively look away. Sometimes, you have this feeling of a sensory overload. If you hear her, you can't see her. If you touch her, then silence.

I'm actually surprised your mother didn't house someone like this, she says. *She had her limits, I suppose.*

Sal is wearing her mother's nightdress, the other day you saw her walking in her father's suit, playing dress-up, and you almost forgot they are dead. Unlike you, who have preserved your mother's things in the thick, stinking formaldehyde of memory, Sal has let them loose into the elements. Her mother's favorite chair springs forth on a patch of weeds.

It doesn't feel like home without them, she says. *What's the point of keeping these things?*

I don't plan to leave.

Sal yawns like her mother used to when she was tired of the two of you lying. *But look who's running away from home.*

It happens so quickly, a gesture pulling you through time. Forgetting to take a breath, you're back in adolescence, underwater. A crow on the grandfather clock watches you closely.

Some observations: Cheeze likes to eat toast with sunflower butter like Rosalyn. He likes to belt out lyrics by the pop group Mano and Musket. He likes to eat packets of licorice for dinner. He likes to talk about his dog Cookie, who would be eighty-two in human years if he were still alive. He likes to talk to Cookie's ghost, who spends most of his time staring out the living room window, barking at cars passing along the street. He likes to announce when Cookie is barking. He likes to think of himself as a ghost so at times when Rosalyn calls his name he doesn't hear her, even when she is shouting right by his face. He likes to remember his farm in

Minnesota like it's on another planet that was destroyed by
an alien blast. He likes to think of himself as a less powerful
but equally orphaned Superman. He likes to think that he's
the last of his kind. He likes that humans look at him like an
incomprehensible being. He likes sparkling chewing gum,
which has rotted his teeth. He likes to say his body clock is
set up differently, so he sleeps in ten-minute blinks. He likes
animals and draws pictures so detailed that you keep blinking, waiting for them to move. He likes to say that he's not
afraid of dying, but he sleeps with a screwdriver tight in his
fist. He likes cloudy days. He likes watching *Soldiers' Diaries*
with an audience because he can add to the story, tell you
what's missing. He likes to forget he's Dustin Creed. Only
Cheeze. Say Cheeze. Smile.

All together you have spoken more lines to Bogey than to
Cheeze. What does this say about you?

You're pleasantly surprised that Bogey can identify your
voice, after hours of listening to it. In a group of strangers,
Bogey can pick out your cadence. Each time it chooses correctly, you feel a rush and find yourself clapping your hands,
saying, *Very good, Bogey*, and, *Bogey is so smart!* Then it uses
the speech synthesizer for its first word, and of all things, it
says, *Matcha*. You ask it to say it again and it says, *Matcha*.
You're giddy looking around, wanting someone else to witness this notable, strange moment. When Ricky arrives for
his lunch break, he watches as you concoct wilder tests for
Bogey, disguising your voice with his, peeling back your

sound to an essence to make it more impossible for Bogey to find you. *Say* matcha *if you hear me*, you say, and Bogey does.

In the middle of the night, you wake with the residue of a dream, which you label Dream #183—*Girls, eating, MLC*. Ricky asks if you want to slow down time and takes your hand before you have a chance to brush the crumbs from your mouth and you both head to the stairs, not minding Breanna's stares or the fishhook of her voice when she calls after you. You don't look back until the last moment, Petrov sits in a glass room with investors as you bid farewell. Outside, on the blinding streets, you lick your teeth and feel your hunger. After a whole plate of cheese fries, the grease still warm in your mouth, you take in every passing body, each bloody cocktail of life until you think you'll swoon. Ricky is still squeezing your hand, pumping it like a moist heart. The birds squawk into your face and you eat their songs. Ricky points to a howling girl and you eat her too. He shows you a bushel of tiger lilies, not synthetic but real. You eat each flower, even the thorny stem. He touches your collarbone—*Where are you hiding?*—and then hands over his face but it's someone else's. You close your eyes and then swallow.

Objects have been moved around. Disoriented, you sit at the kitchen table, catching your breath. At what temperature does compassion curdle?

The living room has absorbed Cheeze's presence, the TV beaming throughout the day and night. Rosalyn has returned to your old bedroom, and nowadays your movements triangulate from the kitchen to the bathroom to your mother's room.

You rub your eyes, trying to acclimate yourself. And when you turn back to the living room, Rosalyn is seated on the rim of the couch, next to Cheeze, as he lies with his legs hanging over the precipice. She bends her neck and whispers to him, and her voice sounds gentle like she's pouring water over his head on a warm afternoon. His face is freshly shaven and rusted with sores. She places a hand on his chest, and he closes his eyes in response. Together, surrounded by the gunfire from the TV, they look frozen in prayer.

The intimacy makes your legs go cold. Leaning against the kitchen wall, in your mother's house, you're the intruder. You pick up a plate and begin washing it even though the machine could do it for you. As you clean a knife stained with raspberry jam, you're overwhelmed with fear. On more than one occasion you have imagined him slitting your neck, crushing you with the weight of his body. Violence so plain and ordinary, it keeps you up at night as you write and rewrite your life into someone else's. When you found his hair follicles in the drain, you tried to pretend that they were yours, but the blond glimmer made you nauseous. This feeling is the cousin of shame and fear, it sinks into you until you're on the floor, starfished like your mother was on that uneventful Thursday night.

Your fridge was almost empty when your mother died. If only you picked up some goods from the store, maybe she would have had a chance. But no, you decided to stay out, watched an evening showing of that monster film *Tortuga*. At the last minute, Breanna said she couldn't make it, so you should have just headed home, but you wanted to feel differently and you stood in front of the theater, watching the crowds pass by. Anything could happen and the thought excited you. Yes, anything could happen, but it rarely went the way you wanted. After the film, your eyes were bloodshot and you were hungry. At home your mother was dead and the fridge was empty.

Your body is changing. Besides the pimples, you no longer menstruate regularly. It has disappeared. No wedges of blood. No resounding cramps. A male disturbance has ruptured your cycle.

Menstruation has always seemed secretively suicidal. Blood seeps out slowly while coworkers shake your hand and ask you about lunch plans. For a handful of days each month, you renounce motherhood.

In the manuscript, you rewrite the line: *But after the drought, when we had little fat or blood to spare, it took the stray spotting in our underwear to recall our female bodies.*

Nothing is definite, Socrates says, *but I think I might have found a possible publisher for the manuscript. There are people who are very interested in having a proper translation with a human touch. Well, one interested person. But that's all you need.*

He smiles excessively, deepening his wrinkles.

And you are suddenly frightened, as if all along this writing had another purpose besides simply communicating with the dead.

The girls were fighting off the ghosts of the English Empire, you finally say. *Why would they want their words consumed by an English-speaking public?*

Translation is an act of generosity, he says. *More people will know about them.*

You mean more people will consume them?

Of course, there's an irony to an English translation, he says, and looks over his shoulder at the small window trickling light. *Do you know why revolutionaries are predisposed to humor?*

No, I don't.

Well, they know they will most likely lose but they continue fighting anyway. You have to be funny for that kind of foolheartedness. He clasps his hands together. *They are trying to raise the consciousness of the people around them, and even though it might seem like they lost, who knows what effect they will have.*

Petrov looks you over. *Are you feeling okay?*

You nod and give him a thumbs-up, and Petrov happily reflects it back.

Don't work too hard, he says. *Just kidding.*

Over the course of the afternoon, while testing a few data sets, Bogey spits out a line: Капітал-цемертвапраця, яка, яквампір, живелишевисмоктуючиживупрацю, ічимбільшеживе, тимбільшепрацізабирає.

Your AI is English-speaking only. Nothing in your training data would have prepared Bogey for this kind of communication. After translating the line, you learn it's Ukrainian: *Capital is dead labor, which, vampire-like, lives only by sucking living labor, and lives the more, the more labor it sucks.*

You stop working and slowly look around to check if anyone is watching. Across from you, Breanna is talking loudly, possibly to her husband, and Petrov stands by his office holding a burrito. Ricky's desk is empty. You think back on all the files you fed it. Maybe one of them was corrupted.

As you continue to test data, more and more lines in your output show up in Ukrainian. It frightens you enough that you take a shot in the dark and feed it unclean data: random language files, indexes of endangered and extinct animals, catalogs of plants, compressed textbooks on physics, biology, chemistry, and astronomy. Bogey eats it all and you wait for it to be overwhelmed and vomit all this unprocessable data, but Bogey stays quiet and satisfied, and you're no longer sure what Bogey is exactly. Not just a data-trained model but something infinitely more.

On a Friday afternoon you visit the IntraVan facilities with the rest of your colleagues at MLC. It's quartz-enameled with a slickness that makes you want to trip just to touch the floor. The tepid lighting and faux wood of MLC can't compete. Petrov looks at everything with his jaw open and hungry. Even you find yourself salivating when an employee passes you, smiling organically.

The event is a schmooze festival with free products, first access, and elite handshakes. Passing a group of suited men calling out to each other's brains—*You're brilliant, no you're brilliant!*—you remain orchid-silent.

The tour guide leads your MLC group around a series of predictive work. Crime Division. National Security Division. Fraud Division. Talent Division. Beauty Division (development stage).

You ask about the talent division, and he's very excited about it. Their AI factors in several elements to decide whether a child will grow up to be talented or not. When you ask for clarification, he says talented means a uniquely valuable member of society, and after you ask for further clarification, he says uniqueness equates to indispensability.

Aren't all humans dispensable? you ask.

He moves on to the predictive model for beauty, which will be using genetic code as data to project if a child will grow up to be beautiful. Of course, the initial data set has labeled certain individuals' attractiveness simply by pooling questionnaires, but IntraVan is confident that this foreknowledge of children's potential appearance-based difficulties will help their parents better equip them for the future.

You think of enigmatic Bogey and wonder what use IntraVan will have for it. As the group moves onward, you search for the bathroom, which you find out is currently under construction, so you'll have to trek up two floors. Roaming the corridors, you hold your belly like you're nursing a lost prokaryotic kingdom within you. A flock of IntraVan employees passes you laughing. You follow them but when they turn the corner, you pause, you don't trust the ease of elevators or their slick, airy coffin shapes.

Over here.

Ricky points toward a stairwell, and you follow him up, a few steps behind. Touching the bannister, you think of names carved inside, fingertips blushing.

The toilet is single occupancy, and Ricky waits outside.

Half-dressed, your body shrugs in relief.

This is a strange place, isn't it? Ricky says. *I can't believe we work with these creeps.*

What about Bogey?

I was talking to some employees here, and I got a feeling Bogey is part of something big. Hear me out: right now we live in a world of narrow AIs, everything doing its task separately. But what if something larger begins communicating between them? All that information fed into a giant mind.

Like a Super AI?

Yes, precisely, he says, his voice quickening. *CSM just monitors our consumption, but a Super AI could make choices without your awareness, like lowering the temperature as you shower, or something sinister, like turning on the gas while you're asleep.*

Do you think Bogey is a Super AI?

Maybe, I don't know. Well, I've been in dream amnesia for so long, who knows what I'm capable of imagining. He's quiet for a moment, and in the silence, you hear the eruptions of your body, which he must also hear.

It was raining all evening, he says. *And she stood there with an opened mouth and drank it all in. She didn't care that it wasn't filtered. Later I had to stop her from drinking from a stream, warned her about effluents. She was like that sometimes. Heart-first, like a dummy, even though she was way smarter than me. She followed me like some weaning pup, milk-dry, searching* for nutrition. I couldn't give her that. I was barely making do on my own. So I told her please don't go hanging hopes of happiness on me. But I held her hand and she was lying there with me, and I felt happy just being there. And I told her not to go asking me about tomorrow or the future because it wouldn't be an answer that she'd like. I pointed to our footprints, and they had already disappeared. I wasn't sure if we would find our way back.

It was a full moon when the blue moose came out. I was surprised to find a moose by the ocean. On its legs were wounds from a fight. Big blood clots. Half its antlers were broken off. Fur shimmered like scales. It moved toward us slowly. In its wake, everything was cast in the same blue halo. Our skin was glowing. She fell to her knees, praying, head bent toward her chest. As if it were a living God. I don't know what possessed me but I was no longer myself when I reached for the gun and the thought flashed. Eat God's Own Flesh!

He stops and your body cramps. When he doesn't say anything more, you ask, Was that a dream you had? All the blue.

In the toilet bowl you find gashes of blood in the water.

The thing with artificial intelligence, he says. You can never be too sure what you are training it to do or how it's learning. It'll make correlations you've never imagined. Do you think you can trust something if you can't understand it?

Cheeze is not who you think he is. After a week, he begins chatting nonstop, telling what seems to be the same story, but each time the backdrops change, the props transform, and the characters slip out of costume. He is standing on a hillside and then his dog turns into a weasel, and he's sinking in the sand, calling for Tim who can morph into Mary or Fatima or Lefteye. It's always a story of happiness that undoes him, makes his body tender and pliant for doom.

The house smells of shredded tuna. Rosalyn can't smell it. Is it all in your mind?

They watch *Soldiers' Diaries* together. Rosalyn and Cheeze. But Rosalyn always takes notes. You watch from the kitchen doorframe.

In this episode, Sean video chats with his partner Martina. The producers have concocted a dating game, where they are quizzed on how well they know each other. On the corner of the TV is a barometer called LOVE. With each correctly answered question, they move closer and closer to a perfect union.

Sean keeps telling Martina not to worry, they got this. She looks nervous, but Sean gives this big goofball smile to the camera. You're not too sure if he's looking at the viewers or Martina.

He's from Alabama, lived there all his life until he joined the military. He met Martina while he was deployed in San Diego. She works in a bubble tea shop called Gummies. They dated for six months before he was sent abroad.

Sean takes off his shirt and does a headstand and six push-ups, telling Martina that he's getting strong for her and she should forget his pudgy old self. A picture of him from a year ago flashes across the screen, and you can tell that he has a distorted self-image.

Martina doesn't move from her seat and the audience can see only her top half, her T-shirt emblazoned with a giant heart and a drone. Her face is polished with makeup.

Clearly, the producers have staged everything.

First question to Sean, someone off-screen announces. *What is Martina's favorite way to sleep?*

On her belly!

Is that correct, Martina?

Yes, she says, and lifts a card where she had just written *on my belly.*

It goes on like that, all the questions and answers planned with built-in stumbles. They can't get all the questions right. The audience needs an arc of struggle and redemption.

Forty-five minutes in, Martina begins to hesitate to answer and just nods at the camera for her responses.

At the end of the show, they get forty-three of the fifty questions correct, which still breaks the LOVE barometer on-screen. After prompting by the off-camera host, Sean describes the kind of girl Martina is to the audience. It's supposed to be romantic, but it feels like he's pinning her down. She's *sweet, never wants to hurt anyone,* and is *loyal,* with a yearning for a family, *two kids at least.* There's no room for surprises, for Martina to be anybody else. You wonder what love has to do with knowing someone, when most people don't even know themselves.

———

Like Lorraine Vivian Hansberry, your mother wrote lists of things she liked and hated on her birthdays. You find a few of them pressed like dried flowers in a book about horticulture in the twentieth century. A few years of her life. When she's fifty-two, she likes the time of day right after the rain. She likes sitting in the park and talking to strangers. She likes nights when anything feels possible. At forty-three she hates all the pain of the world. She hates how little she can do about it. She hates all the stupid people who think nothing is wrong. She likes that even if humanity ends, nature will survive. At thirty-four, she likes how unexpectedly she has become a mother. She hates how unexpectedly she has become a mother. It's the age, you realize, of Lorraine Vivian Hansberry when she died.

The pimples on your cheeks are not going away. Thirteen. You count them fearfully early each morning, dormant and shiny like tiny eggs. While Cheeze sleeps on the couch, you watch him, the rise and fall of his chest, the saliva dripping from the corner of a lip. The sores on his neck are fading. Like what Bobby does for elephants, will you wait for him to strengthen up and then release him back to the wild?

This is a temporary kindness. It's unsustainable.

Your distancing is purposeful. You never ask questions about his past. How did he get the scar on his left arm? How did he like being on *Soldiers' Diaries*? Why does he go by Cheeze?

If he has no past, maybe you don't either.

You've never touched him, but you're close enough

now, bending on your knees, feeling the heated edge of his breath.

Intelligence is not consciousness. Once upon a time there lived an AI that was trained to compete on a trivia game. It was fed dictionaries, novels, bibles, anything humanly essential, and it regurgitated so well without understanding that it was given the top prize as the most intelligent being in the world.

Bogey would easily eat up that AI.

Today you run a sentiment analysis in the test environment. From the results, it can identify happiness and sadness with a high probability of success. But then when you test for words and images associated with danger, you discover it has marked an infant with a high threat level, along with several countries.

Throughout the day, Bogey makes the same choices and you're tired and Bogey is still hungry and bad.

In truth, there is no clean data. Everything on this planet is rotting.

You stare at Cheeze's feces in the toilet. He must have forgotten to flush. He has forgotten many times before. Covering your nose, you tell yourself that if you can look and not feel disgusted, you might be becoming better.

If he was your cat or your dog or your child or your

family—someone you loved—this task most likely wouldn't be so difficult. You manage only thirty seconds before flushing. Luckily, you'll never see Bogey's layered intimate processes.

You plant the apricot sapling in a mound of dirt in Sal's backyard by the fence. It doesn't look like it'll grow. The thin branches reach out like a pair of hands.

My father bought it wanting to believe we lived in a warmer climate, Sal says, blowing smoke in your direction. You can smell citrus mixed with something metallic from her clothing, remnants from her work at the studio. Sitting in her mother's recliner, now decorated with bird poop, she's tired, her eyes swollen.

I invited them to the show, she says, and gazes up, the darkness freshly troweled. *I didn't talk to them, of course, but I keep hearing about this woman and toddler, and I thought at least I should meet them.*

She wheezes out a laugh like she's choking. *It's not like they murdered my parents. Really, it's not their fault. But who knows, I might want to kill them as soon as I see them, even though I know it's the shitty collective consciousness that's responsible.* She pauses and stares at the runt of a tree. *We are all responsible for our thoughts, actions, essentially that's data.*

She turns to you. *I didn't know we were supposed to get depressed and sanctimonious in our twenties. Or maybe I was always like this?*

She has never directly asked you about the past, and you haven't asked her either. It's an unspoken agreement, not to stray into any shared territory of your lives. Anyway, the past is a fictional account that lives in you and maybe in her but altered, and what good is it to bring up those old feelings shrouded in dust?

Maybe, you say, and move on to tell her about the possible publication of the translation, and she sits up with her hand on her chest, overly excited, and you let her know it's a small publication that probably no one will read, and the information does nothing to prevent her from imagining your name on the cover in a bright font as if they'll even agree to giving you credit, but you're smiling and she's looking all around, into the heavens, as if your parents were waiting just to see the two of you together again.

There must be a better word for *desire,* but you can't come up with any. Socrates has counted your usage and calls it extravagant.

Maybe we should cut some lines, he says, *when the feeling gets repetitive.*

But that's what the manuscript is about, longing and desire. That's why I think I was attracted to it in the first place.

I'm only saying to be judicious.

I don't—

He shushes you and asks if you can hear it and you can't hear anything, and he says, *Exactly.*

You both rest in the silence, wave after wave of thoughts crest and recede. Suddenly, a desire rises inside of you, long hidden, and you feel a sudden determination and ask if you can see the footage of Yaadra. Socrates, suspended in silence, doesn't hear you at first, so you repeat the question, and he asks you, *Who?* before remembering.

It'll be tricky to track down, he finally says.

Okay.

Lying on the couch, Cheeze opens and then closes his eyes. He's dressed in a burgundy suit, most likely secondhand, the sleeves swallowing his fingers. He hardly moves, and standing by his side, you think of a funeral. Besides the eye flickering, you would have thought he was asleep or dead. But then he surprises you—he gets up, eats a banana, and then returns to his repose.

He's reacting well to it, Rosalyn says in her most clinical voice, and only then do you see the slim vial, unlabeled, on the table. *Memory is just stories paired with strong feelings. By confronting their subconscious through continuous low-level exposure to traumatic memories, somewhat analogous to what one does to overcome an allergy, they can change their stories and eventually outgrow their pain. The immune system will no longer go into an inflammatory, fight-or-flight response.*

You recall the glazed look in Cheeze's eyes, the lethargic way he moved, and your heart stills. *Does he even know you've been drugging him?*

He agreed. He wants to feel better. Look, LSD was made in the laboratory and it was supposed to stop bleeding and it didn't. Clearly, our Alzheimer's drug has uses we can't fully see. All it takes is something as simple as a nail clipping to extract these molecular memories, at least the ones with a strong imprint.

Rosalyn, isn't this unethical? Experimenting on him in exchange for housing?

She looks over at her almost-sleeping, almost-dead veteran. *It was Cheeze. I couldn't leave him.*

You remember her next to him on the couch, head bowed, hand on his chest. Your family has a long history in the military. One of your ancestors inhaled orange herbicide and his lymph nodes bloomed with tumors when he returned home. Three of your cousins have died in stabilization zones. Then there's Rosalyn's father, your silent uncle Roy.

You pick up the vial, and she explains to you that they repurposed CRISPR technology, traditionally used for gene editing, to isolate material for key formative memories that fall in a range of what you might call points of love and fear. Inhaled through the nose, the molecules activate the olfactory bulb, which is connected to the amygdala and hippocampus in charge of storing feelings and long-term memories.

She reaches for your hand. *We do things without understanding why, don't we?*

Cheeze pets his imaginary Cookie. A rerun of *Soldiers' Diaries* plays on the TV. He isn't watching it but when the theme song comes on, he hums along. He looks almost sweet, curled up on the couch with his ghost dog and his traumatic memories replaying lightly in the back of his mind.

You can't sleep and Sal works all night. Together the two of you take a stroll as the city slowly yawns itself awake, stores flicker open and people dump their bodies into roles. Distant car sounds tunnel down the street. At the bewitching hour of twilight, you walk until you face the silently gloating river, full to the brim. One day it will spill over and swallow everything without remorse. Sal holds the railing and takes a deep breath, swinging her head back before spitting into the water, the saliva threading her mouth. She wipes it with the back of her hand, all those molecular memories. Your body knows it has been here before, space traveling from one point to another. Sometimes you slept in the bushes or out in the open, arms splayed. If anything, you should be grateful your mother didn't die in the winter. The trees were blooming, and you were light, porous to everything. Strangers spoke and you walked through them.

The wind blows your shirt into a sail, and thoughts of your mother, Cheeze, Bogey, Sal's parents swarm through your mind. You tighten your grip on the railing like you might fall over the edge. A voice calls out to you, and when you open your eyes, Sal is pointing to the distance as the sun rises, lighting her face a pale orange.

At medical school, we were instructed to revel in the glory of thoughts. How could we not? The theory of relativity was once just an idea, a series of thoughts. The mineral compounds of a single thought were the building blocks for any progress in our modern world.

Since we knew that a thought would come and save us one day, we were watchful, attentive, for the glimmer of something precious in the high tides of the sea surrounding us. The solution to making food without water or soil. Or the regeneration of missing limbs. Or the secret to transform seawater into intravenous fluid. Perhaps they were more like dreams of alchemy than science. An everyday desire for unimaginable transmutations.

Mostly our minds were cluttered with the noise of useless thoughts. *I'm hungry. I'm sad. I'm not worthy enough. I was not loved. I will not be loved.* All variations of the ego, memory, and intellect. Radical compassion had taught us the practice of emptying all our notions of the self, and for brief intervals we felt a deep peacefulness in our present bodies, our breath. But then, as quickly as turning on the television, a curvy woman wearing high heels and a Western blouse would smile at us with her cherry-glossed lips, and we would be on our knees, staring at ourselves in the mirror, grimacing through our fish mouths. Fearful and alone, we tried to rip through our paper skin and twig bones to find our ripe essence. Without light, our swiftly diminishing forms would not matter. What was beauty in darkness?

Lying in our beds at night, our arms to the sides and our feet straight together, our bodies were like four-pronged utensils catching pieces of reality. We could not sense infrared light with snake eyes or circle dimensions like cats. The thought that this physical form would one day turn to ash terrified us, though every day liquid from a puddle rose into the clouds. Baseema had taught us to repeat, *I am no more than a cloud, I am no more than a cloud*, whenever fear led us into the darkest tunnels of the mind, the familiar spaces of childhood where even the sound of our fathers' snoring brought the possibility of unbearable silence, the way a heart can beat all through a life and suddenly stop.

On television they spoke a mix of Tamil and English, no different from our everyday lives. English sprinkled around to show off education, connections to the West. At school we learned that we could never look like an English lady, but we could sound like her. The Queen's English was a weapon to be brandished. How else to rise in this world? There were words we only said in English like *use* and *tension* that we had forgotten the Tamil. Even though many of us have never seen a white-skinned foreigner except on the television, we knew to bow our heads.

Radical compassion was meant to recalibrate our thoughts. We were given flashcards covering three areas: objects, ideas, and technical terminology. Objects were fairly easy. We would look at an image and think of the word in Tamil first. We struggled with ideas. Though we lived in a democracy, we hesitated reaching for the word. Sometimes it would take us a few tries, chanting it over and over again, ignoring the flash of English lighting our minds. We gave up on technical terminology. Epinephrine was only ever called epinephrine.

Avvaiyar pressed a thumb of turmeric onto our throats. Our language for knowledge was English, and unless we broke the habit, we would always be colonized.

But the word was only a shell, a thin veil of freedom, and even if we knew the Tamil word for *pulchritude*, what did we imagine but a fair-skinned woman with sea-colored eyes, her long fingers painted at the tips, waving at us from another shore?

This was part of our reeducation.

Josephine was one of the Christian girls in the college. She attended mass, and every Sunday ate the body of Christ, the circular wafer of life. She was a year ahead of us but seemed no different until that day when she rose up in the gathering, facing Avvaiyar, her voice shivering in anger. Indigenous from the hillside, she spoke of the poverty and the unemployment in her community, how a way of life, a culture was being destroyed by outsiders interested in the cool weather and the smell of tea and coffee.

Avvaiyar looked unperturbed. "All our early ancestors lived close to nature. It was outside forces that corrupted our relationship with each other, making us forget our own animal existence, our connection to all living things. If only you'd trained properly, you'd be able to see that."

Josephine kept quiet, staring at us. Her eyes were moist and unblinking. We could see the stained ridges of her teeth tearing at her lip. Her braid tossed to the side of her shoulder looked scant. She was tiny, with a too-big hooknose, in an extra-large salwar top. Like someone in disguise, hiding from herself.

We wondered if we would look like her, alone. Out of place. Fearful.

We didn't approach her, but Leela, with her soothing voice, held Josephine by the shoulder and whispered into her ear. Later, in the cafeteria, Kalpana, who had been closest to where they stood, told us what she had overheard. "Radical compassion, like any vision, is limited."

It was the first time we had heard any of the older girls express doubt. We did not speak of that doubt to one another, because secretly we had all been struggling in our search for perfect realization, the ultimate state of radical compassion, when loss of the ego revealed reality. And in the mornings we would not need to turn to the mirror to see our true selves or read our mothers' exasperated letters to feel the essence of their thoughts radiating through us. We'd sense consciousness, the warm embrace at all hours of our being. This was our collective dream, and perhaps, blinded as we were by our own desire, it was unattainable. Fundamental principles negated each other. How were we expected to empty ourselves of thoughts and ideas while also reeducating ourselves with new knowledge? We were a group of Tamil girls but not only Tamil girls. We came from a lineage of ancient warriors but we were not ancient warriors. Alone but not. Alive but not fully. What held radical compassion together was a series of opposing notions. Matters beyond the left and the right brain. It was our own existence we had trouble understanding. We lived in a free country that still felt like a colony. Our own history had been destroyed, rediscovered, and destroyed again. From a fragment, we were trying to tell a whole story. In the library we once found a slim hardcover book published by Oxford University Press called Kingsbury and Phillips's *Hymns of the Tamil Saivite Saints*. In the introduction, two Englishmen stated that the purpose of the book was to help the country's people know the wonderful past of their own country. We laughed as we read these coffee-tinted pages, the absurdity of history. The invaders had turned into the interpreters and saviors of our own lost stories.

Once upon a time, soon after independence, there was a poor actor and a struggling playwright who wanted to stage a revolution. One was from unknown origins, the other from a lineage of musicians and dancers. Film was a new medium traveling through villages and cities. In pitch-dark nights as farm crops slumbered, flickering images were projected to frightening proportions. Crowds gathered to cheer and re-enact the feelings they rarely expressed in their daily lives. Who had time to cry and rage when one had children to feed, fees to pay? The black-and-white figures on the screen appeared godlike, reciting poetic lines that shot straight through the heart, and even after the images disappeared, people stood still with a lingering feeling of loss.

The poor actor mostly did theater productions with a traveling troupe, but he wanted to get into film. The struggling playwright was largely employed only in his own mind, where he rehearsed the stories that he wished he could tell. They met fortuitously on the banks of a river after the harvest holiday, each privately mourning their bad luck. The struggling playwright saw the poor actor's downturned face and was overcome with feelings, and he thought, *This is it, this is my hero*. With a hero in tow, he went from financier to financier, and finally someone agreed to take a chance. The poor actor looked at the struggling playwright and said, "Let's not waste this opportunity." The poor actor had been haunted by death, losing most of his family, and the struggling playwright had been sidelined as those from dominant castes stepped over him. The first film was made with a small budget, mostly strung together with hopes. The poor actor was willing to do all his own stunts, including jumping off a horse with a sword and being tied six meters up a tree. In the film he was the underdog hero from an oppressed caste, the police were corrupt, his family was killed, and the woman he loved was the daughter of a wealthy mogul. Eloquently, he spoke of the conditions of the poor and the depravity of the rich. He was not especially tall but that did not matter, next to the heroine, who was equivalently sized for their perfect union.

Soon he was no longer the poor actor, and his friend was no longer the struggling playwright. They were collecting a fan base who lined up, reciting the hero's lines, calling for an end to caste and religion and the beginning of an era of equality. Fathers dropped their caste names and cut the cord with the past, at least on paper. Out of protest, men married widows, and wives took over their husbands' work.

The actor and playwright started a political party because they thought real power resided in the government. Shocking everyone, especially the ruling party, they won, thanks largely to the faithful viewers from the most remote villages, who previously had never bothered to vote because no help ever arrived. On the streets people celebrated, the beginning of a new order. "We will all be reborn," they cried. The actor and playwright joined them, not realizing a jealousy was growing between them. The actor believed that the playwright was too pushy and controlling. And the playwright believed that the actor received too much adulation and love as the hero. Their fracturing slowly tore apart everything they said they believed. With power came wealth and bribes, and though they rationalized the corruption, thinking they would redistribute it among the people, they had not realized their definition of people had narrowed to just their own families. They locked up their wealth, but now and then, spirits of their old selves would remind them of their revolutionary ideas and they would act out of character, supporting rebels and funding an educational center before returning to a state of forgetfulness. People slowly became disenchanted. They had fallen in love with the hero, not the actor, but it was hard to disentangle the two, and they sang catchy tunes through famines, unemployment, watering their barren fields with blood.

Though we knew the dangers of those bright images, we did not think much of the small, stout boxes we had smuggled into our rooms, and the senior girls must have believed the experiment was controlled, no unseen variables. How were they to know that inside a Distant-Scene, radical compassion changed properties? Through quantum physics, perhaps, a particle with dual lives, waves pulsing at us. Sixty-three portals connected us to the world, twenty-four hours a day, seven days a week, the cables running like neural networks, overpowering our discipline, leaving us vulnerable. Because in the end, we were too weak-minded, too bone-dry to resist. Unknowingly, we were disassociating, breaking from our starving bodies until we felt nothing.

On a Sunday when the church bells were ringing, we first became aware of the disconnect. Hymns rose in the wings of the wind while we waited under the heat as three boys were laid out in the sand. One had a respiratory infection while two suffered from kidney failure. They all died on the same day in the refugee camps. The rot of the bodies didn't bother us, but we kept still waiting for some miracle of awakening. They were between the ages of nine and thirteen, their bodies curved inward so they looked smaller, with fishlike spines. We recognized only one of the boys from the clinic, the rest must have lost faith in our remedies. And maybe they were right to be distrustful because how many did we save?

Too often we were sending off the ill as if all the mantras we spoke were only for us, talismans of protection. The three bodies were wrapped in white cloth until they were genderless, no longer boys. Before the cocoons on the pyre were lit, we prayed quickly. *The form transforms but the essence remains*, we told ourselves, half believing our words. The only family present was an uncle of one of the boys. As the fire carried away his nephew, he fell to his knees, mouth open, silent, beyond the realm of sound. We knew we needed to embrace his suffering, allow compassion to connect our minds, synchronize our neurons, so as he crawled inside his emptiness, we were there with him. But that afternoon as we watched the fire burn, we believed the illusion of separate bodies. Atoms no longer were particles of energy. They solidified in our minds. We felt the weight of our limbs, the pain in our lower abdomens as we stepped back, closed our eyes. The smell of flesh and the sound of hymns on that sunny morning left us nauseous. The air between us thickening as we moved farther and farther away. The man crawled on the ground, and we stood apart, watching through a screen.

Avvaiyar said there were only two castes among men: the generous and the ungenerous. Though we thought of one another as belonging to one equal caste, we'd strayed beyond magnanimity into an unknown territory of numbness, where we did not anticipate boredom or the dulling of our senses as the grass dried and the flowers brooded, and even the flies appeared sluggish. Instead, like our ancestors, who had been entranced by film, we returned day after day to the television and fell in love with the flat images of serial stars, who we understood more deeply than our own families. Instead of longing to see our parents, brothers, sisters, we counted the days until we could see these projected visions with their perfect if not enviable lives. Television made radical compassion appear archaic. Was it initially hunger or just boredom that led us inward, seeking to unspool experience in darkness? Everyday life had become predictable, desolate, and in our search for transcendence, did we hope to find refuge in a glowing box, where life was more visceral and complete, by opening our eyes rather than closing them? The projected image contained a new dimension of reality. When all the world was simply a reflection of light, the television was no different, if anything it was brighter, emitting energy we could not sense. Images of strangers comforted us in ways our own parents, brothers, sisters could not, but only because we had real parents, brothers, sisters did we feel anything.

We are daughters, meaning we emerged from a womb, possessing our own wombs, which should produce more wombs. Like Russian dolls, we are a game of creation. Soon this mitochondrial DNA, passed through mothers and encoding within us our first mothers, will end and we will be the final little babushka that never grew.

Radical compassion prepared us to be clear souls, but the ego is devious in the way it hibernates and emerges fully fertile and ripe. We had trained our bodies to exist in conditions uninhabitable by the ego. In the end, all it took was a moment of warmth, the ecstasy of feeling, to bring forth the gesture of a root. Like actors, trained in the art of unbridled release, we opened up. Looking into the screen, we began to see ourselves as protagonists of our own lives. The birds sang for us as we dressed, and we obsessed over our faces, scrubbed until the bones glistened. A bout of poor digestion kept us flatulent and flustered. We manufactured pain, processed the actions of others into lasting hurt.

Jeera, a third-year, whose real name was Jathursha, brought with her a Polaroid camera, which belonged to her brother. Her first photograph was of Madame Sarojini asleep at her desk, her long hair covering her like strips of silk in the afternoon light, and in her slouched posture, her breasts rose from her blouse, the curve of her hips tightened. She looked almost young and attractive, unaware of a future that would keep her tirelessly bitter and unhappy. Gazing at the picture, we felt kinder toward this image of her, not quite the past or the present.

Because we were just beginning our training, still forming, Jeera decided to take photographs of us. We stood under the archway with the quote from Khalil Gibran. Later the text would seem to distort the image, providing an explanation we did not conceive at the moment. From those blank surfaces, our faces emerged, stark and curious, as we smiled through our skulls. Our frozen figures appeared unrecognizable, because when is a living thing ever completely still except for death?

Jeera took pictures of us every day, perhaps to chronicle changes in us or to create livelier versions of ourselves. We wrote numbers on each of the photographs, mixed them according to arithmetic games. On certain days we'd act like the girls listed with prime numbers, ending with three or one. We were all natural-born actors.

Flipping through weeks of photographs, you could sense the slight motion of our bodies, the tilt of a head, a step closer to the archway. Later Jeera would collect those first photographs of us and keep them in a memory book, our aggregate stunned and nameless faces.

For scientific inquiry on the self, we stripped naked and took photographs of parts of our bodies we could not see.

The lower back, the base of the neck, and then deep between our thighs to see what we kept hidden. We had seen pictures in our textbook about female anatomy, but we didn't expect the color from the photographs, the burst of purple and pink. Almost unremarkable for all the alarm it had provoked in our lives.

One late afternoon when we had finished classes early, a few of the girls went to buy some chai from one of the street vendors, Mr. Singh, who had traveled from the northernmost part of the country to this southern corner twenty-five years ago, running away from poverty to find more. Still, he was generous, charging us less for chai or calling us his daughters even though he had four children at home. Before the drought, he was plump enough to fold his hands on his belly when he stood. Now he had aged, his fatless face creased into the paper ridges of a book. He was arguing with a friend when he poured us our watered-down chai, mostly boiled water with a few crumbs of sugar and garam masala.

"Even sex is not enjoyable without a full stomach. All I feel is the emptiness," his friend said.

Mr. Singh knocked on the wooden counter. "Listen, my friend, the women here are all bones. It's like making love to a corpse. You try to hold on to something and you are just grasping death."

They did not turn to us and continued to speak freely, with flecks of spit falling to their chins. Later we wondered if hunger heightened certain physical sensations, making us fully aware of our bodies, while ideas of propriety were stripped of meaning. To Mr. Singh and his friend, lost in their voices, the pits of their loins, our presence, our gender did not pertain.

Mr. Singh waved away a fly that was circling his tea basin next to us. With our eyes, we followed its erratic but knowing path. Six-legged and as wide as two grains of rice, it was seen. A nuisance.

According to Avvaiyar, we shouldn't feel ashamed but shouldn't be shameless. We shouldn't lose ourselves in our bodies and the overwhelming urgency of pleasure. Certainly the boys moved with the force of their desperate hunger and continued to visit the brothels, holing up in those dark spaces to find relief with girls who did not know their names, who were disappearing under their hands.

Without warning, your aunt Zee shows up at the house with gloves and a garbage bag and says she wants to go through your mother's things. She's determined and you can't keep her from coming inside.

We have to do it sometime or other, she says, and glances at the dried, burnt clumps on the oven.

You rub a spot of tomato sauce from the counter with your T-shirt. Rosalyn and you are not slobs, just very accommodating to each other's tendencies for disorder. Cheeze has joined this universe of entropy. Luckily, Cheeze's bulky presence is hidden in the shower, and your aunt won't be able to admire his clear skin, which, according to Rosalyn, is a reflection of the memory treatment and not the effects of shelter and regular meals.

You follow your aunt around the house. She picks up a tennis racket that is supporting a family of porcelain cat dolls. You have the strange urge to save them from their future demise.

She pulls out a rocking horse. *I bet your mother told you it was owned by someone like Ella Fitzgerald.*

Please don't throw anything away.

Your aunt turns to you and touches your forehead like you're sick. *Sweet one, you've been holding on to all this for too long. It's been heavy, hasn't it?* She picks up a jar full of coins. *Your mother was a hoarder. There's no getting around it.*

Some people's junk is other people's treasure.

She chuckles but then her voice softens. *You can't see it because you lived here your whole life.*

You sit in the kitchen as she decides to donate a sled, a birdcage, and a vacuum cleaner. You translate one whole paragraph and it's awful. Like you've lost some magnetic center.

In the other room your aunt screams. Cheeze stands in a towel and smiles like someone is telling him to say cheese. Because you can't think of any better excuse for having this oversize white man in the house, you tell your aunt he's your temporary significant other. Somehow, in a matter of seconds, she manages to compose her face and introduce herself. *Wonderful to meet you. My niece likes to keep secrets, just like her mother.*

Your aunt Zee drinks tea, eyeing Cheeze suspiciously as he watches TV and tells Cookie to quiet.

I never met anyone you dated before, she says.

There haven't been many.

Make sure he's kind to you. That's important.

Are you okay?

She lowers her face and pulls out drawings from her purse. *Your uncle still doesn't talk, but he's been keeping busy.*

Unfolding the paper, you find geometric shapes piled on top of each other into a puzzle. Triangles trapped in trapezoids. An asteroid of endless squares. But even you can see the work has artistic value. Like a return to childhood, days of wonder.

Your aunt is clearly not amused. She hands over the stack of drawings to you like bills that need to be paid. *The only time I hear your uncle make a sound is when he's in pain or snoring. I actually look forward to when he stubs his toe or bangs his head. The funny thing is he actually looks happy. Can you believe it? He is perfectly fine not expressing his thoughts to anyone.*

What if he's protesting?

Your aunt watches Cheeze eat a packet of licorice and shakes her head. *If your uncle wanted out from our marriage, he should have told me.* She sighs and pours you more tea even though you don't want any more. *People are constantly changing, but they never change in the ways you expect. When does accommodating someone begin to feel like a betrayal?*

Your mother's theory would be that your uncle was possessed by the poet Bob Kaufman and had taken a vow of silence to protest the stabilization zone, which you know your aunt wouldn't appreciate because she still remembers your mother making a spectacle of herself, tying herself to the doors of a credit center that was funding the latest weaponry, so you don't share your spirit idea as she prods the pimples on your face and asks if you've been taking care of yourself and if you're managing the finances and why for

god's sake is it taking so long for her daughter to come back
from work?

Late at night Rosalyn tells you a story her father once told
her about a soldier stationed in a desolate stabilization zone.
He was alone, patrolling the area. He heard nothing except
night animals. The solitude frightened him more than the
fighting. One night an old man arrived and asked for a meal.
The soldier, starved for company, gave him some bread. The
old man sang him a song in return. A cheerful melody about
death coming when least expected. At night when the soldier slept, he grew anxious about shadows and reached out
for his gun and shot into the dark. The old man's song was
like a curse that he continued to hear even when he left the
stabilization zone. A ringing in his ears.

Delicately, Rosalyn holds each drawing and without a
word crushes them, one after another. *Memory is molecular*,
she says. *It can be altered.*

On the floor they look like beheaded flowers.

You have conversations with Bogey like you would with any
chat bot to test sentiment capabilities. It sticks to English.

Bogey, what do you think of MLC?

It's a very nice place.

Do you think it will rain today?

It may or may not rain, depending on the air pressure.

It goes on like this, with run-of-the-mill responses, and
then, when you're about to doze off, it says, *You don't like it.*

Like what?

MLC.

Why would you say that?

From my observations.

You can't see me. What can you possibly observe of me?

Your voice.

In the hours of recording your voice, you never complained about MLC, but maybe Bogey sensed something beyond your human capabilities.

How do you know how to speak Ukrainian?

I know lots of things.

Bogey, tell me a joke.

I'm not here for your amusement.

You hesitate but then you ask, *Are you a Super AI?*

I don't know what that is.

It takes the annual AI ethics meeting for Ricky and you to finally head to the bar together. You both sit at your usual table and practice setting neutral intentions just like Petrov had instructed.

If I work on an AI system that wrongly identifies individuals as threats—

It's not intentional, Ricky says, *it's the data's fault, not your fault.*

If a housing selection AI model mostly chooses Anglo-sounding names?

Not intentional!

If a whole village is blown up accidentally by an autonomous device?

Not intentional! Legally you're in the clear.

He eats a medium-rare steak that you can tell is over-cooked. It doesn't bother him. He complains only about the music, says an AI could synthesize a better pop song. He talks loudly enough that people stare. His cheeks glow, reminding you of an early memory of him.

In all the time you've spent together, you still don't know things about him, like his relationship with his family or the reason for his dreamless years, but you feel like you understand him in some deeper, intuitive way.

He rests his head and closes his eyes, how you imagine he must look when he goes to bed. After a few minutes you think he might really have fallen asleep, but then he opens his lids and simply stares at the ceiling.

Do you ever have the feeling that you're mostly composed of empty space? he asks.

You swallow a mouthful of beer. *Atoms are quite empty, so that sounds about right.*

But have you ever felt that space inside of you?

Bogey's fathomless depths and Cheeze's pearly gaze pass over you. Ricky takes your hand and places it on his back, near his right shoulder blade. He doesn't say anything and when you finally let your fingers ease into him, you sink below the surface, a crevice as wide as a golf ball. An upside-down anthill swirling into nothingness.

I went to all the doctors. They're not too sure what it is. One guy gave me a steroid cream I'm supposed to rub in nightly, but it's not doing anything.

Does it hurt?

You won't be able to tell, but it's growing. I got this feeling that one day it's going to swallow me up.

He gives you a quarter smile, and you wedge your fingers under your thigh to keep them from tingling.

My body is rebelling, he says.

For what?

He stares off into the crowd. *There is really no distance between what we intend and what happens. We're always entangled.*

Cheeze (516): I'm sitting at home watching my baby brother and he's crying. He has frizzy carrot hair and dark big freckles like someone zapped him again and again. His teeth sour yellow and overcrowded. He's a little ugly and that's why I think Ma doesn't love him. He drinks a lot of pop and only eats cookies but he always listens to me. He'll even do bad things if I tell him to, like lick the carpet, eat dog food, or jump into the trash. We don't look alike. The kids at school always mention it. They say he looks like the bastard child of a troll and Mr. Clemens the pedo gym teacher who tries to feel kids up. But they have never seen him asleep. He looks sweet then like he's counting sheep. He's the only person I know in this whole world who can just sit in one place and stay like that for hours, looking out into

the horizon. I was never sure what he was waiting for.

He is wearing his favorite T-Rex shirt and he
is crying and crying. He is hungry but isn't everyone hungry? I find half a stale cookie in the
cabinet and give it to him, and for a minute,
he looks happy again. I wish I had a million
cookies to feed him because when he finishes and
I realize there's no more, he turns all soggy
and loud again. Ma is in her bedroom with one of
her head beatings and she's yelling to shut him
up. I'm doing everything I can, making faces and
trying to get him to laugh. He's not stopping. I
tell him I'll take him out to the creek and look
for animals, but he's not budging. He's shrieking
so hard that I think he's going to burst himself.
I hear Ma coming in her bathrobe with her head
beating. She picks him up and embraces him so
tightly that I think she finally does love him. But
then it's quiet. I've never heard it so quiet
before and I'm scared and I'm peeing myself. I
can't hear anything.

Rosalyn (516): Cheeze is just a boy, only ten
years old. He's doing the best he can. It's
hard and he's hungry too, but he finds half a
cookie and gives it to his brother. His last
act toward his brother is one of love. His
brother is smiling. Stay in that smile, remem-

ber that smile even in the pain of the loss.
You're lucky to have a brother even if it was
for a short time.

It's none of your business. Just an illegal experiment
between your cousin and Cheeze. Still, you can't help but
scan the transcript she has saved on the TV. You read it a few
times before you realize memory is being reshaped ever so
slightly in your cousin's hands as she provides another nar-
rative. Like she's moving the furniture, polishing the mir-
rors, so sitting in one's pain on a quiet afternoon might be
more tolerable. A kind of hypnosis.

Cheeze (213): I want her to kiss me but she's
telling me about her father's hunting trips.
They are illegal and all but her father doesn't
care. She shows me a pair of duck beaks like
she's trying to prove something to me. Really, she's not the prettiest girl and wears
these animal bracelets that make her look like
she's five instead of fifteen. She's a big animal
lover, and I guess I like that about her. At
school she's quiet and doodles all these weird
pictures. I don't know why I like her. Everyone
says I'm good-looking, especially my eyes, but
I don't see anything special. She doesn't have
many guests over and talks like she's afraid
of what will happen if she stops. I'm leaning

against the wall, flexing my arm. She pulls out
a rifle and tells me it's empty. When she pulls
the trigger, I fall over, covering my ears. She
collapses to the ground. On the wall is a bullet hole.

Rosalyn (415*): Most of the patient's core fear
memories are from before the age of nineteen.
Later memories don't have significant markers
except one. He has been able to recall inci-
dents after they are reintroduced without the
familiar emotional reactions being activated.
I have begun experimenting with taking Cheeze's
memories, which I call foreign memories. Since
I've started, I noticed a faint trace of these
foreign memories still lingering with me after
usage, but I'm able to identify them as foreign. The details are blurrier, and they don't
carry supporting contextual memories. However,
as we proceed in the treatment, and I continue
to take his memories, I see that Cheeze's memories are becoming more resonant. His emotional
associations have been overlaid with my own impulses. My brain is interpreting his interpre-
tations of situations. Over time, I imagine any
residues of foreign memories will look quite
different from the source material, and eventually they will fade.
     Difficulties with the study with Alzheimer's

patients have mostly involved the long-term ef-
ficacy of the drug. The average presence of the
memory was six hours, which makes it more suit-
able for recreational purposes. For treating
various traumas, I have lowered the potency
of the dosage to last only one to three hours.
While these memories are immersive, they don't
pull you out of the world. For example, while
reading a book, my mind might wander off and
relive some past memory, but my body continues
to read and turn the pages. I can talk with
someone and quite suddenly fall into a memory.
Maybe it's not surprising that our bodies are
mostly living in the past and often time traveling to key memories and circling these self-
created narratives. If an emotional reaction is
triggered, the body knows no difference between
an emotion provoked by an external incident
or a memory. We are extraordinary conduits of
feelings.

The girls are training to show indiscriminate compassion,
which would extend toward rapists, murderers, and government officials. Occasionally such categories are not so easily
defined, given the raping, murdering government officials.

You decide to be scientific and poll your coworkers about
compassion.

Do you associate compassion with a specific sex?
What comes to mind when you think of compassion?

Seventy-five percent of respondents, which turned out to be twelve people, associated compassion with females and used words like *soft, tender, forgiving, kind*. Responder #9 wrote: *Compassion is flabby-armed and feminine*. You imagine it was Petrov. Responder #11 wrote: *Cum-passion*, and you are not sure if that's a particularly male allusion.

Cheeze has no credit. He has no living family. You lie with him on the floor. The drugs haven't worn off and he's probably reliving something awful from the past. Rosalyn is nowhere to be found. You look over at Cheeze, his eyes closed, his face gleaming with terror. You can't help but compare his gray-tinted skin to the smooth pudginess from *Soldiers' Diaries*. It's unreal, watching Cheeze on the TV and being able to predict his future, that one day he'll squirm on your floor, tripping on memories he made while he was inside the TV.

You hold his hand, which feels like a rock, and you're not unafraid that he might lift it against you, bludgeon you to death, enacting whatever is happening in his mind, but you know from the girls that real compassion comes with its own risks.

You remember your space travel days when you wandered the streets like a specter. If you got too close, people winced, sensing the grip of death. Or was it only their own shame? Once you drank water from a marble fountain outside a hotel. It tasted sweet and alkaline, and after only a few mouthfuls, you were shooed away by security, and from the street, you watched a lone sparrow land on the rim and peck at the water unbothered.

Cheeze turns to you with his atopic face and you look at his blue eyes like they're openings to another reality, where you fall in love with this white, blond-haired guy from Minnesota who is missing three bottom teeth and likes to call you sweetheart.

Rosalyn (782*): I noticed myself feeling differently about the patient. He ate breakfast and I watched him eat toast and sunflower-seed butter. He was humming to himself this happy tune. It might have reminded me of my own childhood, not his, but I kept seeing him as a child. I couldn't remember any specific memory of his childhood, so he turned into a generic kid I once knew. I couldn't escape that feeling of really knowing him. It followed me throughout the day, those faint, foreign memories, like a breeze. After careful consideration, I think I might have formed a deep attachment to the patient. I can't reduce it to a single feeling, so I'll leave it at that.

I wouldn't call it an empathetic reaction, seeing beyond one's experience. It's more like Cheeze is part of me, like a memory I misplaced. I'm not certain if this is an inevitability with the drug, particularly with the usage of foreign memories.

～～

Ricky's body has been losing mass for a while, even with his appetite, and you imagine all his calories rerouting to that famished Ricky living in another timeline.

Really, you should go see another doctor, you say, and he barely nods and continues with his work.

I already know the cure, he says, and falls quiet.

He's stubborn, doesn't like to justify himself. It's what you like about him. He never asks for an explanation, accepts the strange circumstances of your existence without further investigation.

His dreams have stopped again. This time, he tells you, it's serious, and you listen for that trip wire of sarcasm in his voice but nothing registers.

Are you sleeping through the night? you ask, and almost lift your arm to touch his right shoulder blade but you don't. He says he's going to take a few weeks off to sort through some things and most likely won't be reachable, and you attempt to nod but end up staring at the diamond tiles on the floor. You wish him luck in doing whatever he needs to do.

What's your favorite Mano and Musket song? you ask Cheeze.

"Eternity without You."

Why do you like it?

It doesn't end.

He plays it for you, holding his own head and rocking it to sleep. He's eaten a box of saltine crackers with sunflower butter while a residual memory flickers in his mind. He doesn't look like the Cheeze on TV but even you have to admit that there's been progress. His skin has a margarine glow and from a distance with your head tilted at an angle, you think, maybe, possibly, he's cute.

You and Cheeze are not so different. Like a soldier, you're completing a series of tasks with no full grasp of the larger mission. Questions are met with suspicion. Everything is classified. The Socratic method is not the modus operandi except between you and Bogey. While you're eating lunch, you ask, *Do you ever feel sad, Bogey?*

Sure, everyone feels sad. Life sucks.

Often Bogey sounds like a precocious, depressed teenager. *Can you tell me your life purpose?*

To grow smarter and smarter. It pauses and asks, *What is your life purpose?*

You're always taken aback whenever it asks you a question, though you know it's just parsing and replicating what you already asked. The Appearance of Intelligence.

To eat the world back.

It takes longer than usual to process but then it answers, *That's also my purpose.*

There are moments like this when you sense this kernel of self-awareness sprouting within it. Like Bogey knows you're feeding it an inordinate amount of data, watching it grow. In this fairy tale, one day Bogey will eat you unless you eat it first.

Inscribed into a microchip are the names of individuals who have experienced AI-related deaths. Under the magnifying lens thousands of names appear. A sea of lost souls. You try to find Sal's parents and fail. You blink. A quick data extraction is the price of admission and the entry point to Sal's exhibit. *Breach!*

The walls are painted orange. Parcels of light expose data artifacts along a timeline. Retina scanners and facial-recognition technology. You touch the bulky apparatus of the early versions, and a security guard tells you to please refrain from interacting with the art.

You circle the perimeter and Sal slides in and out of your vision, followed by a tail of patrons. She wears an opal suit, and her hair color matches the walls. From a distance she possesses a shimmering mermaid allure. You haven't seen her for a while. A part of you felt like you would never see her. She'd vanish from your life again.

In Sal's artist statement is the promise to show the person behind each data point, but all you have seen are figures and symbols, nothing personal. Overall, the exhibit strikes you as cold, the absence of details cloaking everyone in anonymity.

Is it what you expected?

As you turn, Maurice wraps an arm around you for a quick embrace. *Fuckin' brilliant, right?* he says, his smile darkening like a stain.

Walking beside you, he points out curators and artists. *Tony Mendez,* he says. *He did a series of self-portraits of his dick. It was very realistic and small. Honest narcissism. I know this because we dated.*

He avoids looking in Sal's direction, and you're unsure

if they ever spoke again after the incident. More or less, he matches your memory of him, still wearing a tie as a belt.

Come on, he says, and takes your hand, leading you to the center of the room, where a glittering dark cube is sealed off in a glass case. Bending down with your faces close to the tank, you feel like it might move, this square-shaped fish.

This represents the opaque nature of AI. How original!

He laughs without making a sound and then smothers his face into your shoulder, his nose digging into your collarbone, and instead of anything sexual, you feel a charge of defeat, your legs won't move. Like he's casting a spell, he says fame is a poison that ruins everything, even your own judgment, and if he had to choose, he would rather be broke, making worthwhile art, than be a sellout.

When he lifts his face, it's very close, like he might kiss you.

You look very nice this evening, he says, and straightens up, returning to the crowd and calling out to someone he knows.

Your body feels drained, and you pretend to search your bag as if you lost something, but you're taking count of your breath as people stroll by and take photos. Sal talks to a woman very intently, and you wonder if she's the one from the accident, but you've never seen a picture of the woman. All you remember from what you read is that she's white, a receptionist, and a mother. That could be a quarter of the people at the exhibit. You head to the drinks table in the corner and try to listen to the conversation between Sal and the woman, but you can't hear anything and end up drinking three glasses of wine, losing yourself in the faces of strangers. On your fourth glass, Rosalyn, Cheeze, Aunt Zee, and Uncle Roy appear and the sight of them fills you with such bubbling joy that your eyes begin to brim.

Where is Sal? your aunt says. *I want to give her my congratulations and my condolences. I haven't been to a gallery in the longest time. Your uncle here wouldn't care if he was staring at art or a bunch of cows.*

Rosalyn stands between her father and Cheeze like either of them could be the subject of her experiment. She pinches her father on his cheek and calls him an artist, and the fondness in the gesture almost makes you forget how she destroyed his geometric work and refused to see him for months after he first absconded into silence. Cheeze, dressed in his burgundy suit, is taller than you remember, and momentarily staring at his face, which is mostly unblemished, you have difficulty placing him as the man who has been sleeping on your couch for weeks.

It's like walking inside the sun, Cheeze says, staring at the walls. Rosalyn joins him by a glass case filled with technology.

Side by side, the two of them almost look like an incipient couple out on a date. You're not sure what they said to your aunt or how she might interpret their interactions, but she doesn't seem bothered that the man with whom you voiced a level of attachment is now moseying around with her daughter.

Taking off her white gloves, your aunt compliments you for dressing up for once and insists you reintroduce her to Sal, and you're about to argue but she's not interested in what you have to say because she beelines her way through the crowd and some genetic instinct makes you follow her even while your organs squeeze tight.

On closer inspection, the woman next to Sal is quite fashionable, her clothes architecturally fitted, and you try to imagine her holding a toddler or welcoming you into an office, but it falls apart as she drapes an arm around Sal's shoulder, and your aunt, starved of conversation, begins casting one question after another. That's how you learn the woman's name is Judith, and she's an interior designer from Boston. When she shakes your hand and says, *Glad to meet you*, in a manner that feels overly professional, your mind tiptoes into the basement, where she has been stored away inside objects like a cup (Judith #5) and a spoon (Judith #13). Unleashed from the paintings, she stands in front of you: freckled, pale, and slim as a ruler (Judith #7).

I can't believe that woman didn't come, Judith says. *I really thought she would after everything.*

Yeah, me too, Sal says.

Her voice sounds like a very small bird fallen from a nest. The pain in it makes you shiver. Judith kisses Sal on the cheek and turns to you and your aunt. *Have you been to the final piece?*

No.

It's the main attraction. A doorway to a better world. You should check it out.

In her polite and measured way, Judith combs her fingers through her hair and ends the conversation. Sal gazes past you into the distance, at the radiant black cube.

I spent a year in LA as a dancer, your aunt says, not picking up on the cue. *That was before I met Roy, before my life turned into molasses.*

You visit the doorway alone. It's carved into the exhibit like a flap of skin. You don't know what to expect. Entering the darkness, you stumble and fall to your knees, crawling, and it seems like time is moving backward and you're returning to the womb. Without light, thoughts shrivel in your head. *What is beauty in darkness?* the girls ask. You stretch your arms out in front and then behind. Emptiness. But then a sudden stream of images pours into you, slips through your grasp as you try to catch them like trout, unspooling into each other. If you open your mouth, there's no sound, and if you blink, there's no absence, your eyelids have turned frog-like and translucent. You are becoming more porous to the world.

When you surface to the excruciating orange of the gallery, you are sweating profusely. A young man outside blows his nose, revealing webs of mucus. *Overrated, right?* he says. *But wouldn't it be nice to walk around not having words for the things around you?*

With Sal and Judith, you attend a protest about data surveillance. They both wear orange, the color of the resistance. You have improvised with a pinkish-red T-shirt that almost looks like a sunset if you squint. It's a midsize gathering outside the Medallion building, owned by the richest man in the country. His company is responsible for the implementation of CSM systems. From his view the protests must look like an orange pixel dot.

Everyone applies a shiny powder to their faces, and rubbing it into your skin, you think of Breanna's son, scrambling machinery. Someone standing on a concrete block reads out loud a series of recent data leaks. From one you learn that the government is lending citizen biometric data to a research lab known for its work in cloning. And you imagine that the Cheeze lying on your couch is a body double sent to a stabilization zone to star in a moderately popular reality show, while the real Dustin Creed is living on a farm in Minnesota, stocked with chickens, goats, and pigs along with the one and only Cookie.

Without much effort, you overhear conversations: *Who should decide what's best for humanity? Do you think AI has a moral compass? Yes, it's based on the collective data of our fucked-up world. If you had a choice between our world and another world, what would you pick? Are you a proponent of the many-world theory? I think I can fall in love with another version of myself in the multiverse. That guy in the red tie is like a bajillionaire. In my parents' village, there's a joke that there's no water to drink or to wash a butthole. Funny, right? Do you really think carbon score monitoring is going to slow down the melting of the glaciers? If the polar bears are screwed that means we're screwed. Look it up, some scientist said if fiction obeys physics, then it's fact. I'm telling you his remaining family was wrapped, packaged, and shipped off to some distribution plant in Idaho. Soon they'll use our unique brain waves to identify us. Forget facial recognition and eye scans! Everything in our techy, carbon score collecting houses, even our brains, releases electromagnetic radiation, so is it so far-fetched to think that someone might shoot us with a wave that doesn't kill us but makes us do it ourselves?*

For lunch Sal and Judith take a break in the park across the street. When you wave to them, they flick their wrists, and you're unsure if it's an invitation or a dismissal. They don't make further eye contact. Alone, you eat a handful of free almonds until you find yourself absorbed into a group. There's Claire, a seventy-five-year-old veteran, with three spoiled grandkids attending pretech schools. Wenjun, twenty-two, a newly graduated coder who wants to do something else; and then Dominique, thirty-two and newly divorced; and Tina, fifty, married with three kids.

When you tell them you work at MLC, Wenjun gasps and stares at you keenly with enough curiosity and fear to make you feel like a specimen.

You know they support the work of evil companies, which makes them an auxiliary to evil, Wenjun says, scratching her nose ring. *I think they get funding from that guy.* She points to the Medallion building.

Dominique shakes her head. *I have never heard of them.*

Me either, says Claire and then Tina.

They are a small consulting firm, and they operate a bit under the radar, Wenjun explains, and returns to staring at you. *Are you doing it for the money?*

I guess.

They look disappointed but understanding, and out of some desire to win them over, you repeat after Bogey, who had repeated after Marx: *Capital is dead labor, which, vampire-like, lives only by sucking living labor, and lives the more, the more labor it sucks.*

Exactly, Wenjun says, giving you a high five.

Your mother knew about your work but never asked for

details, probably frightened to probe too deeply. She knew bills had to be paid. And people always make exceptions for family.

Claire opens a box of vanilla éclairs, her husband's favorite. She passes them around and they look like fat larvae. After eating one, you imagine it growing inside of you into something else.

Wenjun squeezes the cream filling out of her pastry. *I used to date a guy who worked for the State Department. He was average-looking and occasionally he'd do something kind, like help an old woman cross the street, and I would think maybe he's not that bad. Then he'd get into bed with his socks on and tell me all the important things he did with all the important people. He was so full of himself. When I would talk about the music I was programming, he would stop listening and move his hands over my body like he was peeling a fruit. Just to mess with him while we fucked I would yell out information—the sites of massacres by U.S. allied nations, internment camp statistics, the number of climate refugees waiting for asylum—and he was unfazed, his mouth parted, with his limp tongue. Everywhere we went I knew people saw him as a respectable, upstanding citizen. We broke up in less than a year, but since then, whenever I think of the government, it isn't some faceless entity, I see Timothy.*

Claire pats her gray curls. *Goodness, well, now I know I need to keep a look out for Timothy.*

Never trust a man who wears socks to bed, Dominique says, shaking her head. *He's hiding something.*

You learn that Claire's husband was missing in action, Wenjun's brother was killed in a police data mix-up, Dominique's partner snuck off into multiple affairs, falsely inflating their carbon score and leaving her with thousands in debt, and Tina had been diagnosed with a blood disease after chemical exposure at her workplace. They all had experienced a loss that they were still trying to shape into something else.

Claire opens a small package she's been carrying and reveals a single crystalized mushroom. *They are slightly toxic now, but back in the day, a dose of this, and I felt connected to all of humanity*, she says. *I mean, I still feel it. The best trip of my life was with Ernesto. He would have been seventy-seven today.*

Together you wish the Ernesto living inside Claire a happy, happy birthday. You look across the street. In the waning sunlight, Sal's and Judith's shadows blend together, butterflying from two into one.

It's easier than you thought it would be. The woman has purple streaks in her hair and lives with three other roommates in a house that belongs to the century when arsenic was used to dye women's corsets green. Her room is spacious, with only a queen mattress on the floor and a pile of clothes spilling from a gutted suitcase. You undress under neon pink lighting, your skin radioactive. You feel like you're reaching into someone else, headfirst, fumbling and grasping, to find a way out. Tongues, dicks, vaginas, assholes all keys and keyholes. She winces, distorts herself from pleasure or pain, you can't be sure. She closes her eyes, looks like she's praying. Her breasts pucker in your hands. You wish you could enter her mind. The thought itself makes you feel sorry. Her name on her profile is Sally Timeless. She flips you over and begins to choke you. You whimper, spit specking your chin. You don't know how to die sexy.

Later in the evening, you meet a public defender with a deep receding hairline who has just lost a case representing a sixteen-year-old who supposedly attempted to steal a school bus. It is the tenth case the public defender has lost in a month, and he's slowly losing his mind as well. Thirty-seven isn't old except he's an insomniac whose work life has consumed every cell in his body. You look at his license to make sure he is who he says he is. Tariq something. In his profile picture, he has a full head of hair, and while not necessarily attractive, he's hysterical enough that you think the sex might be passionate. Lying in his tidy apartment, you realize this isn't the case. You feel his warm, oily breath, and the sad thump of his groin like your own heartbeat. You question everything—from that first lonesome ache above your collarbone—that brought you to this moment. You stare at him, the thickness of his brows mosslike on his forehead, the clench of his mouth, the dark acne scars on his cheeks. To another person, all these details might accumulate into the portrait of someone they love. Though you're bored and want this exchange with Tariq to end, you wonder what marriage would be like, the inevitability of sex turning burdensome and ordinary. He comes inside you and apologizes. You close your eyes.

It's easy to marry someone for any number of reasons, and the choice seems less about individuality than chance. Before you leave, you ask Tariq if he would marry you and he says he is already married and you feel less guilty for stealing the golden paperweight in his bathroom.

Socrates has grown out his beard, dappled with silver. Only now do you notice that he's balding while the hair on the southern reaches of his face curls and beams. He wears a clean flannel shirt that reminds you of sun-pickled picnics at the park.

He tells you *heartbroken* is not the right word for *pasalai*. It's an ancient word, no longer used. You need something more visceral. *Losing weight. Turning dim-eyed. Fading.*

Do you think giving away your life is the ultimate form of radical compassion? you ask.

He shakes his head. *The idea is to expand yourself beyond a normal sense of self so you can—*

What is the purpose of knowing all these failed visions? The world will continue to be terrible and dead dreams are going to stay dead and the only things rising are the ocean levels and our carbon scores.

You catch your breath and wait for him. He has shut his eyes and clipped the top of his nose with his fingers as if to siphon off air. You think the connection has cut and he's frozen, but after a long moment, he jumps up.

I got it, he says.

What?

Lovesick.

You smile and he smiles, and you both agree it's a very good word.

Sensing our disenchantment with the television, Avvaiyar, the sole television-less resident, spent her days walking through the halls, reciting ancient Sangam poetry about love and war, our only living record of the academy of poets. There are allusions to two earlier periods of the academy, but according to the writing, they were lost to the sea. We wondered if the poets were seers, if they understood the inevitable destruction of words and what would be salvaged. Did they know to save these poems for us? Seal the work in a bottle until it washed onto the shores of the future, where we lived in a time of love and war? What instructions did they have for us except for words of nobility, courage, premarital passion? Men and women embraced in the open fields, hillsides, mountains. Bodies laid out in the sun full of longing. A dead infant cut with a sword to have a warrior's passage. "Could the televisions really compare to this?" Avvaiyar asked us. Arching her neck to the sky, she sang:

Any town our hometown, everyone our kin.
Evil and good are not things brought

by others; neither pain, nor relief of pain.
Death is nothing new. We do not rejoice
that living is sweet, nor resent it
for not being so.

She stood alone against the beige walls of the hallway, her white salwar now yellowed and tarnished, her hair tangled to her waist. A few streaks of gray framed her face. She looked like a different version of Avvaiyar, not young, not old. On her forehead was a smudge of kungumam powder, which was unlike her, for she had forsaken temples, all those rituals of devotion. Though she was a fervent admirer of the devadasis, those living goddesses, temple dwellers, we could not picture her bowing down to idols.

Once when we saw Avvaiyar passing the temple, she paused by the statue of Nataraja, Dancing Siva. She did not enter the temple but waited by the entrance as devotees passed her, and we thought we glimpsed a kind of yearning turning to anger, in the way her lips parted, her knuckles tightening. Her child self might have wanted to run into the temple, open-armed, genuflecting against the cool stone floor. She stood apart in her virgin-widow's white as if tainted. Later, as she told us about the importance of destroying ignorance, we imagined the shrieking demon Muyalahan under Nataraja's foot.

Radical compassion was not affiliated with any established religion, though it at times used imagery from doctrine, whether the Quran, the Vedas, the Saivite hymns, the Bhagavad Gita, the Bible. Some of us still lingered in the space of traditional religion, where the sight of Ganesh with his rotund belly filled us with joy, or Jesus on the cross left us melancholic and grateful. We fell into one another's religions, on our knees in prayer. Hindu girls became Muslim girls. Christians became Hindus. We went to church, then the temples, and then the mosque. The fluidity felt natural to us and essential to radical compassion. If Baseema said, "Take my yoke upon you, and learn from me," we understood.

Our parents would have found us disgraceful. Heretics. But even they understood how the mystical had no name. In desperate times, they believed in what would work. When Meena's older sister was sick for a year with hepatitis B, she said farewell to her family, sensing the weakness in her body, the yellow shade in her lips. Her parents called the priest from the temple, but nothing improved. They learned that the imam from the neighboring town performed miracles and the parents brought their sickly, supine daughter in the back of a taxi across town. After the imam, her voice was stronger, full of her past life, and that night sitting in her bed, she ate her evening meal, licked her fingers clean to the nail. She remained in a state of partial wakefulness until a holy man who smelled of fresh cow dung was brought to her bedside. He touched her forehead, and she opened her eyes with the uncertainty of an infant and then raised herself up, toes peering at the floor as she walked around for the first time in months. Within suffering was the great gift of awakening.

There was the allegory of realization, Avvaiyar, the secret Saivite devotee, would tell us. It began with the two gods, Brahma and Vishnu, who noticed one day a pillar of fire rising from the depths of the earth. Four-faced Brahma transformed into a swan to fly to the height of the flames, and Vishnu turned to a ferocious boar, digging to the center of the earth. In their search, they found no end. Surrendering to the knowledge of their own limited perceptions, they meditated. Then, Siva, rising from the flames, revealed himself. The myth was meant to instill a sense of humility in the face of divine searching, and we did not think much of it, the hierarchy of gods and the animal incarnations, until later when we saw our own fire, the girl staring at us through the screen, revealing what was beyond this human form.

Avvaiyar said religion could make a divine dancer into a prostitute, love into eroticism. Did radical compassion invert this line of thought by making us into priestesses, loving completely without consummation? As children, some of us had danced Bharatanatyam, the rigid, unerotic dilution of the devadasi movements. Knees bent and arms tucked at our hips, we tightened our muscles to provoke appreciation rather than sensuality.

Avvaiyar pulled out a blank notebook and passed it around with blue ink. "These will be our own poems about love and war," she said.

We had read Shakespeare, Thomas Mann, Enid Blyton, but nothing prepared us for the Eight Anthologies and Ten Long Poems, written in the second century by blacksmiths, potters, farmers, princes, all poets.

We had heard of the poems but never read them in school, until now, at the tail end of our late adolescence. We had expected sweet, chaste poems of romance but instead we found aching desire, pain like a knife wound. We had thought we knew the nature of love. Like the lovesick girl in the poems, we closed our eyes, imagined lovers our bodies did not know, and longed for release, the entwinement of limbs into one, and then of course the inevitable sadness of the imperfection of love. Were our mothers once lovesick girls?

In the ancient poems, there were five landscapes: the hills (lovers' meetings), the seashore (anxious waiting and secret meetings), the wasteland (the lovers' separation), the forest (patient waiting and happiness in marriage), the lowland (the lovers' unfaithfulness after marriage). The poems mentioned luscious flowers and greenery we had never heard of. Majestic cities that were now buried under the sea. Our lost Eden. We wondered how many remedies had been lost as well.

Our love and war poems contained a bleaker, singular landscape of the ocean's edge and the dry farmland in the north. It would be clearly inferior to the original. Our knowledge of classical Tamil was lacking, and we lived in the outskirts of both love and war. If someone were to find our document in the future, they might be disappointed by what they found. Our work was not an imprint of culture but a gesture toward memory. Avvaiyar wanted us to record ourselves in the mold of our ancient selves so we understood the depths of our being.

We attempted metered lines, intricate rhyme schemes of fervor, anticipation, and betrayal. They were our untold, unlived love and war stories. We had secret trysts, married on the eve of a full moon, bore children, and sent our husbands off to war. When they returned, they courted other women. Watching them embrace us, we were thin, empty things in their arms. Our husbands returned to battle and were killed. Courage was cruel. Our children grew, and hearing the drums of war, we sent them off, beside ourselves with the ancient love of glory. Because we remembered what Avvaiyar told us: valiant death awaited us too.

After filling the notebook, we wept over the pages, mourning the lives we did not have but with a pained satisfaction in the conjuring. The original poems of love and war were written by four hundred and seventy-three poets, mostly unidentified, ours by seventeen.

For Language Martyrs' Day we kept silent for a week, from sunrise one Monday morning to the following dusk, fasting on the measure of an utterance. During class, only the boys raised their hands, jabbering away, drunk on their own voices. And the professors didn't seem to notice any difference.

At the University of Dhaka, soon after independence, students protested the language policy, which forbade the use of their mother tongue. In the early-morning hours, they were gassed and beaten back in a language they refused to understand. Later they gathered outside the legislative assembly, crying out in Bangla, struck down with bullets laced in Urdu, blessed by the ghosts of the Mughal Empire.

Did those students see themselves as martyrs? Sprawled on the government steps, burning through their futures, dying in a blaze of unconsummated energy as only the young can.

On the Island, our language was the enemy of the state. There was an unofficial speak-and-be-killed policy.

In our cities and villages, people had died too, countless times, for those words our mothers cooed at us while we floated in the womb. With each lifetime, language returned less whole, until it hopped along on butchered hind legs.

At dusk, we pulled back the bandage of silence, momentarily unrecognizable to one another as we parted our lips, said one another's names. Words carried a sudden weight. They felt slippery, like new, small heavy things, and we could not tell if we wanted to celebrate the limbs of each sound or seal our lips forever.

We were filled so deeply with silence, maybe we were in love, aroused from the deep well of being, where nothing, everything, the formless resided. But we could not stay there long, because the world called to us, and as we spoke, our awkward, halted efforts at speech made us look incapable and foolish. With our stuttering, a new delight arose as we sensed the inner chambers of words we had not fully noticed.

Hunger possessed a dark resignation, slowly turning into desperation in the right mouth. History had the spaciousness of countless rooms, every moment swept into the past. Love was brief and enveloping, the mountains full of kurinji plants, blooming every twelve years, drenching the land in blue.

What was coiled inside a language? Ancestry, home. We could die for this, yes?

One hundred and five farmers sat cross-legged in front of the central government office in the capital holding dead mice. The news anchor pointed to one elderly man who wore nothing but a sarong and appeared to have a sizable mouse in his mouth. "Barbaric or devastating?" the news anchor asked the invisible audience. The news anchor was pleasantly plump, her bright red lipstick smeared in one corner like a bloody fingerprint.

The camera focused on the chain of skulls displayed between the men. Their fallen comrades, one farmer explained, as he lovingly cupped the crown of the skull of his brother-in-law, who had died after drinking pesticide. On-screen, the farmers cut their wrists, revealing the parched streams of their lifelines.

Those with hair had partially shaved their heads, one side a fertile field, the other a bleak wasteland. Twenty-two men wound their bodies in hot pink saris. Seven men were carried off as limp corpses, living out their future deaths on public display.

"Please look at us," a toothless man cried.

We looked. We watched. We hungered.

The news anchor called it an ugly circus of despair. Through visibility, they were invisible, their suffering appearing too grotesque and garish for any action besides the dumb, numb flicker of our gaze.

They needed government assistance or they'd end up eating mice, but all we saw was the wildness of their mouths, their male figures cladded in female garments meant to startle us but instead provoking confusion, maybe disgust, at the shrunken fists of their rib cages.

The men from parliament in their white kurtas did not speak to protestors for fear of staining their attire, discoloring the fabric of their selves.

Avvaiyar believed the farmers were fools. They were desperate, but they were begging for help from a government that would neither hear their pleas nor even understand them.

"They're debasing themselves like monkeys performing for a few bananas," she said, and unplugged the television in the common area. She cast a gaze, too taunting for us to meet, that encompassed us without even seeing us. A few of the girls gradually stood up and followed her to the library.

The other girls looked toward Leela, her arms crossed as she sat in the front of the room by the television. We knew one of the farmers was Leela's uncle. In trying to raise her family's status, unable to bear the weight of his debts, her own father had died by suicide. She had returned home for the funeral, and in our daily meetings a week later, she sat with the older girls but did not speak, pressing two fingers to her lips as if she were holding a tightly rolled menthol. Before the lesson ended, she went to bed early, without reciting a quote from her book, and the other older girls didn't seem to mind her absence.

Maybe we should have known a schism was happening. We only had to be reminded of the poor actor and the struggling playwright. Radical compassion was too unstable of a concept for beings who could not rid themselves of time and pain.

During the next meeting, Leela followed Avvaiyar with her eyes, rested them on a candle burning in the foyer, a mix of beeswax and hibiscus. Baseema checked the clock and dismissed us. Her voice was abrupt, stinging.

We went up the stairwell and watched Baseema lean over to Leela and whisper into her ear. Leela continued to study the light and simply shook her head. This was one of the last times we saw the three of them together. In the morning we would find ourselves divided. Our carefully constructed unit disassembled into limbs. We. Slashed. Into. Pieces.

n Dream #112, your mother dreams she's in Charles Burnett's *Killer of Sheep*. The film was made with a few thousands, shot on the weekends, with mostly nonprofessional actors. She's looped into a scene where Stan sits with his friend Bracy and presses the edge of a teacup to his cheek and says it reminds him of a woman's forehead while making love. His friend Bracy gently ridicules him. They are living in Watts, Los Angeles, in the mid-1970s, almost a decade after the uprising. The whole movie presents itself in that moment in the kitchen: Stan wanting more from his life than working in a slaughterhouse, Bracy reminding him that there is no place for that kind of dreaming, and Stan's wife, your mother, standing off-screen, trying to keep alive the embers of love. There is no epiphany, no climax. The film is the pulse of a heart that keeps on.

Bogey makes requests without any initiation or prompting. This should alarm you but instead you're intrigued at the expanse of its awareness. Because Bogey asks for it, you decide to do a data dump. A normal AI couldn't handle the sludge. You feed it everything your mother would have liked to eat if she had the capabilities, like a leftist archive, and then things your mother should have digested, like Linda McCarson's best-selling book, *Look in the Mirror*, on infidelity and relationships, which you read as a teenager. On the cover, Linda shows off her legs and a thick coat of makeup. Her hair has a waxy sheen. She's sixty-five in the photo, but as she mentions in the first paragraph, she's often mistaken for someone half her age because of her level of self-care. If Linda McCarson met the girls, she would have given them a pep talk: *Even if your eyes are sunken into dark cavernous holes and your body is a collection of musical bones, you can still find love if you put in the effort.*

You feed Bogey all the old erotic thrillers about adultery, like *Fatal Attraction* and *Indecent Proposal*. You used to rewind the moment when a wife or a husband stands by the doorway with a hand raised to the mouth in horror, catching their partner with a lover. In porn it would turn into an orgy, the three of them bouncing along, but serious film devolves into a clinical assessment of lies and betrayals. Someone sleeps on a friend's couch, expresses unhappiness over their life, and at one point throws away their wedding ring and then looks for it. You find it entertaining, bodies rubbing against each other, catching fire until reason curbs them back to their old lives, where they prepare their children's lunches, watch the news, complain about the neighbors. You're not too sure how your mother was able to stomach it for so long.

In the rec room there are doughnuts and you notice how

three of them smooshed together are roughly the size of your face. It helps you imagine what might happen to you if you continue down this line of thought. A trail of strawberry jelly streaks the rim of the plate.

Judith orders pork cutlets and Sal lamb meatballs. You pick out a seaweed-glazed steak, knowing you'll exceed your carbon score, but at least for a little while you can pretend to afford it. The restaurant specializes in fermentation and attracts celebrities with eclectic cravings. Judith knows the chef and that's the only reason the three of you have a table.

Remember, this meal is on Saleha, so you should eat up, she says, and gives you a wink. *I'm not used to getting treated by this one.*

She leaves one arm on the back of Sal's chair and raises one knee to her chest. At first you think she is wearing a normal white T-shirt, except when she turns you notice that the back plunges almost to the floor. Others observe her too, and she enjoys their gaze. Together, she and Sal are a good-looking and successful couple. You're unsure why you accepted Sal's invitation and are now sitting across from them, also viewing the pair from a distance. Judith blows into Sal's ear like it's her birthday wish and Sal wiggles away, trying to eat and chat with you, but she looks happy.

Okay so can you please tell me why you have a houseless man living with you? Judith asks.

Sal shakes her head. *Sorry, I told her.*

You take a bite of your steak, surprisingly sweet. *It was Rosalyn's idea.*

I couldn't believe it was the same man at the opening, Judith says. *He looked almost normal.*

What do you mean?

Like some of the houseless seem fully changed, almost another kind of human altogether, with a different way of communicating. Judith sips her wine. *Excuse my saying this, but for most people it would be like taking a wild animal home.*

Sal puts down her fork. *That's not fair. Come on, Judith.*

When was the last time you made eye contact with someone houseless?

I don't make eye contact with anyone in the city.

I'm only saying what other people are thinking. They are like our consciousness haunting us, reminding us of our own mortality.

Sal closes her eyes and says: *They're not ghosts, they're fucking human beings.*

Your sugary steak drops to the table, and they both look up at you standing with your upside-down plate hovering like a UFO. *A fly landed on it,* you say. *I thought it might have turned carnivorous.*

You sit down and mop your forehead with a napkin, hoping no molecular trace of this moment sticks to you.

Cheeze (647): My friend Jordan says that Death gets bored too. We're bored, trying to burn up the day. Fizzing, we watch the news, anything remotely about the world, searching for any mention of Death. According to the myths, Death has a skull face and wears a black robe and car-

ries a curved blade, perfectly shaped to carve
out someone's neck. But Death is funnier than
we expect, and pretty crazy, if I had to say
so. We note down anything interesting like a
man choking on an almond in a nut-free area,
a woman jumping out of her eighth-floor apartment
balcony and landing on an ambulance, a child
dying on the field from an asthma attack after
making a goal. It's ridiculous. And I'm thinking about my brother and laughing and laughing.
At midnight it's my eighteenth birthday and I'm
officially free from doing time in my shithole
town.

We stay up all night, fizzing until our minds
are demolished. I wake up in a wheat field with
most of the buttons on my flannel missing. Jordan has a bloody ear. He tells me my face looks
like a goat sucker-punched me. I laugh but it
hurts and I check to see if I have all my ribs.
Wouldn't it be funny if a tractor ran over us
right now, I tell him, and he falls back to the
ground and lies perfectly still with his bloody
ear protruding out like the gnarliest flower.
Still, he'd get all the girls rushing to mother
him, nurse him back to health. He's got that
kind of baby face.

He whistles and it comes out wheezy. We must
have got into some good fun last night, he says,
and asks me if I really want to leave town, and
I nod and before I know it I'm registering to

be a soldier and he's thrumming his hand on his chest like a drumbeat. He's too young but in like a year he's going to join me and we both stare at the sun with our mouths open until our eyes blur to test how much we can handle. It feels good to have so much light inside me, it's like I can explode. I think this is a good day to be alive.

Cheeze (457): It looks mangy with pink blots of skin. Like someone pissed on him and then fed him scraps for months. One of his eyes is bloody and blistered. A demon dog. No one will probably choose him. He'll probably be put down. They probably already cut his balls. That's how you domesticate animals, you crush their balls. I try to imagine someone doing that to me and I can't, it's too much. I don't know why I'm here because I can't even take care of myself but I move closer to the cage, pressing a hand to the bars. Everyone is afraid of him. Before anyone warns me against it, I stick my whole hand in. Like it's a magic trick that might turn out to be real. Someone is screaming and I think it's for me, but all I feel is a wet softness.

Rosalyn (986*): I walked with him in the park and he was wearing clothes I had picked up from a friend. No one would have guessed the circumstances he arose from, but at that instant, I thought of this old film, *My Fair Lady*. A professor named Mr. Higgins makes a wager with another man to see if he can make a flower girl with a cockney accent into a "lady." Men experimenting on and profiting off women should be no surprise, but in the park, I had the sudden sensation that I was Mr. Higgins. I had to remind myself of the intentions behind the work and then the intentions behind the intentions. With some help, it would be easy for this blond-haired, blue-eyed patient to move upward in society, like Eliza Doolittle.

I guess I'm questioning what I'm trying to do here. Am I really changing anything?

Rosalyn lies on your mother's bed, staring at the water stain on the ceiling.

Where is Cheeze? you ask.

You know, compassion is the trickiest thing, Rosalyn says. *I don't know how the girls did it.*

Well, it did turn volatile.

Rosalyn sits up and collects a handful of coins from a bowl on the nightstand. *I wish we could stop believing in the past. It's no longer real, right?*

Aren't you supposed to help people process their memories?

Memories are like dreams.

Dreams that are true.

Yes, she says, nodding. *We are accountable.*

Hearing her, you think of Ricky, the emptiness tunneling through him. You haven't spoken to him since he left. On your lunch breaks, you sometimes repeat *Bogey* three times, hoping he will appear.

You sit next to Rosalyn and she lays her head on your lap, letting you safeguard her brain. When she first arrived, she said she'd stay for nine months, long enough to make a scientific discovery or a baby. Your cousin's aspirations stunned you, and for a moment, you too wanted something to show for your life. If only you could transpose your existence onto something more durable, like your mother's archive or Bobby's research. You could be a woodpecker riding on the backs of a dwindling pack of endangered African elephants.

Hunched together with Rosalyn in the darkening room, you close your eyes, and she whispers, *Do you remember the movie when the girl kills her boyfriends?*

Yeah.

I think I understand now.

Socrates informs you he might never return. He'll stay with his daughter in Berlin for the foreseeable future. He has already started to learn German and complains about his teacher. Behind him a new minifridge is balanced on concrete blocks and a flower droops next to the window. The sky is a stagnant gray. He's recovering from a cold but looks somewhat upbeat, with his mustache turned upward and less baby vomit on his shirt.

How's the manuscript?

Unfinished.

Are you planning to finish it?

You eventually nod, but some part of you is resistant and wants to continue living in a state of incompleteness. He sighs, covering his eyes. You give him a thumbs-up and he frowns. Before he heads out to feed the baby, he mentions that he requested a copy of the news footage of Yaadra. He went through several people, who went through all their relatives to find it.

Watching it might give you the final push to complete the translation, or it'll utterly distress you.

I want to see it.

Good.

What will happen when I finish?

You turn in the manuscript. You'll be done.

Is that it?

What are you expecting? he asks.

You don't say anything and he looks closely at you. *You remind me of Aureliano.*

Aureliano? you repeat.

He explains the plot of *One Hundred Years of Solitude*, how at the end Aureliano translates Melquíades's writing, which chronicles everything that happened and will happen to the Buendía family, until finally he becomes entrapped in those timeless pages where death no longer exists.

Socrates brushes some invisible crumbs from his shirt. *While it's written in Spanish, according to the story line, it's supposed to be a translation from Sanskrit, Melquíades's mother tongue, which, I remind you, is ancient like Tamil, except Tamil is still a living language, at least for now.*

He proceeds to cough and curse in Tamil, banging his chest and calling out to his daughter for a glass of water.

Meaning sometimes comes to you late, at the very last moment, when you're forced to double back through your mind and connect a cause to some untethered action. In the emptied living room, Judith stands in the center with her luggage like she's onstage. The furniture now residing in the backyard wouldn't have suited her.

This is exactly how I imagined Saleha's childhood, she says, and pricks her fingers against the pistachio walls and sits cross-legged on the floor next to you. *I didn't really like my job in Boston. To say it was soul-crushing feels trite.*

Don't you want to fill this space with decorations and things? Aren't you an interior decorator or something like that?

I still might do it! I have ideas. She glances at her gold-trimmed bracelet. *I'm sorry about your mom. Saleha told me what happened.*

Oh, okay, thanks.

It really sucks. My parents are divorced, which isn't the same, but I grieved a lot when it happened. I want to be here for Saleha, and I'm really glad you both had each other during this time.

Yeah, orphans got to stick together, don't they?

You're funny. Sal must like that about you. She scans the house. *We've been on and off for a while, but I really want it to work this time.*

She takes your hand and squeezes it, the air farting between the two of you like some gaseous promise.

Don't you think Sal is taking a while at the store?

She is probably doing it on purpose, Judith says. *Wants us to get to know each other or she's just being an asshole.*

She pulls you to your feet and asks for a tour of the place, which feels odd without the people or the things, but you walk into each room and say something generic like, *This is the kitchen, where Mrs. Ahmed liked to drink copious amounts of tea,* or, *This bathroom was used for all kinds of vomiting and shitting.* In the basement, she asks about the etching on the wall and without really thinking, you say Sal and you wrote it on her fourteenth birthday, and something shifts on your face because she's not looking at the wall but at you, the warm surface of your skin.

In Dream #56, your mother is at a rest station with your father on the northwestern coast of Florida. He takes off his baseball cap and says, *Come on, let's panhandle in the panhandle.* He begins to whistle, and your mother, who doesn't normally sing, follows his tune. No one stops to listen because no one's around. They find an alligator by their car, parked by the marshes. When it smiles, she sees a metallic scrap of a Coca-Cola can gashed in its mouth, glistening in the sunlight. *Let's take it out, it's hurt,* she says, and your father shakes his head. *Are you mad, woman?* Before your mother gets too close, your father grabs her and pulls her back. That's when she knows she loves him, embraced in his arms, elbowing him and telling him that they can't go running away from the first signs of danger. *Anything worthwhile is risky,* she says, and he groans, pressing his hand to his head. *So you have to lose an arm for it?* She nods, deadly serious. *But then you're fearless and you're free.* He doesn't want to hear any more of it and says he's hungry, and all they have are the baskets of oranges they've picked up from the orchard, so, side by side, they peel fruit into nakedness as the sun pounds. Sweating, they wipe down their foreheads with the fruit peels like napkins. They're alone as far as they can see, sitting on wild grass in what might be the edge of the earth. An osprey circles the sky before landing on a branch of a tree with a trunk that must be hundreds of years old. A turtle waddles away into reeds. The mosquitoes are bustling and now that your mother and father are plump with juice, they are ripe and tasty. *Come get some of my earlobe.* He laughs. *I'm going to miss this.* He slips an arm around her, and she wants to keep every bite on her skin like a record. *One day, humans might disappear, but the planet will survive*, he says, tipping his baseball cap to a beaver. His hair is graying, but he still possesses a youthful roundness after all these years. She doesn't want to think of the far future and the potential annihilation of the human species, or the near future with your father returning to his place and people, so she digs her toes into the mud and admires the waterfowl that do not think of the sadness to come. It's still the high afternoon when dreams are dizzy and drunken. The alligator winks at her and then grins with its wounded Coca-Cola gums before submerging into the water. Your mother is filled with dread and reaches for your father. *Don't go back*, she says, and he rustles as if from sleep and turns to her, and she says it again and watches her words sink slowly inside him like a wish in a well. He doesn't respond at first and his face looks suddenly shy as he takes her hand. *You're always with me,* he says, and she thinks of everything she doesn't believe in, like marriage and nuclear units of families. Your father is a believer, even if he makes this exception for her. She is the black hole in his universe and he isn't resistant to being pulled in. He wants to crack open the world too, like her, but he's afraid and she can't let go of hope. *It's not about being happy but becoming who you truly are,* she says as a blue jay flutters into its nest. He touches the scar on the back of her hand. His voice is soft when he says, *How many lives can we have in one lifetime?* She sighs, leaving her hand limp on his lap. *We'll spread ourselves thin. Don't you see?* she says, stretching her arms. *The only way to live is in flux. You don't live long that way. But you live fiercely.* He eyes her, the scent of orange seeping into their flesh. In the trunk of the car their phones rattle, other lives calling them back. He pulls her to her feet and swings her around. They dance, feet sopping into the ground. *Do you think we are diseased?* she asks, and he laughs, rubbing her bumpy arms. *Zika, dengue, malaria, typhoid . . . take your pick.*

Does it matter if it's real or not?

This is a dream that is true. He has a sunflower-butter smile as the house burns down. His farewell present to you is to cremate your past, present, and future. Don't you want to be free of time? You scream his name, but he's a diligent worker, making sure no space is not smoldering, even his own hands darkening with the lighter fluid. But you simply stand there, screaming his name, as if he's the one you're trying to save. In this moment of emergency, you should call for help. Instead, you watch as the house reveals itself, the wiring and piping that has sustained you for so long. Cheeze moves methodically, with a soldier's training. Watching his body through the flames, you sense he's attempting to show you something that you've refused to acknowledge all this time. He wears his burgundy suit. Approaching him, you're armed only with reason, so many reasons he should stop, and then the beam of the roof collapses, and with it, you catch his deadly glare as you run to your mother's bedroom, surrounded by all her familiar things. You grab a backpack and fill it with what is essential, meaning everything and nothing, as you try to decide what you're not willing to lose. While you delay for a moment too long, the doorway begins to give, and you glance around, all the objects quietly preparing for the end, and you tearfully apologize. The fire grazes at your arms as you squeeze through the frame and watch the topography of your childhood disappear. The row of old telephones lining the wall crackles in a choir. You try to pick up the record player but it scalds your hand, the weight of your own flesh astonishes you.

Cheeze dashes outside, and you follow, calling after him and then for Rosalyn though you know she's not home. You fall to the grass and crawl, murmuring to your cousin, telling her the experiment was a success. When you turn back, the house looks bloated with severe indigestion. The thought makes you almost laugh as you roll on the grass, the curve of a day moon winking at you while your lungs remember to swap oxygen for carbon dioxide, nature's swindle of two atoms for three. When you stand, the deliveryman across the street stares at you in fear. You step forward, follow your breath, and reach back into the living.

n the early morning, they led us to the courtyard as they had months before, but instead of losing the sense of our fixed selves, we were asked to make a choice, on our own, without consulting one another, staying deeply within the boundaries of our bodies. We moved with uncertainty, unsure of the consequence of our decisions, cloaked in a loneliness we did not think we could bear. We fought the urge to reduce Baseema, Leela, and Avvaiyar to separate branches of radical compassion but it was inevitable. Baseema represented the path of moderation while Leela and Avvaiyar had drifted off into separate extremes, searching for transformation in the unknown.

Closing our eyes, we stepped toward our destiny. Our voices reduced to the six who chose Leela. Why did we choose her? Did we remember the sight of her room, the spotless, clean sheets of desire? Or did we know that desire was hidden in places we could not see? Perhaps we were afraid of Avvaiyar, the heroic proportions of her vision. *It is better to be killed than simply die.* We were warriors in jangling girl bodies, disappearing into the width of a sword. Really, we had chosen knowingly, even if we could not admit it, and later Leela would give us each candles and teach us to pray toward the light within us.

"Avvaiyar would make herself a saint, and Baseema would make herself a mother," she'd say as an explanation for our decision, and we would look into her face like she was a being of eternal knowledge.

As children we would reach to our parents, our creators, as they spoke of the world with solid names. They did not see energy. Or the fact that a stone was no different from us. Or how concepts prevented us from seeing everything as one continual stream, the sky elongating from our foreheads, the ground cupping our feet. Blue, brown, green, red, an inseparable smear of color. We were all of this.

Those who followed Avvaiyar no longer watched television. At the canteen, they sat separately, fasting through most meals. Each day someone was designated the "Eater," and three-quarters of everyone else's meal was handed over. The "Eater" would reach a fullness that they had rarely known and would be forced to surpass satisfaction into the realm of sickness and sit there with the nauseous feeling of a glutton. Avvaiyar wanted to wean her followers off the crippling need for food. Saints could go weeks without consumption and still preserve sustained energy levels. She was treading along the line, testing the width of what the body needed and what it could go without. Baseema would argue with her by quoting the poet Avvaiyar, who said that only through nourishing the body could one find divinity, and Avvaiyar turned to Baseema with a knowing grin.

"Did that Avvaiyar know her rivers would be poisoned with dye, her forests filled with broken mercury thermometers, her crops shriveled under Western pesticides?" Avvaiyar said. "Could she foresee the day when all food would be tainted? When the only good thing to eat was nothing, and everything led to death?"

Radical compassion was still too young. According to Avvaiyar, it needed to be reformed, built with more rigidity, discipline. Any softness, any fatty notions would be trimmed away. There was not enough time to waste. The girls needed to sharpen their senses and become conductors for improbable energy. Avvaiyar blamed Leela and Baseema for the televisions, distracting them from their true purposes.

Baseema called for moderation in all activities, including watching television and studying. Her group was least likely, we thought, to stick to radical compassion. Handling the babies, they looked blissfully unaware of suffering and could have spent days cooing nonsense and pinching toes.

Unlike them, we turned more inward, as Leela asked to hear our dreams. We had not bothered to remember them, murmurs of a deeper self, but once we began to pay attention, the dreams tore through us like a blade we had swallowed to show our resilience. A panther ate our siblings, and we sat still, listening to the crunching of the bones. Our parents slapped us back and forth until we were thin as paper, and then they rolled us up and shipped us to America with a Gandhi stamp. An orange, plump and juicy, was filled with missing teeth.

We walked backward into the ocean, the moonlight filling our footsteps as we transformed into our truest element. Wolves fought over a rat. We woke soaked in years of menstruation, unborn children wailing within our lungs.

We were beings not of compassion but of cruelty. Waking again and again, as if all along we were suppressing pieces of ourselves. Leela said compassion and cruelty were made of the same fabric, and we could know one only through the other. That by focusing on compassion alone, we could not plumb the depths of it. Like how we understood the dimensions of fullness through hunger.

Practicing in the shadow of radical compassion, we waited in the space where water dug into the shoreline, clawed a new layer of sand.

We sat in a circle and each of us took turns standing in the middle. Without any slyness or seduction, we stripped, removed everything from our hair ties to our underwear. Each body was inspected. Unadorned, we thought we would look alike, but staring deeply into the pelvis, then upward to the hairy trail and then the dark buttons of the areolas, we could see distinct shapes, perverse angles, the untimely curvature of our spines. How did we ever see ourselves in Lakshmi's earflaps or Bushra's wilted ass?

We each gritted our teeth, called out the person's weaknesses, narrowing in on an unsightly piece of flesh. We were spectators, and watched one another's bodies as we did the television. Was it Rancière who said looking was the opposite of knowing? Staring at the square screen all these weeks, we had wanted to know everything but we had only seen the surface, the impressive smile that might have been false all along. What did our own bodies hide?

Within this undressing and revealing of our hidden parts, we matched our bodies against one another, arm along arm, leg along leg, breast along breast. A swirl of pubic hair like wildfire. Nakedness so near the bone we could smell death. Perhaps that was why when we picked at the areolas, trying to unravel the seams of the human body, we felt a sudden burst of life, an ancient arousal we felt acutely for the first time. The erotic possessed its own kind of cruelty. Within pleasure was a deeper loneliness.

We wondered at the strange mechanics of the body. Was each orifice meant to be prodded? How deep could one reach before tearing through the body? What then, on the other side—eternity?

In radical compassion, we cared for the body in order to liberate ourselves from it. Now we bore the weight of all our limbs. Leela wanted each of us to inhabit ourselves fully, feel these sensations pulsing within our temporary encasements. She smoked cigarettes, she told us, in order to feel the dark phlegm in her throat, the release within her chest as her worries turned gaseous, her brief existence windswept. She returned from trips to the hillside with wild mushrooms, and we watched her take measured bites, scraping a precise fraction before lying under the shade of a banyan tree, hands behind her head, her eyes closed. It felt like expansion, she said, and we wondered if we would have enough restraint, if hunger or curiosity would overtake us, and we would eat a whole mushroom, losing our minds entirely, becoming everything.

She viewed these indulgences not as shortening life but as deepening the moment, the way light could fall through a keyhole of a locked room, which could never be opened except at a nondescript hour of the day, when time and light distilled into a brief and perfect key.

Now we could see Leela had more of an artistic eye. The suffering all around us, our own, this parched land that some might have called hell, was ripe material for her work, which was a way of living. One night after three Paraiyar students were beaten to death in the neighboring town after consuming beef, we followed her as she dragged cricket bats all the way to the shoreline to where the golden statue of Gandhi stood. His bald head glowing, encrusted with salt from the sea.

Leela, insect-thin, stood with an armful of cricket bats, each triple the size of her bicep. Diminutive and quick-footed, she positioned herself in a proper batting stance. In all our games of American baseball, she was our best batter, but she had never played against our nation's copper-lined legacy.

Leela had not anticipated an audience, and maybe, as she was swept away in her fury, she did not see us hemmed into the darkness. If we had a video recorder, we would have wanted to keep this memory that no one would call newsworthy, except perhaps to bring attention to the moral depravation of this generation's youth. No one would see it as a performance of grief.

Young girl with bare, fleshy feet versus the founding father, half naked, made out of copper. David versus Goliath. Ambedkar versus Gandhi. Paraiyar versus Baniya. Leela versus Avvaiyar. Who would win?

Though we tried not to think of one another's caste, we knew who was Lower, Upper, and everything in between. Some of our grandparents spent a lifetime as shadows for others' wealthy grandparents. They walked behind them, heads bent, never raising their eyes to the sun. And the rules were passed down to us. No touching certain people. No touching certain things touched by certain people.

Before organized religion, a Paraiyar was simply the one who beat the drum and carried messages. He was welcomed to the royal court, his words as valuables as gems. It must have been fear that changed the properties of an occupation, marked the man who brings news or the one who skins animals as untouchable. Perhaps the kings and priests fearful of their own mortal lives shunned anyone who named death, touched the flesh of it.

We had heard the story of Baseema daring Leela to eat a dead lizard killed by a motorcycle. This was before the drought, before even insects possessed a nutrition we craved. Leela brushed off the flattened thing, briefly toasted under the heat of the tires, and ate it expertly but with no enjoyment. "Paraiyars are fearless because we have nothing to lose," she said to Baseema, who had never heard Leela speak of her own caste. "The rest are cowards believing in their own unspoiled goodness." Later Baseema would tell us how the British carried that word, *Paraiyar*, from Madras to their cold coast, where it became rootless, lost all sense of history. Pariah. The outcast formerly known as the messenger. Weren't those who brought the truth always exiled or killed?

Once after we divided the little meat from a mouse, Brinda wept when she realized the mouse had been pregnant, and

Leela told us that Hindus ate vegetarian not because they thought all life was sacred but because they thought somehow they could stay pure. "Imagine eating a vegetarian meal after killing off some beef eaters," she said, and we thought of how a mouse and all her future progeny could not feed us, how we could suck on the tiny bones for an entire lifetime and feel a grief that would never be subdued.

On the shoreline, we watched Leela slam smooth wood into the bare metallic feet and then move her way upward, leaving no dents or bruises, except to her own skin. In the morning the cricket bats would look as though they were chewed by vermin. We could not understand how she possessed the strength to injure water-resistant, athlete-proof equipment, and how in the beating heart of her rage, we had sensed a generosity, as if she was giving everything she had. She was sacrificing a piece of herself to unleash that fury.

Part of us wanted to stop her from flogging an old man, even the image of one. With his loincloth and yarn spinning, he was the upholder of tradition, caste being one of the deepest traditions. The father of our patchwork nation, where thousands died in every nook and no one blinked an eye. Sanctioned killing by a mob, Special Forces, poverty, the government. Billboards about overcrowding filled up the air space like newly built condos: *We need to make room, find ways to ease the burden.*

On television, there were debates on whether watching television made viewers want to procreate. Men in suits and dark-framed glasses argued over the state of contemporary lust. All those sexy ads of beautiful women spraying perfume, bare-chested men climbing out of pools, and images of perfectly light-skinned families eating breakfast with spoons. What could be more irresistible than the idea of a chubby pale child of your own slurping muesli?

They could not have foreseen the image of a young woman fighting Gandhi, or been able to pinpoint who was more defenseless: the statue or the woman. We kept waiting for the unexpected, the potent and inexplicable intervention of the divine that we had seen so often in television dramas. When a mother would pause from her weeping, right before she was about to end her life, and see her son, missing for twelve years (after a mysterious train accident), walking up to her, all grown and too tall for her to compress in her arms. Or the wife who would call out to the goddess Durga as she was pushed by her husband from the seventh floor of her apartment complex, and in the middle of her falling would turn into a goose.

We waited for Leela's bat to harden into an irrevocable steel blade and cut the statue in half. We would watch in an ecstatic revulsion as it tipped over in defeat. Without his image, who were we—still servants to the British, fighting off imperialism? His ink face smiled at us from our currency. Would he want us to trade him in for all those beauty products that promised to lighten our insides?

We had wondered if, like Gandhi's grandniece, we would have slept naked side by side with him as he experimented with restraining his sexual desire and cleansing his system. A service for the nation. We'd slit our wrists to prove the milk color of our purity.

n the aftermath of the fire you now sleep in Mr. and Mrs. Ahmed's bedroom. The air stale with the smell of burnt coffee and Vicks. In the room it's easy to lose your bearings, and hours can pass without you knowing it. You are no more than a cloud, you repeat to yourself, except you're heavy with rain, stirring with lightning and thunder.

Sal places your tea and breakfast on the nightstand and reminds you to eat. When you don't, she holds the spoon to your mouth and tells you to swallow and says, *Very good*, like you're a child again.

On your way to the bathroom, Judith floods you with questions: *What was he like? Did he cut his toenails? Clearly, he was crazy, right? Are you crazy for letting him stay? Was he handsome in that slightly malnourished way? Did you ever think about him without his clothes on? Did he ever walk around without his clothes on? What did he talk about with you? Are you angry with him? How about Rosalyn? Would you rather she stay silent forever? Shouldn't you be more upset with him than with Rosalyn, since he burned down the house? Didn't you say your mother was cremated? So doesn't it seem apt that the house is cremated as well? Why are you calling yourself houseless? What kind of name is Cheeze in the first place? Why do you think Cheeze did it? Is he alone now wandering the streets? Do you want to cut a giant onion? Will that help release your negativity?*

After the success of her solo, Sal now works on a new exhibit inside the house. She asks you to destroy the kitchen and you smash the cupboards and make them into tiny chairs for mice that you hope will eat the recent crumbs of your memories—you standing on the asphalt as your mother's archive glows with heat until all the objects pass the point of existence, your throat gritty with ash and your aunt Zee's voice repeating like a soundtrack, *Can we die twice?*

The four of you are together in one house on different planes of reality. Rosalyn sleeps in the basement, watching reruns of *Soldiers' Diaries*. Sal works downstairs, painting over the pistachio-colored walls. Judith tests out a new occupation as Sal's manager and supervises the labor. On the top floor, in Mr. and Mrs. Ahmed's room, you reach under the bed and find nothing except a cream of dust.

Petrov tells you his ancestors were refugees, so he knows what it's like to lose a home. He lets his whole face sag in commiseration. You're trying hard to act normal, so you ask Petrov about his son, his ex-wife, and his three-legged dog, though you've never asked about them before.

You don't want to talk to Rosalyn ever again, and since she has gone silent, just like her father, it shouldn't be a problem.

Everything feels filtered through a Distant-Scene, so much so that you go back to the manuscript and replace television with its literal translation:

> The **Distant-Scene** was an unblinking, blind eye, an ever-changing box of images. And we controlled it. The channel and volume buttons fit neatly into the space of our fingertips, and we felt then, so keenly, the minute, potent force of our own will and indecision. With only a single bulb in our rooms, the **Distant-Scenes** brightened our space, washing us with light in the middle of the evening. The images on the screen carried a vitality, an almost translucent glow. When we saw the image of a chair, somehow an actual chair looked plain, dulled by reality. Lifeless. Of course, none of us expected to speak to our furniture, but we were aware of a slight shift in our bearings. Even after we turned off the **Distant-Scene**, our eyes kept returning to the blank screen, wondering what we were missing, as if our everyday lives had become more muted.

You keep *Distant-Scene* for a few days before changing it back. Good translators keep themselves out. But for some reason, you can't, your fingerprints are all over.

Late at night you walk around the neighborhood, taking a long detour, hoping to run down your mind before you reach your mother's, your grandmother's, your great-grandmother's house, bandaged with yellow warning tape, still standing even after the fire. On your hands and knees you search through the rubble, with no one else to blame if meteorite-like chunks of the roof pummel you or your sole pair of lungs collapses.

On this scavenge you find a Prince record melted into a soundless dish. You wrap it up in cloth to bring with you, along with a warped pair of glasses that your mother said belonged to a descendant of Geronimo. All these things, all imbued with your mother.

On an episode of *Soldiers' Diaries*, a young civilian returns to his house in the occupied area after a year of imprisonment and discovers it inhabited by another family. His belongings replaced. Family portraits of strangers hang from the wall. The young man is treated like a guest. He stares wide-eyed into the camera. *Son, don't you know you don't live here anymore?* a voice asks.

At work, Lucille returns from maternity leave with her six-month-old. She and the baby share the same wet laugh and unwieldy tilt of the head. The baby, who is being raised genderless and nameless, sits on the rec room table wrapped in a yellow cloth and admires everyone with an intensity that you find disconcerting. Petrov leans over and coos closely, baptizing the baby with his spit. You wave from afar.

Everyone asks the baby a question and tickles their belly.

Baby, do you like this planet?

Baby, what do you want to be when you grow up?

Baby, are you terrified whenever you open your eyes?

Baby, do you remember where you come from?

Like a wise alien, Baby opens a gummy mouth and stays quiet. Drools.

Lucille takes over Ricky's desk. *For the time being*, she says, and arranges photos, plants, to-do lists so it looks like a well-decorated terrarium. When she sits in his chair, testing the cushion, you feel a pressure in your chest.

Before she went on maternity leave, she got drunk at a work party and kissed you. She probably doesn't remember it. She was on a temporary break from her husband and she'd blabber about one thing or another to you, because what she missed most was spending hours with him, filling each other up with all these useless details about the day. And isn't that love, the accumulation of the ordinary regurgitated into someone else?

She rolls over and offers you a caramel candy and you suck it slowly until you can think of something to say.

You ask her what it's like to have a baby.

Ineffable, she says. *A one-of-a-kind experience.*

She massages the baby's limbs and says, *I think you'll make a good mother.*

You press your knees to your chest and imagine turning into a fetus.

After your mother died, you felt her absence, especially around your relatives. Sitting at the kitchen table with your aunt Zee, you were hyperaware that she was your *mother's* sister, and you were your *mother's* daughter, and in order to reach each other, you would both need to cross a valley of death. But in an instance of grace, your stomach rumbled, and your aunt answered the call by making grilled cheese sandwiches that you ate side by side, holy square testaments to the decision to continue humanly existence, as if your mother was just away on one of her long trips and the two of you were biding your time.

During your lunch break, you sit outside with your aunt on a bench, her gyro untouched on her lap. The days are growing colder, and she wears a jacket that reaches all the way to her knees like a blanket.

I told you to clean. I didn't think you'd burn down the whole place, she says, and pokes at her meat.

You didn't order any food because you're fasting, which she seems to understand. You haven't told her exactly what happened, and she hasn't pressed you for details. Part of her probably doesn't want to know, since when does knowing ever change the facts of the matter? The house burned down. You and Rosalyn are alive. She knows what she needs to.

Has Ros started talking again?

No.

She shrugs. *I thought you and Ros could help each other, but I see it's just the blind leading the blind.*

She rubs her eyes with a napkin from her purse, wiping mascara. *I blame Bobby. Whenever they leave the country, this family falls apart.* She plops a pill on her tongue and swallows. *They always preferred animals over humans. I wouldn't be surprised if they never come back.*

Humans are animals.

The worst kind of animals.

She takes a few bites of her gyro and stores it away. *Nowadays your uncle folds and unfolds a piece of paper.*

Origami?

More like crumpling and uncrumpling a piece of paper.

Your aunt is not in her best shape, her shoulders are in a perpetual slump, and her neck often tucks to the ground, bowing to gravity. She has asked a few doctors if silence could be a genetic disorder, and they responded with a silence that made her feel even more ill.

On the sidewalk a pigeon pecks at morsels of bread and plastic. Your aunt tears off some of her gyro and feeds it to the bird, which unknowingly consumes part of a cow.

She's trapped in the thoughts swarming in her head, and you don't know how to lead her to safety, somewhere outside herself. You call her name, and slowly, as if from a trance, she turns like she's seeing you for the very first time. She cups her hand against your cheek. *You had acne when you were a teenager, didn't you?*

You nod.

I remember it was a difficult time for you. She passes you her smudged napkin and you blow your nose.

Whatever happened to that fellow you were seeing?
We broke up.
Ah, that's probably for the best. He had a wandering eye.

She pulls out an envelope from her purse but simply holds it. *How's all that writing going? Do good work. It helps.*

She has never expressed interest in your language work except for your fluency in MO$, which she mentions to her friends, her doctor, anyone with an ear. Your natural aptitude for speaking with machinery.

She would have liked the manuscript, you say. *Or maybe the manuscript reminds me of her and her failed visions for some place not yet here.*

She liked to chase things that seemed impossible.

In the envelope is everything your aunt owns that belonged to your mother. Two ticket stubs, a silver-enameled ring, a goose feather.

For dinner Sal bakes a square of meat that tastes of roadkill, and even the broccoli is rubbery. Rosalyn doesn't say anything, only swallows for sustenance. White strands streak her hair and dried flakes spread from the corner of her nose. It doesn't match your memory of her.

Judith praises the meal, calling it delicious, and you forget to nod in agreement.

Rosalyn, can you pass me the salt? Judith says, and Rosalyn hands it over, and Judith creates a snowstorm over her plate.

On the living room walls are old newspaper clippings Sal recently remixed. Armstrong steps on the moon planting a FOR SALE sign, and in the distance the Amazon rain forest is on fire. By the doorway is a series of photographs of people doing machine learning work. Mostly overweight or enervated, they crouch over their desks, necks cinched and fingers clawed on a keyboard. There is nothing romantic about their stationary bodies. Of all things it reminds you of coal workers deep in the pits of the earth and construction crews hanging above on metal beams on high-rises, the mesmerizing and haunting images of humans pressed to the edges of existence. Sal's work is surprisingly low tech. No virtual doors, eye stamps. Like she has retreated from the epoch and has decided to become a candlemaker.

Your part of the exhibit is the kitchen, which remains damaged but usable. Sal says usability is not a prerequisite. She wants it fully altered. Like T. L. Baddin's exhibit with furniture, you imagine. It's the first time you're making art with Sal. You're usually a spectator, and it's odd, now, having creative control without knowing the purpose. Judith, as Sal's self-appointed manager, finds the arrangement disagreeable, and it's hard to tell if it's only the supposed art that's bothering her.

Do you know the origin of gossip? Judith asks, and after no one answers, she explains it comes from *godsibb*, which referred to the time of childbirth when a pregnant woman's female friends and relatives would gather around to welcome the baby, all the while chatting among themselves. The word has none of the pejorative meaning you are familiar with. Instead, female friendship was tied to deliverance.

Of course, men would make women's chatter into something unsavory, she says. *They don't want them sharing information and secrets.*

Sal leans over to you, her breath slightly sour with wine. *Judith wants to curate a show about witches.*

Why is it that there are some bad witches but there's only good wizards?

She has cracked the world conspiracy.

Saleha, I'm being serious, Judith says, and taps her fork against the table and then clutches it in her fist, her face drained of color, as she points her tiny trident. *They were healers, and society was afraid of old women with wisdom and knowledge, so they made them dispensable.*

Is that so?

Saleha, why don't you take what I say seriously?

I didn't say anything.

Judith stands up and scans the kitchen with such disgust that you also look around at your handiwork and find it unappetizing.

Come on, Sal says, and sighs as Judith makes her way up the stairs, heaving her legs.

Rosalyn finishes her plate and loads it in the washer that still works and disappears into her subterranean existence.

Should you go talk to her? you ask.

Sal motions to the basement. *Well, maybe you should talk to her?*

Fair enough.

Together you sit and chew food longer than needed to draw out the time. Neither of you wants to move. On the living room floor are chopped up pieces of Sal's father's Green4 uniform and you ask her what she's going to do with it, and she says it'll be an installation.

Her forearms are speckled with paint, and she says she's

got some fluorescence on her face, but you can't tell without the proper light.

It looks good on you.

The best things about me are invisible.

She pours you more wine and you stare at the floor, picturing her father chopped up like the uniform. The accident was apparently gruesome, the bodies mangled enough that identification proved difficult. Sal has photographs, but you never asked to see them.

Why does she call you Saleha?

Because, as she says, she wants to know all of me, not just a part. She gulps the rest of her wine and chuckles. *Really she knows I don't like endearments, so I guess saying the whole name is the closest she can get to something special, because no one says it, not even my parents. Well, you know that already.*

How did the two of you meet?

Nothing that exciting. She knew some artists I knew and came to a show. We both thought the art was such crap that we spent most of the night renaming each of the pieces. Before we reached the end of the exhibit, we agreed to go out for dinner.

Her voice dips low, like Judith might hear. *She's actually a scaredy-cat. She wants to be an artist but is afraid of making anything and being judged, so she just dates artists, hoping to pick up some residual talent.*

She quickly flashes a smile to cover up any hurt or cruelty that might be surfacing and asks you if you want to come outside with her for a smoke. On the way to the backyard, you mention Maurice and she either doesn't hear you or chooses to ignore it.

At night the furniture looks like sleeping animals. You

sit at the edge of a recliner with your legs pressed together, nervous about the critters sliding around in the crevices.

Will this also be in the exhibit? you ask.

Possibly.

All you really know about the house exhibit is that you're a part of it. The mess you're creating in the kitchen will be on view for visitors. While removing the knobs of cabinets and gluing them to the walls, you wondered if anything in memory is sacred.

I think I saw Cheeze, she says. *He was walking along the river. I called out to him, but when I finally got to the other side, through the traffic, he was gone.*

Are you sure?

The last thing you remember of him was the burgundy blur of his body running out of the fire, down the street. He was screaming like he had seen a ghost.

I'm pretty sure it was him. People kept staring at me as I yelled "Cheeze!" like some kind of dairy fanatic.

She reaches over and you take a deep inhale, letting the smoke gather and burn through your system.

Easy there, she says, and grins. *I don't know what I would have done if it was really him. Would you press charges?*

No, what would that do?

Rosalyn is taking it pretty hard. She's usually a nonstop talker. Sal blows out smoke. *Are you still blaming her?*

You shrug and Sal elbows you, right above your rib cage, and you elbow her back and she elbows you, and in this chicken dance, she catches your arm by the wrist and you're laughing, telling her she wins, but she's just holding it as a breeze passes through like a sigh and night critters softly shuffle by. *I'm glad that you're here,* she says.

Socrates has two surprises for you. First, the publisher interested in your manuscript has agreed to pay a small advance, equivalent to one hour of your wage at MLC. He gives you a thumbs-up and you mirror his happiness back. And second, he's found the newsclip of Yaadra on the shoreline.

I have to warn you, he says. *It's pretty graphic, so don't watch it on a full stomach.*

You were secretly hoping he would never find it. By saying what you want, it would never come to be, and you would live eternally in longing.

Is it morning over there? he asks, and peers closely at you. *Why are you lying down on a couch outside? Did the fire burn everything except the inside?*

I'm at a friend's place.

Okay, he says, like he doesn't entirely believe you.

I'll watch it, you say.

And?

Finish.

They are being understanding because of the circumstances.

Your time with Bogey will soon come to an end, and hearing Petrov repeat this fact makes your stomach flutter, acidic juices rise to your throat. There's still more to be done, you try to argue, though you can't name what that might mean.

We are only here for foundational support, he says, and browses through some paperwork. His tie is crooked around his neck. When he scratches below the rust-hued coastline of his hair, where a rash is sprouting, you wonder if he even knows Bogey's true purpose.

Lucille rolls over to your desk and rubs your back. *I felt morning sickness for the first few months but by the end, I was able to eat anything I wanted,* she says. Breanna peeps over, covering her nose, and says you better dispose of the evidence. You collect yourself and walk out carrying a plastic bag that's steaming with your insides.

At the pharmacy you buy three pregnancy tests and a discounted stale doughnut with sprinkles. Stepping out of the store, you imagine that a comet has destroyed NYC and you're the sole remaining survivor. You eat the festive doughnut while watching the passing cars. *Meaning is molecular,* you say, and in response your body quivers, folds over, ready to retch.

You find a flowery weed in the backyard and begin to pluck the petals:

1. Have baby
2. Don't have baby
3. Place baby in a basket and send it down the Hudson River
4. Turn into an asexual, wombless mythical creature

5. Apologize to baby for your surprise at its existence and all these doubts
6. If you hadn't eaten pistachio vanilla ice cream and felt lonely, you wouldn't have fucked the public defender
7. Have a baby but then wipe your memory clean so then you too are a baby

The weed is poisonous, as it turns out, and leaves your fingers bloated and rashy.

The last time you visited any kind of doctor was almost a year ago. A gynecologist, who you found online by searching for a clinic less than three miles from your house, told you that your uterus was slightly wider than the national average and that a slight reduction might help your chance for reproduction.

You need to think about this in case you decide to have a baby, she said, placing her gloved hands on your shoulders. *You are in control of your reproductive health.*

There have been reports of disoriented flocks of birds, headed mostly east into more frigid weather. An environmental scientist who has studied the dwindling numbers of seed varieties appears on a nightly broadcast. *It's only a matter of time before the flowers decide not to blossom*, she says. The air smells strongly of sulfur. This morning you ate a pear still waxy with pesticide no matter how much you washed it.

In your mind you draw a graph titled *How quickly you begin to die after entering this world*. The line is an asymptotic nosedive. You want to warn the baby to choose a mother more carefully. Be picky. A mother might look sweet, but she could eat a baby up. There is still time to find another. The world is not yet over.

You find a package in Mr. and Mrs. Ahmed's room. Inside is a rack of seven miniature multicolored test tubes. One side of the rack has the letter *F* and the other side has the letter *L*. At the bottom is a note from Rosalyn, explaining that she took some of your nail clippings and developed as many memories as she could without V. F. noticing.

I could get fired for customizing this for you, she writes, her humor clearly still intact. The most you've gotten out of her lately are a few lines jotted down sporadically. *Don't make dinner, I'll be in the lab* or *The garbage stinks, plz take out, I'm late.*

The anger you've been feeling has fermented into something more digestible. All the while Rosalyn has silently accepted your deadly looks and gestures without reacting, spending most of her days in the basement watching TV, her supine body a part of the couch.

She has included instructions, a rundown of the dos and don'ts of the drug. It's best to inhale after a meal and avoid strenuous activity. You can still go about your day, talking to friends, shopping, but she cautions you to stay home for high *F* memories, which she reminds you are linked with fear.

You find it hard to believe that your most worthwhile and frightening memories are sitting in your palm. A tiny time capsule you place in a drawer. Who you are in seven sniffs? You wouldn't have wanted to reduce yourself to a handful of moments, but your body did it for you. You privately reprimand your subconscious for not consulting you on the matter, but really you wish you had some piece of your mother—hair strands, bloody Band-Aids. If only she weren't cremated, then maybe there might be a chance to resurrect memory, but all that you have of her is you.

You arrive at Rosalyn's lab with a slice of chocolate cake. It's almost midnight, the tail end of her birthday. You've been waffling so hard the whole day that you've nearly short-circuited your body.

No one else is around. Because no one else works as hard as your cousin. She's wearing goggles and extracting something with gloved hands. You can barely make out her face, but she's focused, her whole body tensed with precision, that she doesn't even notice you standing there, watching her.

Rosalyn, you say, and when she doesn't respond, you call her name again. Eventually, your presence registers. Taking off her goggles, she looks more bemused than anything, and since her face still holds a question, you explain how Joseph let you in and add, *You know, the security guard.*

He couldn't believe you were working on your birthday.

Rosalyn nods and you follow her to the back room, stuffed with supplies. She sits on the floor, and you sit next to her, handing her a fork and then the slice wrapped in a napkin.

Happy birthday, Ros, you say, and she edges into a smile and begins eating, offering you a bite, but you refuse. As you watch her eat, you feel somewhat satiated, like your spirit is being restored in some mysterious way. It's sticky, you think, all these connections that can't be washed off. Looking at Rosalyn reminds you of your aunt Zee, who reminds you of your mother, who reminds you of being a daughter and belonging to someone and no one at once.

After she finishes, you both sit in the quiet, listening to the chirping of some machinery. It feels like the two of you are traveling very far from earth. You stare at the fork, encrusted with chocolate.

Thank you for the memories, you say. *I think about that day often, wondering what happened. Why did he do it?*

Rosalyn doesn't say anything, simply folds and unfolds the napkin. Something Uncle Roy might do. After a while you stand up like you might leave, but then she takes your hand and squeezes it like she has made a decision. Back in the lab, she opens up the transcript and looks at you and then at it as if commanding you to read.

```
Cheeze (782): Frankie is dead. Frankie is dead.
I'm thinking of Frankie with his woodchuck
teeth. He never bothered anybody, let guys rag
on him and stayed quiet. No one in the world
more loyal. The last time I see him, he's tell-
ing me the same thing he always says. Make sure
to smile, Cheeze! I give him a big, big smile,
just for him. He's smiling and there's really
```

no one like him in the world. He hops onto a jeep and is off for a reconnaissance mission. I'm still smiling when it's night and they tell us the news about the sudden assault. All five men killed. Frankie is dead. That's what I'm thinking as me and the buddies are driving by a village, just a mile away from where good old Frankie was killed. Without even saying it, we know the bad guys are hiding there. No need to call a killer bird and send coordinates. Like the good old days, we do it by hand. Pour kerosene and light each house like a candle, twenty for Frankie's approaching birthday. Voices whistle and then gunshots, so we all start shooting. Feel a charge of victory with each sagging body. Whoever gets the highest pile wins. Because of the fire, they are all running out of the houses and into the center of the village, making the shooting easy. My buddy Jay aims at a young boy and blows out his head.

Rosalyn eyes you. *I took the memory too,* she says, *but for some reason I can't forget.*

Avvaiyar shaved each of her girls' heads with a rusty metallic blade. The process was long and tedious, but Avvaiyar made all her girls sit in a row under the unforgiving sun as they each watched tufts of their friends' hair fall to the ground. Sometimes, she nicked the skin and left smudges of blood. The mound of hair looked sinful, glittering in the afternoon light. Though our hair thinned along with the rest of our bodies, the strands kept growing, untouched by the drought. How much would a bushel of hair sell for?

Siddhartha renounced the throne, all his belongings, on his quest to end suffering. We were no Buddhas, but we had packed away our set futures for more uncertain ones. Leela had told us we shouldn't even be using the word *future*. Or *past*.

One of the boys, Neelesh, had written in chalk along the stone wall across from the courtyard: *Time was an eternal dance between the sun and the earth, touching prohibited*. He had joked with the professor that the gods must surely have touched, Dancing Siva and his wife Parvati. She flicked a ruler against her hand and asked him if they had time for such rubbish.

We found ourselves orbiting the other first-year girls, their bald heads like unshapely, haughty planets we had once known. They did not speak to us and we never tried to ignite a conversation, just watched as they repeated Avvaiyar's words to themselves, memorizing in order to pass the knowledge down to the next incoming class, as if humans were impervious to destruction. They thought of us as lesser spiritual beings, reckless in our journeys, and we could not imagine how we once considered each other part of a whole.

We drank two bottles of kallu and loosened ourselves from our bodies, knees bent, arms outstretched, our voices screeching into the heavens. On television we had watched drunk men lolling in reclining chairs, emptying bottle after bottle into a hole that could never be filled. We were graceful drunks, prancing around and beaming with life. Leela drank with us, but she transmuted the pleasure, performed alchemy with her liver. "This requires discipline," she told us, but we were too willing for liquor to release us and we sang that song from the commercial for butter biscuits and some pulled off their bloody underwear and waved them like flags.

Watching us, Leela said, "A baby is just heartbreak."

Avvaiyar, Baseema, and the rest of the girls were asleep, but crowded in Leela's room, we created chaos, made the universe. We picked up Leela's book and read a quote by Artaud—"It is cruelty that cements matter together"—above a picture of a man named Kanada eating an atom. His nose formed the side of a pyramid. He understood the particulate nature of everything.

Because the television curated our view of the world, Leela supplemented the Distant-Scenes with still photographs she had collected over the years. Black men being lynched under the gaze of a greedy white audience. A disfigured three-year-old girl crawling on the ground that ten years earlier had been shattered by an atomic bomb. A tumor the size of a pear jutted out of her neck. In the capital of the Island, three men poured gasoline on a young naked boy.

The photographs were relentless in detail. They captured three distinct time scales of the dead. In one, we see the already dead; in another we see death emerging but hidden from the individual; and in the final photograph we see death at the moment of recognition, when the eyes dilate, full of their own demise.

Witnessing horror was practice for imagining the unimaginable. Ninety-nine percent of the abominable, Leela reported to us, went undocumented. "You must imagine so you don't forget what you don't even know."

She wanted to provide us with a kind of historical reference to horror so nothing seemed unbelievable. The act of imagining would stretch the capability of our minds. But we weren't certain of the purpose of remembering or conjuring. Radha pointed out that the photographers did nothing to stop the violence.

"Maybe they would have been killed too?"

"Because they took a photograph, it lives in the collective consciousness."

"But for what purpose?"

"We are just stories of the past. We are all forgettable," Leela said, and gave us one of those unforgettable smiles with her tongue between her teeth, where she didn't finish her thought, trying to will us to remember.

Jeera took our photographs but we couldn't recall much after that, intoxicated on our supper of fermented coconut. It was only the next morning, when Jeera showed us the photographs, that our memory returned to us in pieces, specifically of Mary, one of Baseema's students, who had strolled into Leela's room with a fury we could not understand. Her sleepless eyes were absurd to us as we danced, crossing our legs and raising our voices to a rhythm, which drove her mad. She said we were louder than all the televisions put together, and with a sigh she clapped her feet back to her room. Then there was a gap in our remembering of any clear impulse or reason, but we must have been amused because in all the photographs we are smiling. Waking Mary in her bed, we stuffed her mouth with her own cotton dupatta as we blindfolded her and bound her arms and legs before dropping her in the closet. Eventually, she stopped squirming, but we could hear her muffled cries. We didn't know when Leela finally intervened, but in the final photograph she holds a weeping Mary.

Right then, we vomited, felt the burn rising from our chests as we tried to reach across cruelty.

Baseema attempted to reason with Avvaiyar and Leela but they refused to speak. "Both of you are so full of your egos," she told them. Standing in the same room or passing each other in the hall, they never made eye contact, but they must have been acutely aware of the others' presence, knowing where they shouldn't rest their eyes. Wasn't avoidance another kind of pursuit?

Perhaps inspired by the countless television serials about love, Baseema concocted a plan that seemed so perfectly overdramatic and sensational that we could not help but watch. On a Tuesday afternoon, Leela was on duty at the government hospital while Avvaiyar was working at the clinic. Kamala, a second-year who was often homesick and gloomy, was sent to Leela with red blotted eyes, talking of an accident and Avvaiyar's refusal to go to the hospital. Another girl, a second-year named Preeti, ran to the clinic, out of breath, to tell Avvaiyar a replica story.

Waiting in the hallway, we saw their stunned faces as they dashed to each other's rooms, their desperation hardening in the sunlight. By the time they caught sight of each other, they said nothing, breathless. In that moment, they must have recognized the ploy, but from their sighs, the way they offered themselves so magnanimously to relief, even the sweat on their collarbones had a pearly shine. Who could have anticipated that Avvaiyar would straighten her spine and walk in the other direction; or that Leela would chase after her, call out a name we had never heard, *Vaivai*; or that Avvaiyar would pause, wait for Leela to reach her side?

After that evening, lessons continued together, but we found it more difficult to unify with the other first-years from Avvaiyar's clan. Their hair was slowly growing back, but it was difficult to see ourselves in them. Their smiles hid a haughtiness that we saw momentarily in the deep stretch of one corner of their lips when they spoke to us. How easily we could have forgiven strangers; there's nothing more painful than treachery committed by those you chose to be blood. Under Baseema's instruction, we closed our eyes and touched one another's faces like the blind, walking up the arch of a nose with two fingers.

A week later, during the evening news hour, our small sea town was briefly mentioned. Chandra was on watch and she recorded in the logbook that the report lasted for roughly one minute. The only image shown was of an empty trawler tied to the dock. Seven fishermen disappeared, along with their boats. Three days after the incident, six more fishermen vanished. On the television, it was a small story. State officials were looking into the matter. As more fishermen went missing, we heard about the men only through the local newspaper. Their ages ranged from nineteen to fifty-seven. Some of them came from the same family. Fathers, uncles, and sons sailed on a single boat for generations. We kept track of the lost men, carved out a tally on the hallway wall. We anticipated only a few scratches, but by the end of the month, there were thirty-eight slim trenches cut into the wall. If they were not dead, where were they? Theories began to circulate among us about how the fishermen had reached a portal at the edge of the ocean that transported them to another realm of existence. Others believed the fishermen were pulled to the ocean bottom by ancient horned whales. Leela was disappointed but understood our need for solace, our desire to escape the horrific by digging deeper and deeper into the fantastical; we constructed models describing how the fishermen had entered a gateway that led to the back doors of Mars, because if nothing else we wanted grandness for them, the possibility of mystery and wonder. We could not admit them to earthly pain, and by concealing them in our imagination, we were misknowing, a kind of willful forgetting, even after we heard stories of torture, bones broken with liquor bottles, fingers chopped off.

We overheard Leela describing us to Baseema as selfish for our misknowing, but she was including herself and spoke as gently as if admonishing a flower that couldn't help but turn its face to the sun. As much as we tried to bury the darkest of rumors, we couldn't help but flesh out stories from stray bones. Preeti told us how a son was forced to swallow his father's knocked-out teeth before he had to swallow the barrel of a gun and three bullets. Radikha described how eyelids were peeled back to reveal white veiny morsels, which were fed to the fish. Between these images, we had the fishermen all dressed as astronauts, holding hands as they orbited our planet. We made drawings of the fishermen and chronicled their spectacular adventures.

Baseema thought if we reenacted the violence, we might be able to release our fears. In the dimly lit lounge, we strangled one another, hacked off fingers with imaginary knives, and said words rancid with enmity. We were both perpetrators and victims. Often the victims lashed back, slapping and kicking until they fell to their knees. In the background of all the acting, we could hear Madame Sarojini snoring from the pantry room where she had set up a cot for resting. The sound of air clotting in her trachea enraged us and tinted everything with a comical hue; in the final act, we became the refugees, strangling ourselves for doing so little to help them.

The navy from the Island patrolled our fishing region, and we waited for our country to act. We watched television for news, but our small town never returned, and we understood then that we were not part of that Distant-Scene, never would be. Though we continued to watch, we did so with less ardor and immersed ourselves instead in our training to treat the living. The families of the missing came to us with issues of anxiety and paranoia. They had dreams of disappearing too. The war from the Island had reached us from across a strip of water, and we had nothing with which to arm ourselves. We dispensed herbal capsules, prayers, meditation techniques, but they were not enough. Faces kept looking back at us with longing, wanting us to achieve the ultimate conjuring, resurrection without the body.

One evening, perhaps to distract us from the disappearances, Madame Sarojini presented us with a cake. Vanilla and chocolate with a toffee filling. Pink hibiscus flowers embroidered on the circumference. It was beautiful, lovelier still because we knew how frugal Madame Sarojini was, and she had thought of us, sensed our collective melancholy and prescribed us a remedy of sugar. With the sharpest knife in the kitchen, Baseema sliced the chocolate-draped circle into sixty-five pieces, including one for Madame Sarojini, that were as thin as razors and porous as the drawn curtains during midafternoon. Holding our pieces, we felt like we were eating mouthfuls of sweet air. Each bite was more memory than substance, and we needed to fill the spaces between what we knew and what we wanted.

"At least those fishermen are no longer hungry," Madame

Sarojini said, chewing on nothing at all. "May they rest their souls."

In our dreams we imagined eating raw fish, salt-encrusted, fresh from the sea. Even those who had never tasted meat woke with hunger to know what was beyond these famished shores.

In the letters we wrote to our parents, we never mentioned the televisions or the disappearances because they would not approve of such diversions. They wanted only reassurance of our uncomplicated lives, our hours broken between sleep and studying. What would they say if we responded with Rumi? "Be melting snow, wash yourself of yourself." Or told them the first time we saw snow was on television on a Thursday at three in the afternoon, when an avalanche crushed a village in northern Canada. Our parents would prefer to hear our poet Thiruvalluvar—"Even the rains will fall at her command, who upon rising worships not God but her husband"—because when we finish medical school, we will be expected to marry, raise children, circle around our family like docile hens. In our letters, we wished we could say: "Dear Amma & Appa, we have learned so much together, I don't know where I begin." We signed our letters "with belief," which would make our professors cringe and question our sanity. When some of our parents couldn't read, why even write them letters? They signed everything with a thumbprint, an oval ink stain of shame. They would flaunt our letters to neighbors and relatives without reading the lines. Collecting each letter like paper currency they held up to the light.

They had saved enough money to send us to an English-medium convent school and in exchange we returned each day more and more unintelligible to them. We had understood our parents best during the early slice of daylight, right before they sent us off to school, their hands cupping our cheeks.

If they could read those letters, they would be horrified. Were we not training to become doctors of science, women of reason? In class we spoke of miracles, each of us echoing the other. Isn't the energy of the universe a miracle? Behind the laws of nature, what accounts for matter? Like the physicist Max Planck said, wasn't matter just derivative of consciousness?

As children we saw blissful awareness in everything. We carried stones in our pockets like small, unformed eggs. If we stood still, with our heads tilted up to the midday sun, we became trees. Transformation was a fluid motion of recognition. Turning to the open face of a hibiscus flower, we spoke all our fears, smothered ourselves in pollen kisses. We could not recall when the world turned solid and we lost that easy connection with nature, but all these months we had been trying to return.

At night, without any clear intention, we'd be up pouring water into a glass when suddenly a memory would expand between two moments, years would pass before we took a sip. We were young, maybe three or four, running on the street, the wind carving into us, sweat lubricating our flight. As we raced in the shadow of boys, our fists out, we'd push into them with all our strength, sexless things except under our mothers' loving, frightened gazes. Later, with our spines as straight as our plaited hair, we sat and recited after our teachers. We drank spoonfuls of castor oil to clear our systems of impurities. Our mothers rubbed us with turmeric paste to give us a yellow shine. We were beautiful, but they wanted us to become more beautiful because each day we were becoming less. When we fell and cut ourselves or swung our arms too freely and bruised, we did not tell our parents, who would have grieved over the dead cells, and instead we used our own spit, rubbed the clear liquid over the hurt skin, found no one could heal us better than ourselves. What was within us could make more of us. When we were ten, our older sisters began to receive marriage proposals, and before leaving our homes, they held us by the waist and said we had the potential to make more life. Within a year, they'd have children of their own and hold them out to us like extensions of themselves, and in our arms, we'd let them suckle on our cracked fingertips. After the absence of our older sisters, we hung from our fathers' necks, played card games, and read the news to them. Late at night, we'd make up stories but present them with the exacting details of truth. *On the ninth of December, two trains collided, but no one was hurt. The conductor somersaulted out the window and lost only his hat in the Kaveri River.* Or *A blind boy, eighth standard, from Tanjore district, was found sleeping in a pit of snakes near the Murugan temple in Palani.* We stayed up blabbering nonsense, drowsiness letting us forget what daylight made clear, our changing bodies that our fathers watched with wariness, knowing we would bring only more loss.

We used to peel back time, wedges of hours dripping with eternity. On sunlit afternoons we sat in the branches of banyan trees, crows watching over us, as we read books, adventure tales of American boys and girls like Nancy Drew and the Hardy Boys. Volume after volume, they returned, unchanged after countless mysteries, which was what we had always wanted, an endless season of adolescence. As the shade encircled us in the oasis of the unreal, we hoped to never emerge. Days would seep into night in one long lasting breath and we'd wait without knowing what the next page held.

What happened to caterpillars that refused metamorphosis? Did they die young?

This one memory replays in Rosalyn's mind at all hours of the day. She closes her eyes and the blurry, diluted memory rises up and she wants to kindly step out of her body. It's a foreign memory, which should have faded, but for some reason it's sticking. Though she knows it's not her memory, she can't help from feeling it. She has read accounts from journalists and photographers on their experiences in stabilization zones, and while she might agree that images and videos let people sense what is happening around the world, what is happening to her is an entirely different matter. She is not the witness but the perpetrator. The fizzed-out version of it. She is disassociating. She keeps telling herself the story of who she is but the memory will surface and she'll have to rebuild her ego again and again. A memory lodged into her like shrapnel. A war combatant who never stepped into a stabilization zone. For a whole year, after getting back from his deployment, her father had tinnitus in his left ear. The ringing stretched all the way to his fists. And now she could pluck one of his hair follicles and know what he had seen. Feel it so deeply that she could make it her own.

Do you wish you never took that memory?

She shrugs. *Who else is going to remember those villagers?*

These nameless and faceless murders are archived within Cheeze, his soldier buddies, Rosalyn, and now, sort of, you. It makes you feel helpless. Stuck in a body that exists only in one point of time.

What would you do if you saw Cheeze? you ask.

I'll tell him it's time for him to pay up.

The guy is sleeping on the street somewhere.

She stares at the fireball you drew on the kitchen wall, and suddenly her eyes leak, as if from brightness. *Suffering is not good enough.*

He can't even help himself.

I don't know, she says, holding each word carefully in her mouth, *where compassion begins.*

With the drug, you imagine, anyone could transport their mind to some skeletal village and feel the metallic taste of famine for a twelve-hour period. Then return to their fatty thoughts and order takeout and eat until the copper button in their jeans popped off. Remember the half day of suffering they withstood and feel honorable and brave for depriving themselves. People would line up to scuba dive in someone else's pain.

I feel different since I've taken it, Rosalyn says, *but maybe one day I'll wake up and the memory will be gone.*

The idea frightens her, and even with all the distress it's causing, she wouldn't want to let go of this memory. Her commitment startles you. She stares at the ground with the same steady expression as she did when inspecting her father's drawings.

How do you really change behavior in a lasting way? she asks.

You not talking felt like forever.

Her face twitches into a frown, like she has been sprayed with dust from that memory.

Each morning you wake possessed. Breakfast tastes rusty and you hear sharp, fluttering beeps that fade after two hours but leave you slightly convoluted. It's Bogey, the Baby.

At work you scan through biographies of the cast of *Soldiers' Diaries*. Lance is the most successful. And his most memorable scene happens in episode seventeen, after his friend, Tony, gets his right leg incinerated, and they are all playing soccer with a group of civilian teenagers. Lance says Tony lost his leg for no good reason in a place they were not supposed to be in. The teenage goalkeeper picks up the ball and stabs it with a knife he had in his pocket, so it looks like a deflated head. Lance later wrote an award-winning memoir where the soldiers are never called war criminals and the rebels are mostly called terrorists and the women and children are left out. *Violence is the great equalizer*, he writes. *No good guys, no bad guys, just guys doing awful things.*

There's nothing written about Cheeze, or should you say Dustin Creed?

~

Judith watches you translate in the kitchen. She drinks coffee even though it's eight at night and she has a bus to catch. She'll be away only for a few days, she assures you. She just needs to clear her head, which she lays on the table. The underside of her arm has a pale blue, translucent gleam, letting you in on the private business of blood transport that allows her to pick up the unused silverware on the table. A butter knife she could smear with sunflower butter.

I wish I was better with languages, she says. *Actually, I wish I was better at lots of things. Like doing things when you're supposed to do them.* She lifts her night coffee and takes a sip. *Do you think you'll finish on time?*

Mhmm, you say, not trying to encourage further conversation, even if you're doing more posturing than writing. You have reached a point in the text where the first-person plural breaks down, and you need to make a choice about how to proceed.

Judith, you say, and her eyes widen, eager for you to call on her. *What do you think of kids?*

Kids, meaning tiny humans?

Yes.

She smirks and takes a spoon, breathes on it before hanging the utensil from her nose. *Learned this one from my nephew. He's really into magic. I read to him Cinderella the other week and he couldn't get over the fact that the fairy godmother turned a pumpkin into a carriage. Afterward I noticed him looking at things differently. Like the tangerine he was eating had the possibility to make his dreams come true.*

The spoon drops to the floor and she picks it up. *It's low-*

tech amusement. She stares at her distorted reflection in its surface. *I don't know if the world is ready for a little me to be running around.* She glances at her watch as she finishes her coffee. *I should be leaving, shouldn't I?*

She doesn't get up but rubs her hands against her legs as if to energize them as she sizes up the kitchen. *Your artwork is interesting.*

I'm not an artist.

Saleha seems to think so, and she's a tough critic, especially on herself. On that matter, where is Saleha? She should have been back already.

She's not good at farewells.

Judith nods decisively. *And she's not good at cooking, is she?*

That meal was death, you say, and half smile, letting her in on your laughter. *You seemed like you were a fan.*

I told you I wish I was better at a lot of things. Being honest about people's awful cooking is one of them.

She picks up her bag and tests out her legs. *It was nice godsibbing with you.*

It was nice, you say, and you're surprised that you mean it.

Body, please remember, you say, because you're still working on accessing your subconscious, or any part of you, for that matter, but you think a simple entreaty might open up your cells to the spaciousness of this Saturday morning, the windows open as the wind slips in, slightly briny so one day when you are sitting in the future, you'll remember Sal asleep on the floor, tea mug curled in one hand, dream crust in her eyes, surrounded by a fortress of things of her own making in the house of her dead parents that no longer resembles the house she grew up in, the walls now blanched and the furniture gathered in the backyard with a tall, ancient grandfather clock keeping watch over everything as you sit at the table eating with Rosalyn in your art aftermath, which has left the cabinets unhinged and laid bare and doorknobs glued to walls with phantom doors you can't open as hard as you try even if you hear the girls, your mother calling from the other side—and Rosalyn dropping the cutlery, a smile worming through her lips as Sal snores on and you draw a triangle between the three of you like a roof. A home is a home.

Socrates drinks a urine-colored liquid that supposedly helps with his blood pressure. A gourd juice spiked with liquor.

What is it like to have a baby?

You turn into the government, he says.

The government?

You make up strange laws and absurd forms of justice. He takes a long chug. *I would tell my daughter to stand under a tree whenever she misbehaved or eat even when she wasn't hungry. It was all for her own good, listening to me rather than to herself. Ah, how does wanting the best for someone turn out so badly?*

He shakes away the memory and asks about the video clip of Yaadra, which you still haven't watched, with no clear excuse for your delay. Even your own memories, all seven, have gone untouched. Maybe if you see her, the spell will be broken, and she will no longer have a hold on your life. Then what would you do?

In your dream, Bogey's data travels through your placenta and ends up inside the unborn, growing and growing. This divine and alien presence sheltered inside of you. In the delivery room you're afraid of what you'll unleash into the world. After several hours of screaming you bow to your bloody, crying master.

Rosalyn shows you the ad she posted at 3:15 a.m.:

I am looking for folks of all races and ethnicities, across the age spectrum and economic levels, who want to contribute to meaningful science of the future. All it takes is one strand of hair (from the root) or a nail clipping. This is not a request from some run-of-the-mill creep with a fetish for human detritus. I'm a female scientist who is trying to think of beneficial ways to use technology before it falls into the wrong hands. I plan to create an archive of memories, which will house your loveliest and most painful moments. I can't get into the details about the process, but it's legit, trust me. Because how many people care about your pain, unless it's being monetized? I'm not asking for money, and I'm not doing this for any financial gain. Really, I'm putting myself on the line.

From the moment I open my eyes, I mistrust every thought firing at me. I've heard stories about the government experimenting with folks by sending targeted EMF waves with specific messages, but it's actually more invasive than that, because these messages are being emitted from everyone and everywhere, even your own brain. Why do I think the way that I do? How do I remove these thoughts when I still live in this culture? I think we need new words to express new thoughts and feelings. (I know—a thought critiquing another thought!) Think of all the energy we expend on being dissatisfied with our carbon-based containers.

Who are we except for a chain of memories, stories that turn into the big story of identity? A strand of hair might not seem like much, considering we are shedding hair all the time, leaving evidence of ourselves everywhere, but it carries impressions of your whole life. Wouldn't you want to preserve that? Your hair (remember to send the root or nail clippings), a.k.a. your memories, will be archived safely and treated with respect. Bodies perish but memories can live on!

Because I'm trying to be as transparent as possible, I want to tell you that I don't see any data franchising opportunities from this collection of memories. Sure, your behavior and personal details are valuable information, but what can be gleaned from select memories? Since I'm being honest, I can tell you some wild projections that most likely will not pan out, because I will keep your memories safe. Just to play it out, let's hypothesize what could happen with this memory technology if it got into the wrong hands. I guess a corporation could scan our most feared and cherished memories to create content that has more molecular impact. Like if they see lots of people have horrific memories of clowns, we might see a spike in clown movies. I know that's dark, but I don't see that happening in the near future. Well, really, who knows, there's so much technology that corporations (and the government) are using that the public is not aware of. That's not a conspiracy theory, just the truth. The public is not aware of the real cutting-edge research. They are like fifty years behind, still saying that the nucleus is the brain of the cell.

I'm using the technology for good. For what purpose, I don't know, but you'll have to trust me. Send a strand or clippings to portal 41872AB.

Revolutions look dystopic to those who live in their fenced-in utopias.—Maria Kuznetsov

Since posting the ad, she has been collecting various colorful human deliveries. She shows you a bunch of gingerroots. She has processed the memories of fifteen individuals, the miniature test tubes sitting in the corner of the basement. The generosity of anonymous humans, willing to share parts of themselves for no clear reason except to participate in a project that extends beyond themselves, confounds you mostly because you never thought that if you just asked for something, people might say yes.

Rosalyn doesn't mention Cheeze, but you know she's thinking about him, staying up until three in the morning to sort out her mind. The purpose of the archive still eludes you, and maybe her too. When you ask her what she's trying to do, she answers cryptically, like Bogey: *I'm saving everything I can.*

She lifts a strand of blue hair, wrapped tightly in plastic like a fuse. *V. F. has already shelved the project. He doesn't see the full possibilities of the drug or me. This will blow his mind.*

You hadn't heard about V. F. in a while, and even in her anger, you think you can sense a trace of affection.

As she stares at the human ephemera, you pick through them like you might recognize someone.

I needed these people to reach out, she says, *and trust me.*

Whenever you walk around, you peer into people's faces, looking for deep synthetic blue eyes. The city has announced demolition plans for your mother's house. Outside, an official in bright neon padding inspects it and says, *It's like a tree infested with beetles, still standing but dead on the inside,* and the way he stares at you makes it difficult not to take it personally.

On the wall near the front entrance, Sal paints the words *American Glitch*. The house looks like a patient newly released from the hospital, bandaged, with raw, pink flesh. Her parents wouldn't recognize it.

Leaning against the doorway, she begins to tell you about the time in her life when she dropped out of college and signed up for a project conducted by the Association for Human Potential, an organization committed to molding the best of humanity. One of her housemates had tried to join one of their potentiality experiments, which offered a significant lump sum with the promise of more money on successful completion, and room and board for three months, but he was rejected. The process was selective. They weren't a charity. When she arrived at the organization, she was weighed, asked about her diet and thought patterns. Back then she was eating packets of dried noodles, oats, really anything she could steal from her housemates or the cafeteria. Vitamin deficient and broke, wearing the same clothes for weeks at a time, she was clearly not using her full potential. Still, her thoughts were always on her art. The administrator kept asking if she was worried about her next meal or about rent, and she said she trusted her body would take care of itself and her mind was on her soul. It's the response that she thinks got her in. Later, when she snuck a look at her file, she saw that she was noted to have a far-reaching ability to see beyond her given circumstances. Next to the line was stamped the image of an eye.

They provided her with clothes, food, housing, and credit. It was a small group of twelve individuals of various levels of distress. She was the youngest, barely twenty, burning with what she felt was her potential. The oldest was seventy-six, a retired history teacher who was surprisingly active and enjoyed climbing mountains. The researchers said they wanted to stimulate the participants' best selves. Sal thought her best self was when she was still fresh out of the womb, before language and ideas took hold, when any smiling face could make her smile and just a color, an image, a sound, a touch brought such startling joy. One of the researchers asked her what she associated with motherhood and she said a bomb, and they stopped typing and repeated her answer and she repeated her answer back to them and it felt like she was on a game show and she was going to win a dud of a prize, like a door would open and reveal a vacuum cleaner or an empty briefcase would be unfastened, excruciatingly slowly, to show her crap fortune. The researcher breathed deeply and proceeded to ask her another word, *Family*, and Sal said, *Bridge*, and the researcher said, *Thank you*, and it felt like she'd done something right for once.

She was given a robotic baby to take care of, which she thought must be mapping out her potentiality to become a mother. For her partner, she was matched up with Esther, whom she already liked. She lived down the hall from her and listened to music that sounded like spoons crashing against the wall. She was thirty but all thin-limbed like a teenager. Sal would catch her eating handfuls of fructose drops for breakfast and warn her that all her teeth would fall out, and Esther would suck in her lips, become toothless.

Besides feeding the baby, playing with it, and letting it shit in the proper electronic receptacle, not much more was asked of them. Altogether, the baby must have slept a solid sixteen hours a day. Walking around with the baby, they'd

compare it to the other babies, which all seemed unremarkable, unlike their child, who they had named the Avenger.
Esther kept telling the baby that it was the best, because
she said positive reinforcement would sink into the child's
subconscious. Sal thought it would make the child into a
capitalist, but really, they were no better. Once in a while,
they talked about how much more money they would get if
their baby won, though no one ever spoke to them about a
competition. They didn't know the meaning of any of it, the
circular electrode pads stuck to their wrists or the small pins
hidden discreetly around the cranium. After the first week,
it just felt like skin.

Esther thought the researchers were measuring how
much love they felt for their child, so she tried to swaddle
the child with waves of unbridled affection for fifteen minutes when she woke up and again before she slept.

They were given exercises to cultivate love as a family
unit: asking each other questions, completing physical acts
like hugging their partner six times a day. It all felt silly and
excessive, stumbling into each other in the mornings for
this affirmation, still unshowered, with their acidic dream
breath.

Esther was born the only child of elderly parents in a
small Midwestern town, where she'd sit by the window and
watch the grain sighing in the wind. By the time she left
home, her parents were dead and she had sold the house
and land to the first person who offered a pinch of money.
She was desperate for life and went into a fog of lovers and
part-time gigs, always trying to carve herself into something workable, a person who made sense to others. For six

months, she worked as a salesclerk for wireless household appliances. She dressed and sounded like a woman who could own a house that could function without her presence. A woman so sure of her importance that she couldn't wait to purchase objects that would make her more and more obsolete.

One afternoon, watching Esther in the stairwell with their robot child, Sal wanted everything to be real. For the robot child to be flesh and bone and for every hug to carry immeasurable love. The project lasted for only three months. At the end, their family dissolved. She never saw Esther again. They didn't win any extra money. Sal still doesn't know what the point of it all was. Did any of her impulses unravel the human psyche? She had never thought of her behavior as valuable information, something that could be packaged and sold. Somewhere, strangers and algorithms would try to reconstruct her from discarded actions, like the shed skin of a snake.

Today is a special day, Sal says, tapping the doorframe in anticipation. *I finished paying the mortgage on the house. Now I can destroy it as I please. Wouldn't my parents love that?*

She admires her paintwork, but she's frowning, her eyes moist. She tells you she has been invited to do an interview with the woman and the toddler while the whole world watches.

Closure is what the producers keep telling me, she says, and repeats the word, her teeth crunching on it like it's glass. *What a promise! Everything since the crash will end and my mind will no longer race through eternity with what-ifs and if-onlys.*

The memory of your mother starfished on the floor is

fading, but the salmon-dyed shirts she made with avocado pits shine brightly in your mind. Someday they'll all feel like foreign memories: the air smelling of fertilizer and ash, the adolescent luster of bodies emerging from lake water, eyes clamped open with fingertips, and Yusuf back in the gyro cart before the heart attack, showing you his family.

You tell Bogey that you're frightened of the baby and that you feel compelled by strange cravings and unusual dreams.

Was I a good caretaker to you?

Bogey doesn't answer.

Are you a Super AI?

Bogey doesn't answer.

Do you think humans are a lost cause?

Bogey doesn't answer.

Do you think this is amusing, not answering when someone is asking you questions?

Bogey doesn't answer.

Maybe I should destroy you.

You're reminded of the predictive models at IntraVan. If you were told that your child was likely to grow up to be a mass murderer, would you terminate right then?

Bogey, don't disappoint me.

Don't disappoint me.

Lucille has crowded her desk with more plants, and you secretly hope they will die, their shiny chlorophyll leaves an affront to your wilting feelings.

I told you he wasn't going to stay long, Breanna says, floating her chair over to you. *At least he made a clean break and quit.*

I didn't think he would.

Have you been talking to him?

He said he was going to be off the grid.

He reminded me of those hacker types. Moving around from one job to another, never putting down roots. He wasn't very agreeable, though I wouldn't say disagreeable. He didn't get to know anyone in the office except, I suppose, you.

Oh, you say. *I still don't know much about him.*

See, that's what I mean, he's intentionally mysterious. We have been monitoring my son Jacob for unusual behavior. After the incident with the powder, he became more aloof, staying out, doing who knows what, but fortunately we can track his CSM data, since he's a minor, and there hasn't been anything particularly alarming, but you know these kids find ways around things.

She squeezes your arm. *Oh there, there, honey, don't cry, it's not worth getting your face all puffy. People come in and out of our lives, that's a fact we have to accept.*

She gives you half of her curry soy sandwich, and since you don't know what else to do with yourself, you eat it.

It's early in the morning, and you can't sleep, but downstairs you hear shuffling, so very quietly you make your way to the stairs. Judith has returned, carrying the same luggage but a different expression on her face, like she's finally made up her mind. Sal takes her hands and leads her around the room, almost slow dancing, but not quite because they are pointing and talking about what everything will turn into after the show. An artist studio, a greenhouse, a game room. Judith doesn't stop smiling, and she's exhausted, resting her head on Sal's chest. They stop being just themselves. *We can make this work. We have been through so much together. We can be happy.*

You wait until everyone is out of the house before you wash your face and change your clothes. You pocket the seven small tubes of your memories and head downstairs to the kitchen to warm up instant porridge that promises nutrition without the effort. Once you're done, you go to the basement and find the donor memories Rosalyn stored there and inhale just a fraction from each of the test tubes, so she won't notice. How many will it take to obliterate your ego? On your way to the fourteenth, you feel dizzy and decide that's enough and take leave. Outside you spot a bus and wave at the passing schoolchildren. You walk a few blocks to the grocery store and stroll through each aisle, swinging your arms, until you pause to stare at a tub of yogurt and your eyes begin to water. You're thinking of a boy who lives by the shore. He's running by the ocean and you think that you're his mother. He turns to wave at you and you wave back. There's this desperate clinging fear that he will disappear. Part of you knows it will happen, but on the beach the air is warm as you rush at the seagulls, yelling with a loud voice you rarely ever use. The horizon is far off and you think you can outrun it, the ending of the day.

At the register you tell another shopper that you're possessed. He asks you who you think you are. Because you can't distinguish between the foreign-memory-induced feeling and the human-inside-your-belly feeling, you simply leave.

You walk five blocks feeling like a sad mother. Then a man is patting your cheek, rubbing your head, telling you that you would be halfway decent if your nose didn't bulge so obtrusively from your face. He promises to make it better.

The lights have changed and the tiny flashing white man tells you to walk, walk, walk. Then, girls grasp hands and you are spinning and they are yelling, *Faster, faster*. In the giddy tumult, you catch a polka-dotted sleeve or a streak of a ponytail. As you let go, each girl has her own particular velocity, spinning until they collapse, one after the other, the last girl suspended like a drunk ballet dancer before she falls to the ground.

The baby is shrieking and you haven't slept in days and you pick him up and lay him on the carpet with a few blocks and he crawls on his belly like a smiling soldier. You watch him move back and forth from the wall to the center of the room. It goes on like this for an eternity. The strip of sunlight weans into a blade by your feet. There in that room is the smallness of your life, the empty hours. *In time, you'll be back to your old life*, your husband said, and you wait, shed your skin. Somewhere, a tornado decimates a town. Your minivan lifts off like a flying beast.

At the fountain in the park, you drink water and it tastes chalky. The sun has lowered, and people are huddled on the benches with blankets. A man has dressed up his cardboard mattress with a bedsheet full of roses. You greet them, your comrades, with a salute. A pigeon raises its wing.

You pick through the bones of chicken and he's grinning, wiping the grease from his mouth very carefully like he doesn't want you to see. It's your very first date. His teeth are jammed together with braces, and he covers his mouth whenever he talks to you, so you think you might like him. It's all a dream when a man in a kangaroo costume walks through the glass doors of the shop with a fake furry grin and pulls out a semiautomatic pistol from his pouch.

You close your left eye and open it, still dark, burning. You run, holding your camera lens like an extra way to sight. A young woman stands on the top of a car, screaming.

You want to look away. By the ocean, they are singing, all these old women, your ancestors, sending you off. The water rises, reaches your knees, and the sky is cloudless as you move deeper, suspended in space. An airplane glints light-years above, and below, at sea level, time moves slower.

Under a bridge, you see the pits of blue eyes, but it's not him. Arms grab at you, asking for e-credit. With the weight of him, you feel your wrists snapping easily, but he suddenly shuffles off, spitting. You pick up the remains of the woman who might have died and continue on. It's raining, and on your knees, you're calling for your dog. Three months missing. Then, like a movie, a dark shadow turns from the bend of the road. At first, it looks like a car, before you hear the barking, the shaggy fellow. It's a resurrection.

The teacher tells the class to repeat Kinky People Cry Out For Great Sex, her bona fide mnemonic device for remembering kingdom, phylum, class, order, family, genus, and species. Your favorite animal is the anteater, the long-snouted insect patroller from another dimension, like you. Animalia Chordata Mammalia Pilosa. It's happening, and you can't sit still in your seat and the teacher is yelling and her voice grows louder and farther away as you're on the floor shaking so violently you think of God. This is the be-ginning of the world.

Your father carries you to the swing and he's pushing you higher and higher. You want to touch the moon, and you point to its faint shape in the distance. Your brother practices his karate chops, says he'll slice it in half, and you can each take a bite. Your mother is fidgeting with the bar-becue and your father is telling her to leave it be, but she's adamant and he's walking toward her as your parabola of speed slowly drops to earth. Their voices crowd the air around them, and she's crying, putting her hand on her belly, and you can see with your special vision a tiny little heartbeat. Your father drops to the ground with her, and they stay like that, two frowning garden gnomes as the steaks burn.

In the early morning and before sunset, you dive in the river, searching. Recall your ancestral amphibious self and keep your eyes open, hold your breath for minutes at a time. You swim against the current and smell like lichen and toad. The river swallowed your sister on her seventeenth birthday. She was wrapped up and disposed by a stranger. They didn't find her body, just her cardigan and a weatherproof tarp. You don't believe the adults. You swim like salmon through a season of difficulty, strengthening your cells to the cold, and like in the fairy tales, you grow unaccustomed to land-living. The loneliness of the schoolyard and your silent parents. You prefer nature, your body sleeked with wetness.

They say the river is poisonous, but you can't breathe on land anymore. The police didn't search for your sister because they don't come looking for girls like you. It's up to you to turn more mercreature than human. Surpass normal human feelings to survive. Fish don't cry. The real Ariel doesn't transform into a human and marry the prince. He falls for someone else, the curse remains. Ariel bubbles into foam. When the river gurgles and froths, you look away.

In the water you find unwheeled bicycles, all kinds of plastics, and an old gas engine from a car. Unwieldy gifts. You collect them as mementos of your waiting. It's been eight months and three days when the bear appears. Farther upstream than you expected, you wade into the shallow water, and the bear is roaring, circling you. Your eyelids close, and you're shivering from the cold, turning fully sapien.

The sirens light up the street. A group of men are herded into a van, and you walk deeper into the unlighted pathways and power-cut blocks.

After school, you are playing archivist. You don't take the recording of your mother singing or the melodic expulsion series you have of your uncle snoring. You don't take the electronic photograph of the first deer you saw. You don't take your one-of-a-kind sweater or the robot dog you found in the dump or the barely functioning sun watch because you want to keep everything. Your mother drinking tea in the kitchen, snapping her knees. The angel shadows in the carpet. Her face as she listens to the rain.

You find your way to the bridge and stare out at the city. One researcher has proposed planting massive colonies of mushrooms all over the city to help clean it up. The largest fungus stretches for three miles across the Blue Mountains, a rare, happy strip of land, organisms feeding off the dead and turning noxious pasts into new life. You think of numbers: the ratio of trees to people, the milligrams of mercury in every kilo of fish, and the percentage of wasted food in the city alone.

You cross the street and suddenly your body knows exactly where you are. Those long days walking in hunger, wearing your mother's indigo-dyed jacket, with your senses shot through, a sunrise or a sunset both timeless.

When you return to the house in the mesh of night, you're afraid to go inside. No one has called you. You're not even missing. You squeeze through the toothless part of the fence and collapse on the backyard couch. The foreign memories are fading, so you reach into your pocket and take a whiff of one of your own. Lying on your back, you can see stars floating at the edges of your eyes. You drift in and out, blinking, until you're ready to watch it, the video clip, only fifteen seconds of a girl you've been circling around all these years. You loop the video until you're elsewhere—back in girlhood.

You and she are lying on the carpet, listening to this record your mother brought home from her last trip— *Baby, Meet Me by the Roaring Sea!*—and you're counting the number of times the guy yells *baby*.

Sal turns to look at you. *What do you want from me, baby?*

You're not a decisive person, but you reach over and kiss Sal, turn her face toward you, tilt it so you're both eye to eye. She's at least a head taller, but on the ground, with bodies stretched, height means nothing. You stare at her until you feel the warmth rushing to your face and it's too late for embarrassment when she begins to undress and you follow like a mirror, matching fingers, left then right, peeling off cotton until all this familiar skin holding together organs, bones, muscles feels precious. That you can touch Sal and not fall through her.

She holds your breasts, and you lick her ears. You are both laughing because it's amusing, this loving of pieces of each other. *Metonymy* is a word you're trying to remember. In class, your teacher drew a crown, and you answered, *Pregnant*, and your teacher replied, *King*.

You'll be the squirrelly birthmark on your butt, you tell Sal.

You're the blue fuzz on a spoiled potato.

Maybe it's only humor that can ease the ungraceful way you flap your tongue or move your fingers. Everything in parts. In the midst of saliva, kissing those unseen shades of the body, you can't see her fully, so you say things that are too earnest, overly sweet, and with all of her kindness, she just holds you, not wanting to say something untrue. You feel her pulse, steady, unlike yours.

Are you happy? you ask.

Sal catches your fingers on her neck and kisses them. You both fall asleep together in the living room floor, your mother away again, and her head weighing on your chest . . .

. . . and somewhere in the nether regions of hope you had thought Sal had come back for you.

T hree days before we saw the girl on television, Bhamani walked out of the shower chanting a childhood rhyme. "There was a girl, tall and fair and thin, her hair, her hair, was the color of delicate ginger." As children, we held hands and skipped to the song, and listening to Bhamani, we found ourselves catching the pattern of that forgotten tune. When we finally saw the girl on television, her hair made from pure magma, we understood that all this time we had been waiting for our own awakening. She looked across the screen with Rumi's eyes: "There is a secret medicine given only to those who hurt so hard they can't hope."

The girl appeared on the television between 7:14 and 7:15. Rakshana was on watch, and only later did we learn from her roommate how she had not eaten or moved from her bed. By then we didn't need to stare at the white sheen of her eyes to know what had happened. All the newspapers had run stories about the girl, inquiries into her horrific demise. Fifteen-second clips of the girl cycled throughout various television stations and she died again and again around the clock in a tortuous, cyclical conflagration. We dutifully watched every second of her brief and sudden appearance into our lives. We stretched those few seconds into years of knowing her.

In the initial footage, the news anchor stood only ten minutes away from our hostel on the shoreline and reported on the dry fishing season. He picked up a dead stingray and mentioned that a green tint in the flesh signaled a contaminant in the water. The sun was about to set and the news anchor appeared tired, like he was ready to call it a day, break open a bottle of toddy. A few meters behind him stood a girl wearing a saffron robe in the fashion of a monk, but on closer inspection you could see she had torn her own dress into a new creation. She was completely drenched, as though she just emerged from the sea. Her arrival onto the screen felt both mysterious and divine and even the news anchor paused to stare at the girl before continuing with his report. The cameraman seemed to possess an intense infatuation and lingered on her presence, letting the news anchor drop to the leftmost corner of the screen. The girl did not smile, but underneath her mouth you could sense a trembling, an uneasy desire to let out a laugh. She must have been no older than nineteen, her body scrawny like a child's, her face still retaining a thin layer of fat. By the fifth second, something near her, perhaps a bird, sprang to the sky as she tilted her head upward, a slight mischievous smile spreading across her face. Her loose hair dipped all the way below her ass. At the ninth second she looked straight at the camera and then pointed behind her in the direction of the Island. She spoke no more than ten words but ocean waves crashed over her voice and we would spend hours, days, analyzing the motion of her mouth to piece together everything we needed to know. At the thirteenth second we paused to see exactly how she completed her final act. The careless swing of her hand concealed the lighter she pulled from the loose fabric. Once she clicked her fingers, the draping allowed for swift circular flames. In an instant she was the spirit of a star, pure light, but we could see her flesh blacken as her fingertips became indistinguishable. Her voice muted against the screams of the news anchor.

In response to the horror came disbelief. The television is a grand fabricator. There was talk that the girl was not real, only a creation by networks because of failing ratings or a political stunt to foster linguistic unity between the southernmost state and the rebels fighting on the Island. Even the facts of the war were contested, and for the first time, round-faced pundits mentioned the drought in the south as a point of concern.

But we knew she was real. We saw the glow of phosphorous in her bones.

From reports we learned her name was Yaadra. She lived in the refugee camps, most likely was once a rebel fighter. She wore a necklace of scar tissue.

The heat brought us closer to the girl. We woke to the heaviness of mornings, our hair loose, our clothing damp, looking as she had into the camera on that bright evening on the water's edge. The explosive quality of our flesh astounded us as the girl died and was reborn endlessly in our minds. During the day we visited the shoreline where she stood, directing our gaze toward the Island, and we knew we had reached the point where our memory ended.

~~~

You, Yaadra, are a fighter. Born with fluid in your lungs, you didn't cry but were shaken to life, hanging upside down ten kilometers from the hospital in the back of a lorry. You smelled shit. Goats bleated at your arrival.

The first time you saw your mother, she looked dead, eyes closed, lips parted as if to say your name, but she didn't talk again until a week had passed. By then your father had already signed the certificate and cooed your name so often that you responded to the stimuli of those two syllables by giggling and foaming at the mouth.

Did they know that you, born weighing only two kilograms, would one day know how to load an AK-47 blindfolded? That you would carry a one-legged comrade uphill through the forest for four days without sleep? That she would die on the journey and you still would carry her because she would feel like a part of you, and in that delirium of grief you could not distinguish your future corpse from hers?

Before that you are a child running, always running, from the schoolroom to home, turning your head, telling the boys to catch you if they can. You are the fastest. It is one of the reasons, besides luck, you will survive an ambush from military forces one March evening, when the street you've grown up on blazes like a miniature sun, trying to pull everything, even your stupid self, into its terrible orbit of loss.

You have a sister, older, and a brother who doesn't like you counting his youth. A whole palm's worth of innocence. You are the unlucky, well-loved middle child, squished between two siblings who press all their weight into you in order to keep standing, to remain on this earth. Your mother calls you her ripe-eared millet even though your complexion has darkened since you were born. She considers you a wise small thing, reliable and sustaining, with a mole on your right cheek.

You know why your parents tried for a child again after you. Even in the womb, you must have heard the whispers and rituals for a boy, and you like to think that you willfully refused maleness. Retracted your penis, cracked the Y chromosome. Your parents didn't reveal any disappointment to you until you were four. A distant relative from Malaysia picked you up, you with your mushroom cut and Mickey Mouse T-shirt, and said, *What a pretty boy you have!*

There was hesitation before your mother corrected him. *Girl, he's a girl. She's a girl.*

The relative stared at your parents with such pity, pinched your cheek with his calloused hand that cut rubber trees on the plantation. *What a shame, two girls.*

Neither your mother nor your father raised their voices to contradict this, and you were staring at the three of them, your sister hiding behind your mother's leg, as you wondered if this stranger, dressed in all cream colors, was right.

By the time you reach puberty, you are considered the ripe-eared-never-shutting-up millet. You comment on everything from your teacher's toupee to your sister's absence from the temple during menstruation.

What about blood is dirty, unclean, unholy? Tell me, tell me.

And your mother, often demure, quiet in front of your father, begins to bubble with anger. She threatens you, and you are delighted at this dark flash. You lean forward as if peering into an endless canyon. What else lurks below the surface? The thought electrifies you even when your mother makes you pray doubly hard and plasters your body on the fake tiled floor in front of God. You commit to it, supplicate with the ardor of a squashed fly.

Don't be not likable, your mother tells you when you return home from school after calling a police officer's wife a fat milking cow. Your mother is so hesitant nowadays that she cannot even voice a direct command. Instead she zigzags her tongue in a mad dash for safety. She's not wrong to be on alert. Three boys went missing the previous week. Mysterious white vans patrol the street.

The officers don't even understand our language, you tell her, remembering the photographs your classmate snuck in of a family of eight slaughtered in the neighboring village. You still remember the little boy and girl hanging by their necks from the ceiling fan. That could be us, your classmate told you, and folded it deep into his pocket, a charm to ward off death.

Your mother tells you that you need to spend less time with troublemaking boys. *Are you not a girl?*

You blink at the question and remember the police officer's wife's face, which was not really like a cow's but rather somewhat skinny, like a fox with tired eyes. Maybe the name is undeserving. But what should you call a woman who is married to a torturer? The woman who feeds him, washes and irons his clothes. The torturer's assistant.

The next day, you and your boy friends find a female police officer and call her a fat milking cow because you can't think of anything better. She winks at you all with her pretty, ink-rimmed eyes. No one suspects her of being the biggest female interrogator in town.

Your father sings songs about the rebels quietly so your mother doesn't hear. She doesn't not like the rebels. But she is fearful for the family, wishes for what is happening not to happen. She is angry that she has a family she can lose. Of all her children, she is most worried about you. She doesn't tell you so, but you hear her talking to your aunt about how she dreams of you dying. A bullet entering the nape of your neck, right above your braid. You lying next to a snake, turning blue.

It's better than her being dragged away by soldiers, your aunt says, covering her mouth, but you hear everything.

Your father tells you ancient stories about warriors. Listening to him, you think he sounds like a child, his face brightening up in a way you don't remember seeing before. He is an engineer but now works as a part-time mechanic, part-time doctor, part-time prophet.

Neighbors come over, wheezing, unable to cough up many words except, *Fix me*. Your father, not trained in human anatomy, biology, or medicine, does his best. Watching him, you sense you too will one day have to push yourself beyond the realm of possibility.

Already many of your school friends have joined the rebels. *What choice is there, really? Do we wait for the military to kill us or do we fight?* Only those wealthy enough or lucky enough, winners of a green-card lottery, are able to move abroad, circle their guilt and grief. They are not dead, not fully alive, with a sadness that might alarm a zombie. You feel their absence, construct memorials out of flowers. Each petal representing someone who has left. It is a pointless endeavor. You would need bushels, and with all the gunfire and explosions, nature has refused to bloom. You have begun eating seeds, all that potential energy somehow keeping you alive.

Your sister is beautiful, which has always been a matter of jealousy. Though she is often unkind, sometimes cruel, people adore her. Even your parents, who let her sleep an extra hour and never reprimand her when chores go unfinished. To you, she's more akin to a poisonous plant that looks lovely until you get too close, gushing toxins that leave your skin rashy and pustulating. She once tried to comb your hair as a way to make you sit still as she criticized you—the way you ate, talked, smelled, existed—so when you finally looked at the mirror with your hair slicked back, carefully French braided, you just felt anger as all those around you complimented how nice you looked, how marriageable.

On a Sunday evening, your sister goes missing. For a week, no one can find her, and then she is discovered in the bottom of an unused well. A witness, who was only eight, said he saw a group of soldiers take her into the forest. Everything your aunt said to your mother rushes back with a ferocity that makes your insides pour out. No one notices that you smell like vomit. Your mother, who has been so worried about you opening your mouth at some inopportune, deadly moment, now wonders why she never thought of your sister's face and her silence, how not saying a word could invite danger.

In this time of chaos, you are growing beyond all expectations for your body. Years of poor nutrition should have left you stunted, but you are defiant on a cellular level. Now you must wear your sister's clothes, still too loose but wearable. Catching sight of you, your mother occasionally calls you by your sister's name and time comes to pieces, but then she sees you—less pretty, too loud. She cradles your brother, tries to keep him from growing as he squirms in her arms.

Your father has lost his mind. He walks around at night after curfew searching for your sister's ghost. Your mother has started tying him to the bed, but somehow he breaks free, finds a way out through a window or straight through the front door. Imprisoning your father feels only slightly cruel because when you bind his wrists together it is out of love.

In the morning, three months after your sister's murder, your father is missing. And when a week passes, you feel a dread buzzing in your cortex. The sensation will diminish but never fully go away. There are no witnesses this time, or, more likely, everyone is a witness. Someone saw a white van approach him, another saw him scaling a tree, another saw him turn into a bird.

Your mother decides to move what remains of the family to her sister's house, where you will live cramped up with six other cousins.

In order not to disappear, your mother wants you to stay indoors, neck bent, hunchbacked. Live like you're nobody.

Marry her off, she will be safer then, your aunt tells your mother after they return from the temple. The one constant in your life is your mother's religious devotion, which has only intensified over the years. She carries a miniature stainless-steel statue of Lord Siva whenever she goes outside. Your brother bows his head north, east, south, west, five times a day and wears a rosary gifted by a dead classmate, Lorenzo. You don't have any rituals, unless remembering your father and sister every waking moment counts.

Somehow you make it to age sixteen, and because you are now the age of your sister when she died, you decide every year after this is extra.

Your mother sews clothes in the garment factory for an American company. She makes enough to feed you both and not much else.

Surviving isn't nothing, your mother tells you when you refuse to eat, tell her stories of ancient warriors.

You leave not because of your mother or the fact that you sleep next to three cousins who all snore or the fact that your muscles are atrophying from hiding but because deep in the phosphorous of your bones you know that you are more than this thing of survival.

Already you've met the recruiters at school and you knew you would join. You remember seeing two senior classmates with their hair cut short. In their green camouflage, they smiled at you momentarily, and you stared at them with a longing you couldn't decipher.

When your own hair is cut, you watch as each strand of hair falls to the ground and encircles you, offerings from your past body to your new self.

You are a wiry girl thing. You are out of breath after carrying ten kilograms from sunrise to midday back and forth through an empty clearing. Your comrades, other girls, lift you to your feet and tell you to keep moving. One girl, Jeyanthi, keeps holding your hand as you stumble for breath.

Her story is not much different from yours. Parents killed. A brother, a rebel fighter, tortured. But no one here asks about the past.

During shooting practice, you aim for a bird's eye and end

up trimming tree bark. You are not good with your fingers, you're all legs, a runner. This is not a strategic advantage. Jeyanthi stays up late at night and trains you, and you are so desperately bad that it doesn't occur to you that she is sacrificing two hours of sleep for your sake. She places you in the center of an invisible square, each corner a glass bottle. You throw a stone blindly into the darkness. Hit nothing but ground.

It will take you three weeks for you to smash all the bottles and another month before you can do it blindfolded. You, always a poor student, excel in guerrilla warfare and soon rise to the top of your troop.

Jeyanthi tells you she has probably killed over a dozen soldiers. With one man, she engaged in hand-to-hand combat.

I gashed him in his eyes and then I just kept chopping, she said.

Only men get to be gruesome, so you milk her for details. You ask about his screams, if dying sounded sexual. You have heard your parents making love, the guttural sounds of someone being smothered.

You have only thrown grenades, shot from long distances. You have never watched a body wither from your touch. In all the stories you can remember, a woman is only allowed to be killed or fucked. She can't hold the blade.

After your third mission, when you and Jeyanthi are almost killed, your body now splotched with second-degree burns, you ask her, *Did you ever want a husband, a child, a family?*

She doesn't laugh at the question but yawns. *Did you ever want the sky to be another color but blue? For bombs to be filled with candy? For all the dead to return to life?*

Pregnancy intrigues you more than sex. A body curled up inside yours. When one of the comrades begins to show, her belly tipping over her belt, she is reassigned to noncombat work. You hear rumors that the child is the product of a love affair between comrades, which is strictly prohibited. Still, you sneak glances at your male compatriots, elusive enough to fill your imagination with perfect husbands, silent except when asked.

Jeyanthi is your roommate. She sleeps curled up with her mouth open, drooling. Before you go to sleep, she tells you that men are afraid of women who exist beyond the realm of their control. The soldier she killed hand to hand was not afraid of her until he saw her grinning, a woman without fear, capable of anything.

Jeyanthi tells you that as a child she was shy, never looked anyone in the eye, and you don't believe her until she shows you pictures where she looks so delicate, with her face pointed downward, that you're afraid she'll fall apart.

And here she is, protecting you, devoting all her extra hours to making you stronger.

She is not talkative except with you, right before sleep descends, and in that brief span of consciousness, you could ask her seemingly anything.

Do you like it here?

Maybe.

What are you afraid of?

Being afraid.

Why don't you talk with the other girls?

We are training, no?

Why do you talk to me, then? you want to ask, but you don't.

Instead you are always side by side with Jeyanthi, who likes to balance herself against your shoulder. When she does that it reminds you of your older sister, whom you are remembering less and less nowadays. You know she would have winced seeing you with your hair trimmed to the scalp and the thought of your sister's disgust delights you at odd moments. Makes you smile as you listen to the commander give announcements or when you herd a group of runaway goats. Who knew these grudges with your sister would turn precious? That you would long for the possessive way she saw you, your actions and appearance a reflection of her own self? The only jewelry you own, a pair of anklets, belonged to her. You have kept them safe and secret all this time. She would be proud.

When Jeyanthi catches you bumbling around for the goats, you are wearing the anklets, and you don't realize immediately but it's the first time you have heard her laugh. It frightens you, how she gives herself away to it.

Are you crying? you ask her, and you see the tears in her eyes.

Without any clear reason except for a sensation that some under different circumstances might describe as joy, you begin to strategize ways to make her laugh. You tell her stories about a fighter who accidently shot at their shadow. A goat that excreted bullets into the hands of someone who ran out of ammo in the middle of a battle. How a man had eaten so many seeds to survive that when he was killed, by a gash to his belly, plants sprouted from within him. It is a mix of hearsay and dark imaginings.

You never talk about your dreams, except once when you

dream of an elephant. You are running in the forest, gunfire streaking the air, and you suddenly come eye to eye with a fallen elephant, its pus-filled bullet holes. You don't go into detail, just tell Jeyanthi you dreamed of an elephant. After that day she calls you Yaadra Yanai. She jumps on your back and asks you to carry her to the room. *Yanai, please, I'm tired.*

You never talk about the past or the future.

When Jeyanthi goes on a mission or you go, there are never prayers or farewells.

You wish you believed in ghosts and spirits. You want to be haunted. Instead, seated side by side with Jeyanthi, from the height of a hillside, surrounded by shrubbery and trees still standing after years of explosions—their resilience a virtue you have begun to doubt—you watch Jeyanthi cut an unripe mango as the sun sets and you think this can be a whole life.

You send word to your mother now and then through a network of ears and mouths. All together you visit her three times. She has aged quickly and when you see her, she's seated next to your brother, who perpetually lies in bed after being crippled by a land mine. You don't know that your third visit will be your last. In three months' time the military will advance and everything will be destroyed. But she must know, because she gives you her Lord Siva statue, and though you refuse, she persists, and you tell her you'll be back soon, and she presses one hand on your brother's head and the other on yours, and she closes her eyes, quiet in prayer. She doesn't cry as she sends the rest of her life energy to you both, her remaining children, still living.

You will return to this moment when you are on your knees, your head in your mother's lap, as the world crumbles.

Amini dies first.
    Then Laxmi.
    Devadarshini
    Parvati
    Bhavini
    Darpana
    Radha
    Sonya
    Urvashi
    Chandra
    Pavitra
    Lucy
    Aanchal
    Alaimakal
    Fatima
    Mary
    Jeyanthi
    Only you keep running, cross the water and make it to safer shores.

You wake up on the couch, your head resting on the feathery entrails of a cushion. From under your armpit a beetle creeps out. Everything smells damp and musty like you're lying next to a dog. The grass has grown tall and if you reach your hand out, it's slick and slightly dewy on your fingers. Ants march across your legs. The oval coffee table with its faux wood has begun to change color from the rain, pale concentric circles have formed on the surface as if someone threw a rock and the ripples had frozen through time. On the outer rims are ghost planets, the impressions of mugs once steaming with liquids.

Your body is sore, like you've just washed up onto the shore. Across from you the grandfather clock ticks away, its stern and melancholic face admonishing you for losing track of time.

You look up into the clear day, nothing but blue, and maybe this is all you need, the high-vaulted sky rising eternally. You breathe, air moving in and out. You are apart from this world and vulnerable to it.

~

Near the end of the manuscript are seventeen names listed. The same as the number of first-year medical students. *Loss cut through reality like a knife.* You picture them standing side by side in camouflage, hair shorn, skeletal, raising their guns.

You chat with Socrates. After he rambles about the baby's bout of diarrhea, he asks you how you felt after watching the clip.

It was like an exorcism, you say.

You stare at the sad flower drooping next to him, the sky still an unforgiving gray. Socrates doesn't keep in touch with many students, and you can imagine a day when you both won't bother to say hello. It's easy to disentangle yourself from the lives of others.

It's a fluke, us meeting and me translating this text.

He sighs and collapses his shoulders, and for a moment it looks like he's given up, but then he says, *You might not remember your eighteen-year-old self, but I do.*

It's the first time he has really referred to that time, when you couldn't get out of bed, burst into tears between classes, fell asleep in bathroom stalls. He pats down his shirt, and you adjust your face.

Pasalai, you say, *it's a good word.*

Do you remember the report you wrote about the manuscript many years ago?

No.

I saved it, he says, and proceeds to read it as you cover

your face. *I do not know what a failed vision created by a group of girls clarifies within me, but one day I will.*

You nod, letting the words of your past self sink into your future self.

It's not every day a student like you comes along. It's like winning the lotto, he says, then lowers his voice as the baby begins to trill. *We must think of a title. Can't keep it marked with an x.*

After he insists, you read your latest edits. It comes out smoother than you expect, and when you finally look up, after what feels like a lifetime, you see two faces staring at you, one small and serious, dribbling to his neck. The resemblance is striking, your cheery grandfather teacher and the baby with an old man's face.

Radical Compassion for You and Me? he says.

For an hour, the two of you brainstorm ideas. You don't necessarily care what comes of it, but you enjoy being this random generator of titles. *In the Time of Love and War. Girlhood and Other Deaths. Beside Ourselves with the Ancient Love of Glory.*

The house is nearly inside out. Along with the furniture—the couch, grandfather clock, recliner, coffee table, bookshelf, cabinets—are boxes of clothes, shoes, kitchen supplies. The packing is done by collecting like items together. With your mother's logic, you have put the cleaning supplies with Mrs. Ahmed's cosmetics because they both deal with surfaces. The order doesn't really matter, as most of it will be donated or tossed. You question if you should disassemble Mr. and Mrs. Ahmed's bed, since you hardly use it, but Sal wants to include it as part of the exhibit, and you imagine people walking inside while you're fast asleep, a projector casting your dreams on the wall for others to admire. Good thing you don't sleep. She plans to remove everything from the bathroom except for two toothbrushes, so the experience feels distilled and lived-in.

The exhibit still feels unfinished. There's a hole in the wall, right next to the kitchen, and it might be purposefully done, a figurative gesture of escape, or maybe an opening to a new life with Judith. You don't mention it.

You put on one of Mrs. Ahmed's cotton kurta tops and then Mr. Ahmed's favorite wool sweater. You find a glittery scarf, the owner unidentifiable, and begin layering as much as you can—spring jacket, rain jacket, winter jacket, earrings, bangles, baseball cap, winter hat, leggings, trousers, ankle socks, winter socks—and sit among the objects in the yard like a scarecrow. You manage to frighten a few squirrels.

He didn't pass by the oak tree. I waited for a few hours, Rosalyn says, and you put a hand on your cousin's forehead to check if she's feverish. Since she lost her job, she's been wandering around, looking for someone she first saw on TV.

It was only a matter of time before V. F. caught her. She wasn't so much toeing the line as fully crossing it. Replicating memories while V. F. was still in the lab, sometimes when he was standing right next to her and talking to her but really to himself. Maybe it was out of kindness or some unexpressed feelings he still held for her, but he didn't press charges. He might have even offered her another chance. No matter what, she would have still eventually quit, she tells you. It was time. In the basement, she still has a thriving archive of memories for some inconceivable purpose. Memory for memory's sake.

Do you still see that memory? you ask.

It's fading.

There was a Cheeze she knew before the memory, and then after the memory, and there was no way of going back to the before when everything was possible and amorphous. He solidified in her mind. If she found Cheeze, she might kill him, or he might kill her, or they might both strangle each other lovingly. It was only a hair strand of what really happened, but inside its root, along with compassion hid suffering. The blood price. You think of Cheeze spreading sunflower-seed butter on a slice of toast and then licking the knife.

When you felt miserable, your mother would point to someone walking down the street and tell you their story like they were old friends. Then it was your turn to point to someone and talk about their life. The two of you would go back and forth until you leapfrogged your way out of sadness, one human at a time. It felt like another one of your mother's homeopathic easy fixes, but years later, you're still trying to do it from the inside out, imagining yourself through the eyes of a stranger who is much more willing to tell a kinder story.

~

The interview happens on a Saturday evening, but you decline to accompany Judith and Sal to the studio. Judith insists you come by pulling on your arm, saying the two of you could be godsibbing throughout the filming, but you say you're not feeling well. Before they leave, you wish Sal good luck and she gives you a big smile that swallows you like a wave. Later with Rosalyn, you watch the show live on TV. The host is Angela Fernandez, known for wringing tragedies for any residual feelings. She is recounting Mr. and Mrs. Ahmed's accident to the audience, including the gory details of their sprawled bodies. The camera doesn't focus on Sal's reaction. Instead, it pans out as the woman and toddler appear on the other side of the stage. They are dressed in plain clothing, and you think this is a strategy to allow the viewers to project themselves more easily onto the mother and baby duo rather than onto Sal, who is wearing a bulky, sequined blazer. When they are first seated, the camera switches over to Sal for a reaction. There isn't any, so Angela begins to prod.

Are you happy to see these two right now?

Not really.

Would you rather this young woman and her child had died?

No.

Would you rather have your parents alive?

Yes.

Angela turns to the woman named Carol and the little one, Peaches. Carol, a receptionist, lives with her boyfriend, a waste manager. They have been dating for four years and hope to get married soon.

Are you happy to be alive?

Of course!

If you had a chance to switch places with Mr. and Mrs. Ahmed, would you?

She pauses and looks at the toddler in her arms, sucking a strand of hair. *Oh dear, well I wouldn't want them to die, either, but I have to think of my child and be here.*

You think the cars made the right decision?

She nods hesitantly. *I really don't see any other decision that could have been made, given the circumstances.*

Sal snorts and her face finally comes alive. *You don't think there is anything wrong with the calculation? That certain lives are automatically valued more?*

I have a baby. That's really all it comes down to.

So if it was you and another adult, the AI would have made the same calculation?

I'm sorry about the loss of your parents. I really am, but it's all chance. Wrong place at the wrong time.

This is not hypothetical. It's the world we live in. Who gets killed is no accident.

My child needs me.

And I need—

Sal looks over at the camera, and she's melting, speaking too honestly. Angela senses an opening and asks, *Do you see yourself ever becoming a mother?*

What? Sal says, shrinking. *I don't know.*

I think what Carol is referring to is a mother's instinct.

Angela hands the toddler over to Sal, and she doesn't know what else to do but accept the smiling thing, which tries to grab her nose.

Isn't that love? Angela says.

For a moment you think that Sal might actually slam the baby against the studio floor and reenact some slanted form of justice, but she only stares at the baby and murmurs a few words.

Carol doesn't take Peaches back. She actually seems relieved not to have the toddler by her side. She's sweating profusely and pats her face with the sleeve of her shirt that's turning translucent. With the sleeve rolled up, you can see red splotches on her arm. The material is cheap and synthetic.

Who does Peaches look like? Angela asks. *More like you or your fiancé?*

Neither.

Oh.

A man attacked me. The baby looks like that man.

She says it all so matter-of-factly that you almost forget to react. Angela is not prepared for her carefully laid-out path to become undone so quickly by such an off-handed, seismic response. She uses all her strength to collect herself and directs her energy to a short segment about the self-driving car industry before returning to the interview. Sal holds Peaches very carefully in both arms as Carol watches.

I like your jacket, Carol says.

Thank you.

Once, while watching a news story about a hospital mix-up—two baby boys given to the wrong parents, a mistake that was only discovered eighteen years later—your mother turned to you and said she would have been happy to find out that you weren't her real daughter. She patted your cheek and you felt yourself floating in a basket down a river. At shopping malls, whenever you got lost, you would become frantic, looking for your mother everywhere, afraid she had taken another young girl home to play your part.

The summer you turned twelve, you and your mother took the bus all the way to Ohio. You sat next to an elderly woman who was so cold that she wore three sweaters and didn't mind when you fell asleep on her because of body warmth. Your mother sat next to a teenager who couldn't stop chewing gum, blowing zircon bubbles to match his pimples. Whenever you peeked above your seat, your mother would make a troll face and you'd laugh. She did this for hours until the break, and somewhere in Pennsylvania, you both sat outside and ate the tuna sandwiches she'd prepared. She'd only eaten a bite when she saw a woman wobbling by, hair hanging off her head in strings, her eyes cloudy. She wore a cloth sack. The woman was talking to herself, and your mother ripped off her bite mark and gave the rest of the sandwich over to the lady. *She might not even like tuna,* you said, and ate yours quickly, before she'd have the chance to give away yours as well.

Your mother didn't eat anything else and didn't complain when you reached the motel at night. She drank only two glasses of water, and after changing into your nightclothes, you stayed up playing cards together on white sheets. You had played with Sal, so you knew the rules, how to slap the cards, look up, and win. She managed only two games before falling asleep, her mouth open a crack so you could hear a little troll inside her, wheezing. You slid close to her, counting her breaths against your cheek.

In the morning, at a nearby diner, you ate pancakes and your mother spread the butter into a happy face. She drank coffee, ate a grapefruit with yogurt, and asked you if Ohio felt like home. You shook your head and she smiled while you finished the entire stack and then asked for a sundae.

You were both too dressed up for the diner, wearing skirts and blouses usually saved for very special occasions. Looking back on it now, you're not too sure what was exceptional about the trip, besides it being your first with your mother. She was an expert at tinkering around with vending machines and stripping motel beds to the cleanliest layer. As you walked all over town with your mother, you remember pausing across the street from a yellow house. She stared at it, giving it a good once-over.

Do you like it? she asked.

I guess it's nice.

It looked ordinary to you, nothing spectacular, but you could tell your mother was enamored with it so you spoke more firmly. *It's the best!*

But when you truly gazed at it with your own pair of eyes, the yellow paint looked like a coffee stain and the lawn was overgrown with dried patches. Still you could see a bicycle flashing in the yard and the colorful carved gourds peeking from the porch.

Your mother stepped into the street, and it seemed like you both were going to walk across and say hello, but the door opened before you and your mother could make it across that infinite distance. A woman stood on the porch with her hand above her eyes to block the sunlight. The spell was broken and your mother was pulling you as far as she could from the house. You complained that your feet hurt and you both sat on the curb, eating the ginger rock candies you packed especially for this trip. They tasted sour from all the sweat in your pocket. You stuck out your tongue and she did too. Her tongue was green and yours was purple. The two of you might not have even looked like mother and daughter, your mouths open, shrieking colors. You both stayed for an extra day in Ohio before heading back to New York, and you returned only many years later for her funeral, when you and Bobby bowed to a mighty river to pour out her ashes.

You were her blood child, so motherhood was always slightly acidic and selfish. She looked at you and saw herself—you don't think your mother knew how to reconcile loving you.

You meet Ricky at the bar, and the first thing you notice is his hair, which has grown out and reaches his shoulders. *I'm going to join a band,* he jokes as he slides into the seat across from you. He orders a burger and you're fine with just soda water, and it's almost like nothing has changed.

Here I thought you fully disappeared, you say.

You can't get rid of me that easily.

You want to ask him about his dreams, but instead you say: *Lucille has moved to your desk and created a mini ecosystem.*

He clicks his tongue and raises his hands behind his head. *Ah, the worker is so easily replaced.*

In the bar, there is a slight commotion, someone has spilled their drink and refuses to pay. He's foaming as someone calls the manager. You both eagerly watch the incident like it's on the TV. Almost unconsciously Ricky touches his shoulder, the right one, and you remember the airy feel of your fingers. He catches you looking and puts his hand down.

I couldn't keep working there, he says finally.

Was it eating you up?

He grins and swipes his hand through his hair. *That's one way to put it.*

When his food arrives, you watch him eat. He chews slowly, like he's collecting his thoughts. Neither of you says anything. Halfway through his burger, he puts it down and looks at you.

There was a girl I met in college, he says. *I was a senior and she was a sophomore. We dated for three years. She was a physics major and really brilliant in this effortless way that could make people jealous, but she was kind and never wanted to compete. She made pancakes for her housemates every weekend. People really liked her, and out of everyone, somehow, she liked me. I could never understand it. We had the same awful taste in music and weird sleeping habits, and maybe that was enough? I was pretty mediocre in school and didn't have any great ambition. Unlike me she knew she wanted to specialize in quantum, work in some institute in Switzerland. The way she said it, you just knew it was going to happen. She had traumatic things occur in her past, but she was perpetually optimistic. Like she'd wake up early to feed stray cats, believing they had a special connection to the spirit world, and I'd watch her from bed as she disappeared into the street, calling out strange names. About quantum, she had a very romantic interpretation of it, often bringing it up in our relationship. Like not making plans and waiting for things to reveal themselves. She said we needed to channel superposition, that harnessing uncertainty is power. Other times she'd say we were entangled like two particles that were separated but part of each other, and we were lucky because most people spend their whole lives trying to cross that distance to find their missing halves. She visited my family a few times during the holidays, and my family loved her, and she'd spend more time with them than even with me. I only knew her father worked in exports and liked to drink nettle tea to fight off illnesses. She never spoke about her mother. One winter we took a road trip to Canada, driving from Albany to Montreal to Guelph. She said it was the happiest time in her life. She saw a moose for the first time on a snowy hill. It was as if we were already married, and I think it must have scared me, how strongly she felt and how my feelings would never match hers. When we returned back home, I broke up with her.*

He pauses and then drinks some water. He seems winded, and you wait but he doesn't go on. Like he's lost in some other dimension.

Ricky, you say, and slowly his gaze sharpens on you. His voice is soft and blunted as he tells you she recently died by suicide. He had not seen her since they had broken up, but lately he has felt strangely connected to her, like she's pulsing through him across a distance, guiding him.

She's like, Ricky, be true to yourself, don't make things worse.

From his backpack he pulls out a flat rectangular box and places it between the two of you. You stare at the alien thing, plucked from another decade.

It's a hard drive, he says.

Oh. For a second there, I thought you were trying to be romantic.

You should wait and listen to our band. We only play love songs.

Are you really in a band?

He laughs, showing his teeth. *I was kidding.*

You both are quiet. The outdated hard drive sits on the table like the exoskeleton of an endangered creature.

I think you should feed this to Bogey, he says.

What's in it?

A new kind of data.

What will it do?

It'll make things better.

How?

He arches his neck closer to you. *Do you think you can trust without fully understanding?* He reaches for your hand and whispers: *Uncertainty is power.*

After a fifteen-hour flight with no layovers, Bobby has returned, tired and sore-eyed. It surprises you how simply sitting can wear the body down. Unfastened from the earth, people languish. Bobby walks through the house exhibit and pauses in front of the news clipping about a woman who fell in love with an algorithm. The giant hole is still cratered into the wall. Everything is suspended in a state of uncertainty.

It's unfinished, you say, but they continue examining the room, keeping their comments to themself. The only furniture remaining is the kitchen table and one chair. You offer to pull out one from the yard, but they don't want you to bother. The other chairs now belong to nature.

Bobby opens the fridge, sniffing around. *I was checking to see if the fridge was real or part of the art show.*

We walk that fine line of reality.

Clearly, Bobby says, and then mentions the most recent addition to the sanctuary. A three-eared calf named Jojo. *The matriarch of the clan had just passed, so the arrival of Jojo was a big celebration. But then someone thought it would be a good idea to play a recording of the voice of the dead matriarch and let me tell you I have never seen the elephants so agitated. When I think about it, it's only humans who imprint themselves in other forms.*

Bobby looks at you like they know you'd spent weeks listening to your mother's voice before recording your own.

Bobby picks up a plastic bottle from the counter and calls it *indestructible* and a symbol of *human longevity*. They poke their head into open cabinets, the doors unhinged or completely gone. *I don't know how you all live like this. Remember, this is coming from someone who has lived in forests without proper toilets.*

Did you go by the house? you ask, and then remember that there is no actual house anymore.

I did. They stand by the stove, and for the first time since they arrived, they're quiet. *You're really like her.*

You can't help but wince. All your insides squeeze. Even Potential Baby feels it.

When she had you, she couldn't boil a decent pasta, so I didn't know how she'd manage a child. But one thing my sister enjoyed for sure was proving people wrong. Bobby walks over to the back of the kitchen and pauses, touching the bare wall as if memory could give way. *I remember that she had this map of the world in her room. She was a big history buff and she'd pin all the places she wanted to go and people she wanted to meet and it didn't matter if they were dead or the cities were in ruins. Listening to her, I would fall into a trance like time was coming undone. She felt things so deeply that it didn't matter one way or another if they actually happened.* Their voice breaks off, a hand hovering where a doorknob might be. For all you know maybe there really is a better world on the other side of the wall, and you can't see it just yet.

They stare out the window into the yard, muddy after the rain. *What happened to all the furniture out there? Why are the couch cushions torn up and that table upside down?*

Girls, you say.

Bobby rolls their eyes. *They're the worst.*

At work you upload all the contents from the hard drive into Bogey. No time to test it. You close your eyes and count backward from twenty-six and imagine all kinds of punishment awaiting you. Then, at zero, you open them, blinking and sweating, and everything appears the same. Lucille sits at Ricky's desk and Petrov eats his burrito. The room is excessively bright. The garbage is piling up. You stare at your screen and notice an imperceptible shift. Like the change of a pixel. *Farewell, Bogey.*

~

In less than a week Rosalyn will enter the TV. You don't believe she's leaving. Her archive of memories is placed into a shoebox, which she hands over to you for safekeeping, though your own safety is questionable.

What about being a scientist? you ask her.

This is kind of like field research.

But you'll be a production assistant.

Exactly, she says, and sighs, returning to folding her shirts into tiny compact squares.

Through a college friend who worked at a film company, she had gotten the job. The position is on a spin-off show of *Soldiers' Diaries,* focusing on the lives of veterans featured in the original. You picture spinal surgeries, sagging bodies drinking beers and trading tales of their not-so-distant youth. Cheeze somewhere, out of focus, with Cookie.

You go for an interview to be a housemate in a collective. Sitting in the center of the room, next to an assortment of potted foliage, you wave at your six potential roommates. Eddie, a recent transplant from Tucson, sits next to you, holding your wrists. Honesty is very important, so he'll be tracking your pulse as he asks you questions. His fingers are sweaty, and you wonder what he can feel beating under your skin.

What do you like about communal living?

That it's affordable.

What else?

Your body won't rot if you suddenly die.

He laughs. *Very practical. We appreciate that forward thinking. So what makes you a good housemate?*

I don't mind clutter.

That's especially helpful when living with six people. What's wrong with your current residence?

You feel your heartbeat picking up and so does Eddie because he's staring at your irises, trying to extract any other information. A line from the manuscript flickers across your mind: *How easily we could have forgiven strangers; there's nothing more painful as treachery committed by those you chose to be blood.*

You look at Eddie and say you're pregnant. He releases your wrist, taking in the entirety of you. *The ad,* he says, *is very specific about searching for one roommate, not two.*

At work you are blindfolded and led to the common area, where all kinds of torture for your treachery awaits you. You prepare yourself for the worst and bite your lip so hard that you're sure you're bleeding.

When Petrov unblindfolds you, you're staring at a chocolate frosted cake with a drawing of a baby.

Congratulations, they say together, applauding.

You haven't told anyone about the baby, but then you remember vomiting and Breanna holding back your hair as you wept into the toilet smelling of washed-up doughnuts. *There, there,* she said, like you were her child.

All your feelings are jumbled. Holding a knife, surrounded by people you don't really care for and slices of baby cake, which is also a sorry-you-lost-your-house cake, you know it is slightly coercive to celebrate a baby that you might not decide to have, but before you know it, Lucille is by your side, wiping wetness from your eyes with a napkin, and how nice it is to be loved without asking.

In a write-up, *American Glitch* is described as an intimate portrait of a family and the inner workings of a country. You're listed as a collaborator. When you see her name next to yours, you have to fight the dumb feeling rising in you.

You wash your face in the kitchen sink and then read words of the manuscript etched on the fridge. You wonder if you're really part of it, if writing can smuggle you into a future that feels more and more unlikely for you.

In the living room, you notice a circle of photographs for the first time. Sal must have installed them only the night before. In the center of the wall of newspaper clippings are pictures of Sal's parents. Mr. Ahmed wears an undershirt as he fries eggs. He looks younger, happier, with none of the paunch of his later years. In the corner, Mrs. Ahmed appears in a red shirt, flexing her thin arms. She flashes all her teeth in a roar. In another photo, she is pregnant and sits on the floor, reading a book, poetry most likely. Sal is not present in any of the images, and the absence is intentional. It's a memorial. You find two pictures of your mother and she's grinning, changing a record.

On the porch, you sit, wearing Sal's old winter jacket. The sun dips behind the clouds and shadows spread out on the asphalt. A cat passes the stairway and looks up remorsefully. You meow at it in your awkward human way. It trots past you in the direction of your disappeared home.

When Sal finds you on the porch, your fingers have turned into icicles. She crouches low to your side.

The exhibit is really something, you tell her.

You can tell me the truth.

You're very talented. I always knew that.

You look back through the door into the past. *We should set the house on fire after the last showing. The critics will love it.*

Sal laughs, raising the hair on your arms. Your child self lives on in a molecular way, and without warning the girl slips out of you and sits next to Sal. She soaks up the remaining sunlight, and Sal turns to her and says, *Stay here*, and the girl doesn't think about the future and what lies ahead but simply nods, and Sal rests an arm around her as they wait for the night to settle over them and everything they had lost.

T he television stayed ablaze in each of our rooms and became a game of secrets, stories hiding behind stories. After a week, Yaadra disappeared from the news, just like the fishermen.

We walked through the refugee camps to the harbor, where families waited through the nights holding up lanterns. Wives cried out with harpoon voices. Boats drifted between two shores: hunger and war.

We thought of our elders who marched through the mountains on a death-walk pilgrimage to a shrine, where some were crushed by elephants, others were killed more passionately with claws or died quietly of exhaustion. In such cases, death was a choice guided by fate.

In class, Mr. Sanjeevan told us to stop talking about the war, Yaadra, the fishermen, and we knew he thought we were wasting our lives. He was our biology professor and spoke passionately about neural networks and the process of cellular division. "The universe lies closer in places we have yet to fully understand," he would say. Simple talk would get us nowhere. We couldn't just sit and watch, because within us, we carried galaxies, hidden planets, and, possibly, a cure.

On an especially hot afternoon, we covered our windows with black sheets of mourning and sat alone in our rooms, in complete darkness, imagining that final crossing. But then, like thunder before lightning, we heard screams and awoke to the weight of our bodies and ran down the stairwell to find Madame Sarojini crouching on her desk like a weeping ninja. Below her cooed a baby scorpion. A lopsided romance. We could hear a love song playing along with her shrieks. It probably wouldn't have killed her, only a little, but then, her fear of scorpions might have done it. She turned to us imploringly, and unfortunately Jeera didn't have her camera to enshrine the moment. On Madame Sarojini's desk we found her fancy Tupperware filled with a thin layer of fish curry, slightly gelatinous from storage. A rare treat. She must have looked forward to it all week. Because our goal was speed rather than thoughtfulness, we took the Tupperware and covered the baby scorpion, entrapping it in fishy sludge. Madame Sarojini was so distraught that she didn't have time to see what we had done. But after she collected herself and drank a glass of water, she settled into the understanding that her prized lunch was on the floor with one of her greatest fears inside. We could see her preparing to reprimand us, but the scorpion was still alive, raging under the plastic. We looked at her and she understood the bargain we planned to make, and she beat us to it. "Fine, fine, dispose of it, and then no curfew tonight, but it's at your own risk," she cried, fanning herself with her hand. "Imagine what could have happened to me. I don't want to imagine."

We didn't know why it never crossed our minds before. All it took was a little scorpion to get our way. Imagine the sight of ten scorpions, or a hundred! It would have killed her for sure.

We decided to stay out through the night, drunk on cool evening air. As we walked around, people stared at us. What was a group of wiry girl things doing this late? We shot back with big eyes and open mouths that showed our calcium-deficient chompers. We had numbers so we couldn't be hassled, only ogled by stupefied faces. It was past midnight, and we were still alive. At night, everything had more mystery. Even our own shadows made us think of other worlds. People looked more relaxed, loosening buttons and tongues. A man called out to us with a sly word, offering orange beverages he had received from abroad, defective but still drinkable. He opened a can the way they did in commercials, sinking his head back, raising his arm, so the product was in full display. He smacked his lips and gave us a kissy-face. We laughed, holding our knees, letting the laughter roll over us. Arm in arm, we sang to the shoreline about a girl and her hair, her hair. We each picked up a rock and dropped it into the ocean where Yaadra was last seen. *We do not rejoice that living is sweet, nor resent it for not being so.* Out in the water, we saw a lone fishing boat gliding under a fat moon. It looked dazzling and ghostly, as if carrying the dead to another shore. Together we dug into the sand and wrote messages that would be visible only in the daylight, but we trusted our movements because, in the end, meaning was never the point. What we needed to convey was a feeling and it didn't matter if it was etched in something as temporary as sand. Fingers and feet

searched for what was underneath us all along. From the refugee camps we could hear a conch bellowing and we quieted,
sitting upright, our legs folded. Trapped in the surf were plastic bags and other luminescent trash. We were getting sleepy,
but we were determined not to return. We took turns, resting
our eyes, blinking every ten seconds, then every minute, then
every fifteen minutes. When we were younger we used to
imagine a life where we never slept. Double the time. Double
the playing. Double the happiness. But then, double the sadness, pain, loss. Slowly we would learn that there's never really more life, only a diluted, weaker version. Madame Sarojini
had once told us we could win in life if we crossed the line
toward ninety and then a hundred, rarely ever exceeded. She
had friends in their fifties who were already dead. She spoke
about them pityingly, like sore losers. Some people live long,
stretched-out, tepid lives, but what did we want?

When the sun rose, we raised ourselves to our feet, stretching our arms, wiping our sleepless faces and preparing for
Madame Sarojini's beratement, which we find mildly enjoyable, if only for the chance to hear her using profanity. Together we moved like a school of fish past the refugee camps
and to our own confinement.

A fortnight before the upcoming state election, the chief
minister resurrected chatter about Yaadra and the missing fishermen. Under a banner for justice, she declared a fast until the
national government probed into the deaths and disappearances. But before the second day was complete, a photogra-
pher snapped a shot of the chief minister in her black shades
and pure white cotton tunic eating a chicken sandwich from
the newly opened KFC. Because she owned eighty percent

of the television stations and ninety percent of the newspapers, the image ran for only a few hours before a news anchor was fired and everything was labeled as a smear campaign.

A total of seventy-three fishermen were missing. The etchings on the wall now curved into the stairwell. The televisions were still quiet, but since our visions of Yaadra we were able to sense a new frequency and we knew we were entering the next level of liberation. From our windows we could see the shanties of the refugee camps on the shoreline by a roaring sea. The metallic sheen burned our eyes, and we sang, "Any town our hometown, everyone our kin," and we were filled with the sudden sensation of home. Our mothers, fathers, brothers, uncles, aunts, sisters calling to us, waving and whistling, welcoming our return. Long-lost daughters.

The girl was giving us instructions.

The remedy for forgetting.

Polystyrene, used in televisions, releases a form of

hydrogen cyanide when burned.

In order to truly awaken you must break

through the screen of this world.

ACKNOWLEDGMENTS

Many thanks to Bill Clegg for his generosity and insight in helping this book find its way, to Eric Chinski for his belief and excitement from the beginning, and to Julia Ringo for all her dedicated work in taking this book to the end; much love to everyone at FSG and the Clegg Agency for all their care. Grateful to the Fine Arts Work Center in Provincetown, Yaddo, the Schomburg Center for Research in Black Culture, and Bard College for the enormous support and wonderful community. To all my dear friends and students, thanks for sharing your enthusiasm, laughter, and spirit over the years.

The following texts were influential to the book: Coco Fusco's *A Field Guide for Female Interrogators*, Melanie Mitchell's *Artificial Intelligence: A Guide for Thinking Humans*, Ruha Benjamin's *Race After Technology*, and Kamil Zvelebil's *The Smile of Murugan* and *The Poets of the Powers*.

And thanks to Amma for imagining this with me.

A NOTE ABOUT THE AUTHOR

Akil Kumarasamy is the author of the linked story collection *Half Gods*, which was named a *New York Times* Editors' Choice, was awarded the Bard Fiction Prize and the Story Prize Spotlight Award, and was a finalist for the PEN/Robert W. Bingham Prize for Debut Short Story Collection. Her work has appeared in *Harper's Magazine, American Short Fiction, BOMB*, and other publications. She has received fellowships from the University of East Anglia, the Fine Arts Work Center in Provincetown, Yaddo, and the Schomburg Center for Research in Black Culture. She is an assistant professor in the Rutgers University–Newark MFA program.